The  Xavier

By John A. Ashley

Cover art by Richard K. Green

Copyright © 2012
John A. Ashley

ISBN-13: 978-1481227445

Prologue

The instant rush sucked the air from my tense body. Fighting the extreme G-forces that were pinning me to my seat, I managed to turn my head and look out the ship's back portal. The earth seemed like a street sign in the rear view mirror of a car, becoming smaller and smaller until disappearing from sight. I turned back in my seat and tried to relax, tried to slow my pounding heart. Almost twenty minutes later, a voice came over the speakers, startling me slightly.

"We are now exiting the solar system," it said.

Even though the technology had been around for sixteen years, I was still shocked by our speed. The science behind dark energy travel was unfathomable by all except the small group of men and women who'd nurtured it to reality. However, that which I could understand was incredible. By 2067, we had finally visited a world that, for over a decade, we could only watch in admiration. Sometimes, however, the only outcome of mankind climbing higher up the mountain of achievement is that their fall hurts that much worse. Charting alien worlds is no different

My name is Captain Michael Dawn. I am aboard the military craft *Pandora,* named after the mythical box that when opened unleashes all the evil of the world, just as we have unleashed the evil of other worlds.

Chapter 1

"Run!" I shouted.

The agonized screams of the captured scouts echoed in my ears as I forced my legs into a crazed sprint. Bizarre underbrush flew past me, ripping at my suit with their thorns. Our troop scattered like mice, tripping and stumbling through the rough alien terrain, trying desperately to escape their vicious attackers. All around me, I heard the clicking and hissing of the Scorpion tribe, followed by the short, muffled cries of their victims. My lungs felt like they were going to explode. My entire body was cramping up, but I kept running; slowing down meant death. Suddenly, the forest broke, giving way to a rocky ledge that jutted out over a sickening drop. I slid to a stop, coming so close to the edge that I sent pebbles and dust tumbling off. Whirling my rifle back towards the forest, I fired a volley of blind shots into the brush. The rounds zipped through the foliage, knocking down leaves and sending shreds of bark into the air. I heard the smack of a bullet impacting flesh, followed by the dying shriek of a Scorpion, then turned back to the ledge. Just as the first of the menacing creatures materialized from the bush, I jumped. Air rushed all around me, reminding me of the day I left for this hellish planet. I closed my eyes and clenched my teeth together, just before hitting the ground.

Slowly, I regained my senses. Fear that I'd been captured overwhelmed me, but as my vision came into focus, I saw the bare, plastic lined rooms of the base's Combat Support Hospital. I shuffled slightly, expecting to erupt into pain, but instead felt nothing but a nauseating wave. The door to my room suddenly opened, and a nurse walked in. She was slender and well fit from treating the ever-growing list of wounded. She had fair skin and curly blonde hair, and dark circles outlined her eyes. Forcing a weary smile, she walked over to my bed.

"Just came to give you some antibiotics," she said, producing a needle from her coat.

Despite her gentle appearance, she was quiet rough in giving the shot.

"How'd they find me?" I asked.

"Your monitor of course," she said, just before leaving the room.

I sighed, feeling foolish for not remembering it. When we had first arrived on Xavier997 (the name of this God-forsaken planet) we had been injected with a microchip that monitors our location, heart rate, speed of travel, etc. I was not surprised this device had saved my life; it had done so more than once. I let out a tired sigh and turned my head until I was facing a small window at the room's left outside wall. The sun was shining, the wind rustling through knee-high stalks of greenish-yellow grass, and the shrill chorus of birdsong floated through the walls. The world beyond this hospital, Xavier997, was humanity's last hope—a last second resuscitation for a race that was all but dead. Yet this world, so full of the resources we must have, was a deathtrap. The creatures here were unlike anything our military has faced, and reality has hit us hard. The five tribes of Xavier, with technology thousands of years behind our own, have fought us with a ferocity we could have never expected, and after two grueling years of trying to make this planet habitable, it was starting to look like a pipedream.

The door opened again, and a man I recognized as Dr. Clemson came in. He had slick grey hair and a clean-shaven face. A clipboard was cradled in his arm, and he was clutching a worn down pencil.

"How are you feeling?" he asked, preparing to write down my response.

"Fine Doctor, how'd you do it?"

He scribbled something across the clipboard, then looked back at me.

"Let me start by saying you're lucky to have been brought back outside of a body-bag, I got the report from your rescuers. They said your suit detected that you were falling and deployed a small parachute. Otherwise, you would've been brought back in *multiple* body-bags."

I smiled a little.

"Now, you did sustain several broken bones but we fixed those with hydroxalite precarrium. Are you familiar with the compound?"

I shook my head, once again feeling ignorant.

"It looks a lot like shaving cream, and, when you apply it to a break, it causes the bones to fuse back together within an hour."

I nodded.

"Any other injuries?" I asked.

He shook his head, "Other than sustaining a few considerable lacerations, that's it. Though I must remark on how well you took to the procedures. Most people take at least three weeks to recover from something like this. You've done so in barely two days,"

"Two days?" I said.

He smiled, then wrote something on his clipboard.

"My apologies Captain. I tend to take things for granted sometimes. Let me explain," He said, and set down on a small chair beside me.

"We injected you with a more potent anesthesia to keep you out longer. We always do this when applying hydroxalite precarrium. It keeps you from stressing the bonds before they've had time to strengthen. I hope it's not an inconvenience for you, Captain."

"No, none at all," I said, "I was just surprised I'd been here that long."

He smiled, then handed me what I assumed was my release papers.

"Well, you're good to go now. Again, it's truly remarkable how quickly you healed. I don't know if I've ever seen anything like it."

"I've always bounced back quickly," I said.

He smiled, then rose from his seat, "If you will excuse me Captain, I have other patients to tend to."

He jotted a few more things down on his clipboard, and then left the room.

Once he was gone, I started building up the strength to get out of the bed. I slowly swung my legs over the edge, and stood. I saw my uniform hanging in the corner of the room and started walking towards it. It was painful at first but slowly I regained my strength. After changing out of the hospital gown and into the familiar fabric of my uniform, I headed out the door. Not five feet outside, I

4

stopped and shuddered. The stench of death filled my nostrils, and screams of pain reverberated along the cold concrete walls. Two nurses passed me, pushing an operating table with a dead soldier lying on it. He had been completely disemboweled, and his left arm was gone. No amount of medical advancements could save someone with such mortal wounds. I picked up my pace, eager to get out. Finally, I reached the front desk. I handed the nurse my release papers and quickly headed out the door. Fresh air rushed into my lungs and I inhaled it gratefully.

"How ya feelin', Captain?"

Slightly startled, I turned to see who was speaking. It was Private Hawkins, a short muscular kid with dark skin and sharp brown eyes.

"Pretty good, Hawkins. Pretty good."

"That's great. I heard you were hurt bad. How did they get you fixed up so fast?"

I turned back towards the rugged hospital.

"As bad as it is in there, those doctors know what they're doing. They're the best the world had to offer."

Hawkins smiled. "Just like us, right, Cap'n?"

I smiled, "Just like us."

I turned and started to walk away, but Hawkins stopped me.

"I almost forgot. Colonel McBride wants to see you."

"Thanks, Hawkins."

Colonel McBride, Logan as I knew him before the service, had been my friend long before he or I ever donned a uniform. The fact that we would wind up in the same battalion, on the same sector, whether lucky coincidence, or gift from God, was one of the best things to happen in my life. I started off at a walk that quickly turned into a jog, gaining strength with each step I took. The cool morning breeze pierced through my clothing with ease, but after being in the stuffy hospital, it was welcome. In only a minute's time, I reached Colonel McBride's quarters. I trotted up the steps and walked through the open door. Instantly, I was gagged by the overwhelming smell of cigar smoke.

"For cryin' out loud, Colonel," I said between coughs, "Your lungs must look like charcoal. I'm gonna get cancer just from walking in here."

He chuckled dryly, then blew a puff of smoke into the air.

"Trust me. Of all the things on this planet that are trying to kill me, these cigars are the least of my worries."

I smiled "Can't argue with that. Hawkins said you wanted to see me?"

"Yeah, have a seat, Dawn."

He leaned forward and kicked a small rolling chair from beneath his desk. I stopped it with my hand, then sat down.

"First off, I wanted to know how you were making it after your fall."

I raised my hands, "I suppose I'm doing fine."

He chuckled, "Glad to hear it. That was some hit you took."

I gave a smile that quickly turned into a concerned frown.

"How many men did I lose, Colonel?"

He sighed and coughed a little.

"Eleven confirmed KIA. There's six more MIA."

I shook my head, "Those six are as dead as the other eleven and you know it."

He stamped out his cigar. Ashes floated to the floor, before flickering out on the cold cement.

"Don't lose faith, Dawn," he said, "We're making progress."

I shook my head, "What progress? Show me one thing we've accomplished. The only good we could do for this place is to eradicate the tribes, but so far they're eradicating us."

"That's not true," he said.

I didn't feel like arguing with him. There was no point.

"Is there anything else, Colonel?" I asked.

"Yes, actually there is."

He reached across the desk and handed me a crisp piece of paper.

"Just came in today," he said, as I began to read.

Attention
Soldiers of the Eighth Ranger Battalion need to report to Sector Three, earth date, September 3rd at seven-hundred hours. General Dwight Stacks will be presenting information relevant to the battalion at this time. Attendance is mandatory for all units.
Colby Scott,
Private first class and secretary of General Stacks.

I looked up from the letter and grinned. General Stacks was one of four, well now three, men in control of the entire Xavier Project. What he wanted with us was beyond me.

"Should be interesting, huh?" I said.

Colonel McBride laughed, then lit another cigar.

Chapter 2

The next couple of days passed by rather calmly, but I had a feeling that was about to change. Yesterday had marked the arrival of General Stacks, and according to the letter, he was to be speaking in two minutes. I walked out of the barracks, savoring the warm morning air, and began jogging towards the center of the base. By the time I got there, a crowd of soldiers had already gathered. A wooden podium, with three microphones extending from its top, had been set up, and two guards stood at either side of it. The sun glinted off their erect rifles, and I could tell by the sweat on their faces, they had been there for over an hour. I saw the general exit his personal quarters and slowly make his way to the podium. He was a large, well-built man with short, grey hair and a long, scruffy beard. Every move he made screamed efficiency, and, judging by his scars, he was battle hardened.

He eyed the crowd for a solid minute before speaking.

"Soldiers of the Eighth Ranger Battalion. I am here to personally condone you for your accomplishments in the Scorpion territory."

Already, I was confused. It went against all reason that General Stacks would travel halfway across Xavier just to recognize a Ranger battalion.

"In the past five months, this unit has managed to secure three, ten mile sectors. That, boys, is remarkable. I would also like to recognize the medical staff of CSH 123. You ladies and gents have been patching up our boys with a survival ratio that any unit would be jealous of. Every man and woman at this base has been doing a mighty good service for your nation, and, for that, I thank you. Having said that, there is one man in this battalion that has been going beyond what's expected of him for five years now. I would like to present Captain Michael Dawn with the American Alliance Medal of Extraterrestrial Combat."

I was shocked. There was a round of applause, through which, I replayed what had just happened.

"Come up here son," he said.

I made my way through the crowd and towards the elevated podium. During this time, General Stacks was continuing his spill. "To date, Captain Dawn has led more successful engagements with the Scorpion tribe than any other combat commander on Xavier. On average, he brings at least seventy percent of his force back with him, and that in itself deserves respect."

While grateful, I didn't feel deserving. My accomplishments only stood out when compared to other combat commanders. In truth, little over half of my assignments were considered a success a number that, before Xavier, would have been shameful.

I made my way up onto the platform until I was standing face to face with the general. Just before he shook my hand, he reached up to straighten his tie. This, however, was not the only thing he did. Before bringing his hand back down, I saw him switch off his microphone.

"Listen close son," he said as he shook my hand, "I want you to meet me in my quarters at eleven hundred. Don't make it obvious and don't talk to anyone about this exchange."

The general handed me the medal, then saluted. He paused for a second, his eyes still boring into mine, then turned sharply and walked away, his guards following close behind. I was stunned. The walk back to the barracks was full of congratulations and handshakes, however, I was far too bewildered to celebrate. Once inside my quarters, I set my alarm and crawled into my cot. Going to sleep, however, was practically impossible. My head was spinning, still trying to process what had just happened. For three hours, I lay there, but sleep never came.

At eleven hundred hours exact, I was outside the General's quarters. I nervously marched up the metal steps that led to the building's entrance, my boots clanging with each stride. My heart was racing and my throat had gone dry. After a deep breath, I knocked on the door. I heard the movement inside, and suddenly the door creaked open. General Stacks stood at the entrance.

"Come in, Captain." he said, ushering me inside.

I walked into the well-decorated room. Soft light poured from a

9

crystal fixture hanging from the hardwood ceiling. At the rooms center was a mahogany table, lined with cuisine I hadn't seen in over a decade.

"Sit down and have a bite to eat," he said, "That right there is the only lobster within three light years."

He erupted into laughter, then sat down, slowly sinking into the cushioned seat. General Stacks had already started in on his dinner. He looked up at me, chewing on a mouthful of potatoes.

"Go on, eat, you act like it's that slop they usually feed you."

I took a few bites of the lobster. After washing it down with a drink of wine, I pushed my plate aside.

"I don't mean to be hasty, General; after all, this is the best meal I've seen in twenty years."

He smiled, "That's what happens when you get that fifth star. Anyway carry on."

"Well, I've got so many questions; I think my curiosity is overpowering my appetite."

"Fair enough," he said, wiping his mouth on his napkin, "Let me start by apologizing for the way I set this up, but this is by far the most classified assignment I've ever dealt with, and that's saying a lot. Don't get me wrong, the recognitions were genuine, but they're not the primary reason for my coming here."

"What is your primary reason, General?"

He took a deep breath before replying.

"Three weeks ago today, the American Alliance, the European Alliance, and the Eastern Empire decided to embark upon a joint-task operation to recover five key objects."

"What does this have to do with the Eighth, sir?" I asked.

He started to speak, but stopped as if reconsidering his words. After a long pause, he continued.

"This mission's association with the Eighth Battalion is that you have been chosen to lead it."

I sat there, not sure what to say. My pounding heart felt like it had stopped entirely, and I started to sweat.

"Si-sir, I'm not even the highest ranking officer on this base." I said.

"Stars and bars on a uniform does not win battles, Captain. We need someone who can lead from the front lines. Not some high-brass givin' orders from a base fifty miles away."

10

I sighed, trying to grasp what this meant.

"I hope your right, General."

"I believe we are."

"What does it entail?" I asked.

He propped his boots up on the table and pushed himself back to the point of almost tipping. After adjusting his hands into a headrest, he sighed and began talking.

"You are going to be searching throughout the territories of the five tribes, looking for particular...objects of interest. They're going to be hard to find and hard to get out, but get them, and your mission's complete."

"Pardon my confusion, General, but what are the objects, and why the effort?"

He paused and inhaled deeply before responding.

"I suppose you need to know. Four months ago, an explorer got himself lost somewhere around Glacia. He was stumbling through the ice, didn't have a clue where he was. Then all of a sudden, the man stumbled upon an entire city! I mean skyscrapers, hundreds of buildings, lights, the whole nine yards, right in the middle of nowhere. He managed to sneak into it, and how he did, I'll never know. Anyway, he stumbled upon a massive globe. It showed all of Xavier, and only four locations were denoted with any significance, represented by symbols that were unmistakably scrolls. Luckily, the explorer had the good sense to video log the entire thing, and when he was found three days later, dead as a stone, we were able to recover the recording."

"Has anyone else seen this city?" I asked.

General Stacks cleared his throat, "No. President Young and Prime Minister Chambers both ordered their respective recon units to turn the place upside down, but neither attempt uncovered anything but a lot of ice, and a very angry Wolf Tribe."

"Maybe the video was faked." I said.

He shook his head, "No. I had every tech team at my disposal analyze the recording. They assured me with one-hundred percent accuracy that it was the real deal."

"So why go after the Scrolls?" I asked.

"We have reasons, which I am not at liberty to discuss, to believe that the documents on that map hold the key to finding out who or what built that city, why we can't find it again, and how we should approach it once we do."

He leaned forward and took a drink of wine.

"Is it clearer now?"

"As clear as it's gonna get," I said.

He chuckled then stood up.

"Good, you leave tomorrow morning at daylight. I suggest you get some rest. I'll see to it that your gear is packed for you."

"Thank you, sir." I said, as I stood and exited the building.

The night breeze sent goose bumps down my skin. Lightning flashed off to my right, followed by a booming clap of thunder. A strong gust of wind blew through the trees making an eerie howl. By the time I got back to the barracks, it was pouring down rain. I lay there listening to the drops pound against the tin roof. My thoughts ran wild. Once again, rest did not come easy, but after lying there for quite some time, I began to get drowsy. My eyes fluttered shut and I was enveloped into a sleep plagued by nightmares.

Soft beams of daylight filtered through the barrack's single window, stirring me awake. I got up and after getting dressed, headed out. Fresh puddles lay scattered everywhere across the base, and a cool mist still hung in the air. I pulled my jacket a little tighter and trekked towards the LZ.

Private Hawkins was waiting for me, my gear in hand, standing on the edge of the chalked out landing zone.

"You didn't forget anything did you?" I asked.

"No sir. I packed everything on the general's list. I swear you got more firepower here than a Gunship."

"I may need it, Private."

"Well, I wish ya the best of luck, Captain."

"Thanks, Hawkins, I may be needing that too."

I heard the blades of a helicopter churning through the air. Off in the distance, I could see it rising up over the mountains, heading this way.

"There's my ride."

Hawkins nodded and gazed up at the incoming craft.

The helicopter hovered down, until its shiny landing skids gently

12

bumped the center of the white H. The craft's twin rotors were deafening, drowning out my thoughts and sending dust flying into my eyes. Hawkins quickly helped me throw my gear on board. I ducked beneath the whirling blades, far lower than was actually necessary, and slipped in through the cabin door. As the chopper ascended, I gave Hawkins a final salute, holding it until the base appeared as nothing more than a child's toy.

"Welcome aboard, Captain," I heard loudly through two speakers on either side of my head, "This is your pilot, Lieutenant Richards, speaking. We will be cruising at a speed of two-hundred and twenty mph. Our destination is Fort Celtic. It should take about an hour to get there, providing we actually make it that far. Anyway, just settle back and enjoy the flight. You Army boys don't get off the ground much."

I leaned back against the worn seat and scanned the forest below. Thick brush, dotted with small ponds and streams flew beneath us. A flock of red and white plumaged birds sailed up and out of the dense timber, obviously startled. I watched the scenery rush by for the entirety of our flight, letting the beauty of the landscape enthrall me, something that on the ground, was too dangerous to allow.

After an hour of silence, the pilot spoke again, his voice jolting me out of my wistful trance.

"We are now landing at Fort Celtic."

I looked down and saw the landing zone, growing closer and closer until the circle of white seemed to engulf us. The chopper's skids nudged into the asphalt, bringing the craft to a stop. The pilot flipped a switch and the cabin doors slid open. I threw my gear over my shoulder and leaped to the ground, once again being very cautious of the craft's whirling blades. Once I was a safe distance away, the pilot gave a quick salute and lifted off into the sky. I scanned my surroundings, taking only a second to locate the fort's main entrance. With gear in hand, I took off towards the gate.

"Can I see your orders, please?" asked a middle aged warrant officer in charge of commanding Fort Celtic's main entrance.
I handed him a pair of crumpled papers I'd shoved in my back pocket. He frowned as he took them, obviously displeased with my

storage method. After taking great pains to straighten them back out, he flitted his eyes across the page, digesting the information far quicker than I thought possible.

"Barrack thirty-six," he said, pointing to a line of dull grey buildings not twenty meters from the entrance, "Your squad's waiting for you."

I nodded and walked through the gate. All around, soldiers were training in everything from distance shooting to hand-to-hand combat, reminding me of my own stay at Fort Celtic. All recruits were required to train here for three grueling weeks before being deployed. Even though they had years of military experience on Earth, it was nothing like what Xavier could throw. I walked past the line of barracks, scanning the doors for the number thirty-six. It only took me a minute to find it. I made my way up to the thick metal door, somewhat anxious about going inside. I had no idea how foreign soldiers would respond to being placed under the command of an American. I straightened my cap and took a deep breath, before pushing open the door.

The room was overwhelmingly dull, consisting of nothing more than concrete walls and twin-sized cots. Soldiers, representing all three super-nations, were spread throughout the room. A few were playing cards, some were lifting weights, and others were simply resting. They all ceased what they were doing, staring awkwardly for a few tense seconds before rising to attention.

"At ease," I said, "Now, I assume you have all been briefed."

"Yes, sir," They said unanimously. "Good then, we can skip right to introductions."

I nodded in the direction of a tall, muscular African American clothed in Navy whites.

"I am Corporal Luke Jackson, SEAL Team Eleven."

"Glad to have you along."

I pointed at the next in line, a short, stocky Russian literally covered with scars.

He spoke with a thick accent, "My name is Armon Yakutsk, Spetsnaz."

"It's an honor to fight with you."

Next was a bit lankier man with short blonde hair.

He spoke in an Irish accent, "I'm Corporal Rodger O'Brian,

14

IRA sniper."

I saluted and moved on. I paused for a moment on the next in line. She had long red hair and flashing green eyes. She wasn't dressed like the others. She was outfitted with more of an urban warrior's attire.

She announced herself, "Agent Ashley Collins, head assassin of the CIA."

I once again paused for a second. "Can I ask you something?"

"Maybe," she said

"What's a pretty thing like you doing out here?"

She looked me in the eye and smiled roguishly, "The prettier the rose, the sharper the thorn."

I nodded, not entirely convinced. "Very well. Glad to have you along."

The next soldier in line was the strongest looking thus far, with a shaved head and medium height.

"I'm Sergeant Peter Stillworth, Israeli Commando."

I continued moving down the line to a tall tan kid with steely eyes.

"I'm Private John Rice, Green Beret."

Next was a man who looked to be in his fifties with short grey hair, a scruffy grey mustache, and an air that screamed strict military.

"Sergeant Daniel Smith, USMC Seventh Division."

I nodded, still having to get used to hearing divisions that, before the Xavier Project, did not exist.

Next was a thin, but muscular Englishman with a happy-go-lucky smile.

"Private Jim Roberts, RAF paratrooper, at your service, sir."

The next in line struck me as odd. He didn't look a bit like the others. He was of an average stature, but didn't seem as hardened as the rest. He had wavy brown hair rather than a buzz cut, and his attire was that of a few explorers I'd seen.

"And I am Charles Gatling, ER physician."

"May I ask you a question, Doctor?"

"Certainly, Captain."

"Do you have any idea why a combat medic was not chosen in your place?"

He shook his head, "No sir, I do not, but if it is my ability to keep up your questioning, I believe I am more than capable. I have three years experience as a planetary field researcher and explorer before the military so thoughtfully coerced me to resume my medical practice."

"Do you have any idea what this assignment entails?" I asked.

He exhaled loudly, "No sir, but I do hope it doesn't involve blood. Being a surgeon and all I really can't handle the stuff."

I frowned, not pleased by his sarcasm.

"We will see just how much you can handle, Doctor."

I paused for a second, before continuing.

"My name is Captain Michael Dawn, Eighth Battalion of the Army Rangers. As I am sure you all were informed, we have been entrusted with the most shrouded, and arguably most important mission in the history of the Xavier Project. You also know, if you've had any experience on this planet at all, that past those gates is hell. Everything that walks, crawls, swims or flies wants to kill you and is very good at doing so. I know some of us here aren't used to being on the same side. In fact, I was doing a little research the other day, and I found out that this will be the first joint operations undertaking in over twenty-one years. That being said, we *must* operate as one if this mission is to be successful."

I paused, "Any questions?"

No one said anything.

"Well, that's all I've got to say. Get some rest."

I noticed a second door at the far end of the barracks.

"What's in there?" I asked.

Private Roberts spoke up.

"That's your private quarters, chap, er Captain."

"Agent Collins, you can have it if you'd like." I said.

She smiled and started walking towards the door as soon as the words left my mouth.

"Thank you, Captain."

I found a cot that was unoccupied and tossed my gear beneath it, before crawling on top. I pulled the digital map of the Scrolls locations from my pocket and scanned it over. We were to start in the territory of the Scorpion tribe, then move on to the Brute's territory, then to the Spider tribe, then the Marsh tribe, and finally to the arctic domain of the Wolf tribe. After linking the coordinates to my GPS, I folded the map back up and put in my pocket. I rolled over and closed my eyes, needing rest. There was no telling what tomorrow had in store, and even with the world's best soldiers and a doctor to take care of their wounds, the likelihood of our success was slim.

Chapter 3

Sunlight filtered through the barrack's single window, slowly stirring me awake. I stretched my arms and rose, surprisingly eager to start the morning. Upon exiting the cot, I saw a small scrap of paper, pinned to its edge. Scribbled across it in pencil was a short message.

Captain Dawn,
Meet me at building eighty-two at six-hundred hours.
Colonel Farris

I glanced at my watch. It was already a quarter 'till, putting me in a bit of a rush. I threw on my uniform and quickly laced up my boots. Corporal Jackson and the Spetsnaz, Yakutsk, were up as well, but neither of them bothered to ask where I was going. After strapping on my sidearm, I creaked opened the barracks door. The cool morning pierced my clothing like an icy needle, sending chills down my arms. I quietly shut the door, not wanting to wake those still asleep just yet and began jogging across the base. Loose gravel crunched beneath my boots, generating the only sound that penetrated the tranquil morning. The soft glow of daybreak settled on the base, reflecting off the stainless steel buildings like a signal mirror. I remembered from my own time at Fort Celtic that building eighty-two was the quarters of the fort's commanding officer, and while Colonel Farris was not in this position three years ago, it was not unlikely that he was now. Units on Xavier tended to go through commanders often, as their failures were both common and unaccepted. I could see the building in the distance. Its larger size and upscale furnishings made it easy to spot. I jogged up to its wooden door, the only building I'd seen to have one. After three hearty knocks, it opened. A middle-aged man in standard issue trousers and a sleeveless shirt stood at the entrance. He eyed me from behind a pair of worn glasses before inviting me inside.

"Have a seat," he said, pointing to a cushioned chair at the edge of the dimly lit room. I eased into the seat, taking in the colonel's overpowering sense of militaristic decoration. On the wall hung original photographs from every war in U.S. history, along with rifles from each era. Next to me was a bookshelf, stacked with manuscripts on combat, ranging from Sun Tzu's *Art of War*, to biographies of General Patton.

"You said you wanted to see me, sir?" I said.

"So I did," he said, sitting down in the chair across from me, "Consider this a second briefing from a man who knows a lot less about your objective and a lot more about this area."

He chuckled after saying this, but I could tell he was frustrated that a captain knew more about *anything* than he did.

"First," he said, "Let me tell you that the sole reason Fort Celtic was chosen as your point of deployment was its proximity to your first, um, object of interest."

I was slightly surprised that he'd not been briefed about the Scrolls, though I suppose the only reason was my unfamiliarity with knowing more than my superiors.

"How are we going to reach our destination?" I asked.

He sighed and leaned his chair back.

"You'll have to march."

"What?" I said.

He paused, and I could tell he was pondering the best way to explain this decision.

"Captain," he said, "Have you ever been in an unsecured sector of the Scorpion territory, or any territory for that matter, when an aircraft landed?"

I shook my head, slightly embarrassed that I hadn't.

"Every hostile within miles watches the thing until it touches down, and then ambushes its occupants by the hundreds. The same goes for ground transport except it's far worse. There is simply no way we can safely get you where you need to be. The only option is for you and your men to go on foot and try to lay as low as possible until you've retrieved whatever you're supposed to. After that, you can guarantee there will be a craft with guns blazing to get you out of there."

19

I nodded, now much more apprehensive about the assignment.

"In the meantime," he said, "You will be monitored by weapons equipped satellites, as well as a PredatorIV drone, but they won't be able to intervene unless you're really in a tough spot, or else we're back to the same problem."

I sunk back into the chair, my eagerness to get started entirely shot.

"Anything else, sir?" I asked.

"That's all I've got," he said, "Except that if the Scorpions care anything at all about what your trying to retrieve, they're sure not gonna give it up easy."

"I didn't figure they would," I said.

"My men will see you out the gate," he said, "After that there's nothing more I can do."

"Thanks, Colonel," I said as I headed for the door, "You've already helped a lot."

By the time I arrived back at the barracks, the rest of the squad was up and dressed in full combat attire.

"We had a feeling we'd be moving out before long," Private O'Brian said.

"You were right," I said.

I slid my pack from beneath my cot and unzipped it. The GX5 combat suit was on top, neatly folded into a compacted rectangle. I picked it up, letting the shiny black fabric unravel in midair. The GX5 was made of carbon-reinforced fibers, was equipped with a parachute, communication devices, and night vision optics, was waterproof, fireproof, and was, overall, a soldier's best friend. I pushed my legs into the suit, then pulled the rest over my shoulders. After taking almost five minutes to secure its seemingly endless fastenings, I grabbed my pack and headed out the door. By this time, the alien sun was fully above the horizon, sending beams of warmth raining down. I could see Colonel Farris and a small escort waiting for us by the fort's entrance. With troubling reservations, I took off towards them.

The unnerving chorus of alien insects rang loud and unending as we neared Colonel Farris and his men. The luscious vegetation of the Scorpion territory was all that I could see beyond the sparking wires of the fort's electrified fence. As we passed him, the colonel extended a salute to each of us.

"You guys have everything you need?" he asked.

"I hope so," I said.

He nodded, "Good luck,"

He pressed a quick combination into the gates electronic lock, then stood aside. The mechanism beeped, then unlocked, causing the gate to swing open. Colonel Farris and his men stood by until we had exited the fort's security, then, after locking the gate shut, he saluted and left. The world beyond the safety of Fort Celtic looked treacherous. I had the impulse to turn back, but this feeling was not new. I took my rifle from its sling, then after making sure it was loaded, headed into the brush.

"You've had run-ins with the Scorpion tribe before haven't you?" Jackson asked, after thirty minutes of fighting through the rough terrain.

"Yes," I said, "Have you not?"

"Nope," he said, "SEAL Team Eleven has never performed operations in their territory, sir. We've spent most of our time trying to secure sectors of the Marsh territory."

I brushed aside a thick vine, laden with deep red flowers.

"Well, Corporal," I said, "You've got to keep your eyes open for ambushes. The Scorpions may not be the most advanced of the tribes, but I believe they're the craftiest. Not only do they... "

"Hey, Captain," Private Roberts said, "You need to see this."

I turned back around and saw him pointing at the sky. I traced my gaze up until I was looking at the top of a magnificently tall tree. The bark was black and lined with thorns, the leaves dark green, just like a million other trees on Xavier. However, from its uppermost branches hung a grisly array of corpses, ranging from a cattle-like species known as minwors, to human beings. They were dangling from their feet, bound by strands of vine that were woven together into crude ropes. All of them had been skinned, some stripped of their flesh entirely. Large flies swarmed around them, landing every so often to enjoy their gruesome meal.

"This is a butcher tree," Gatling said, not looking up from a strange symbol carved into its base, "The Scorpion tribe hunters store their kills at the top of designated darkthorn trees. The lower

21

ranking members of the tribe are then tasked with dressing the kills and preparing them for consumption."

Agent Collins stepped forward. Her face was stern, but just as Dr. Gatling, she did not seem revolted by the sight.

"If these trees were merely a means of storage, the bodies wouldn't be displayed like this."

"She's right," Gatling said, "Before humans arrived on Xavier, the Scorpions stored their kills at the bottom of pits, then covered them over with dirt. Now though, they hang them from trees as an intimidation factor…and at times a trap."

I heard at least three safeties click off after he'd said this.

"If this were a trap, they'd have sprung it long before now," I said reassuringly.

"Still," Gatling said, "This means that the tribe is in the area, and between hunters bringing fresh kills and workers coming to clean them, these trees are visited at least a dozen…"

A small pebble bouncing off his head silenced him.

"Use your mike before you get us killed," I heard Smith say through my in-helmet radio, "Do you want every Scorpion out there knowing where we are?"

Gatling frowned, then switched his communications on. I started to resume our march, but a small whisper stopped me.

"Hostile located," it said.

I turned to see O'Brian, lying on the ground with his eye pressed against the scope of his rifle. I could see movement in the direction he was pointing, could see sunlight reflecting off razor sharp scales. I immediately recognized the source as not only Scorpion, but also one of lower rank. No hunter, much less warrior, would have been spotted so easily. I motioned for everyone to get down, though most had already done so, then lowered myself onto the foliage-covered ground. The Scorpion was not twenty yards away and coming closer. In his clawed hands, he was clutching a sack, made of sewn vines and covered with blood. His large frill rippled with each step he took, and his barbed tail flicked back and forth. His reptilian eyes darted left and right, but as of then, he did not see us.

"Permission to engage?" O'Brian whispered.

"Negative," I said.

I lay there, trying to remain as motionless as possible, both my

22

heart and mind racing. Taking him out would have been easy. He was a juvenile, armed only with a small knife used for skinning. Yet the sound of gunfire would bring every Scorpion in the area down on us. Before I could think of a solution, I saw Stillworth inching his way towards the tree's base. In his hand was a knife, no shorter than a foot long and with deep serrations running down its back. He reached the tree without a sound, the only evidence of his movement being a slight sway in the grass that could have easily been blamed on the wind. The young Scorpion drew closer, his yellow eyes focused on the tree's top, having no warning he was walking into a trap. He reached out his hands and grabbed hold of the tree, his raptor-like feet inches from Stillworth's face. The nimble creature sunk his claws into the bark, preparing to hoist himself up, but fate had other ideas. Before the unsuspecting Scorpion could even begin to scale the tree, Stillworth bolted up, bringing his arm down in a full arc and driving the blade of his knife deep into the creature's skull. The dark green juvenile convulsed once, then fell to the ground, his legs slowly kicking in a nervous response. I was both amazed and pleased with the Israeli's skill. Anything less than a cut to the brain would have sent the Scorpion into a shrieking frenzy that would have been just as detrimental an alarm as gunfire. Stillworth tugged his blade free, then wiped it clean on the grass.

"Come on," I said, "We need to get away from here."

Chapter 4

After twelve hours of clawing our way through the thorns, vines, rocks and underbrush that were the signature of the Scorpion territory, the sun had regrettably sank. I glanced at the GPS and shook my head. We'd only lacked two more klicks reaching the approximated destination, and, while I knew it would have been almost impossible, I'd hoped to have retrieved the Scroll and been picked up by sunset. An overnight stay with the Scorpions was something I could do without. Now though, with the first stars slowly twinkling into view, it was unavoidable.

"We'll make camp here," I said, "I want two sentries on duty throughout the night. I'm willing to take the first shift. Any volunteers to join me?"

After a second's pause, Sergeant Smith stepped forward.

"I will, sir."

"Good," I said, "The rest of you can figure out the order after that. It doesn't matter to me, as long as after three hours, there are two more to take our place."

They slid their packs from their shoulders and began making a crude campsite. Gatling passed out MREs and the rest began unfolding their sleeping gear. Tents were a luxury we'd not been given, and I could only hope that over the course of the mission, the weather remained tolerable. Me and Smith slowly trekked to the edge of the makeshift camp, and sat down. A slight breeze blew wispy clouds across the night sky, covering and uncovering Xavier's twin moons, the blood red Advenacruor and the lunar-like Albus. I lay my rifle against my lap, then rested my head against the base of a small tree. Smith came and sat down beside me. He put his weapons down, and began rummaging through his gear.

"Jerky?" he said, offering me a foil package.

"Thanks," I said, taking it from his hands.

Insects chirped all around us, as if they were serenading the moons above them.

"Why did you come to Xavier?" I asked, after a minute of silence.

He sighed and paused before answering.

"For ten years I fought in the Great War. With every battle I was in, I told myself that I was making earth into a place where my children could live in peace and safety. Finally, I realized this wasn't true. So, here I am now, trying to do the same thing, trying to make this killing pit better than the one I left."

He looked over at me, "What about you?"

I stared up at the stars watching them fade in and out.

"I had nothing on earth. I was nothing on earth. I guess I saw the Xavier Project as a second chance."

He nodded, "We all did, sir."

I smiled, but my thoughts quickly morphed into apprehension when I considered where we were. The surrounding woods looked just as forbidding as the ones outside my house as a child. Every shadow appeared to be a Scorpion with weapon in hand and ready to attack. Every rustling of leaves reminded me of the same. I clutched my rifle a little closer and prepared for a very long night.

After two hours of sitting motionless, scanning the woods for creatures that move like ghosts, Roberts and Jackson came to relieve us.

"Come on, chap," Roberts said, "You look like you could use some rest."

I nodded and stood up. The others were lying in a tight circle, tossing and turning constantly. I quietly unraveled my own bedding, then lay down beside them. Even though the inch of blankets did little to shield the rocky ground, or the wind, to merely relax was a blessing. Before I could even kick off my boots, I was asleep.

Warm sunshine streamed down on my face. I slowly opened my eyes and stood up. Looking around, I noticed that the area was much more welcoming in the daylight. Large red and purple flowers lined the ground, and a coating of dew glistened on the grass. I took a deep breath, inhaling an aroma of coffee that was drifting through the air. Dr. Gatling was huddling over a small fire,

25

stirring a pot from which the scent came.

"Good morning Captain," he said, "Want some coffee?"

"You sure the fire's a good idea?" I asked.

"Don't worry," he said, "There's no smoke."

I looked down at the fire, which was blazing, but not producing even a wisp of vapor.

"What's that you're burning?" I asked.

"Carryfall bushes." He said, "They're a smokeless wood."

"Hmm," I said, "In that case let's have some coffee."

He handed me a tin cup full of the steaming brew.

"You sure know a lot about this area, Doctor," I said.

He smiled, "And there is the answer to your question."

"What question?" I asked.

"You were wondering why they chose me instead of a combat medic. There's your answer."

I chuckled, amused that he'd remembered.

"Glad to have you along, Doctor."

I stood up, intent on waking the others, but realized they were already up.

"We'd better get moving," I said, "Waiting here isn't going to accomplish anything."

The squad grabbed up their gear, then followed my lead back into the woods.

"Where do ya suppose we'll find the bloody thing?" Roberts asked, after twenty minutes of marching.

"What do you mean?" I asked.

"The Scroll," he said, "It's not like whoever placed it is just going to leave it out in the elements to be destroyed."

"So?" Stillworth said.

"So, have you seen any such place?" Roberts asked.

Stillworth spat on the ground.

"Not yet. But we're not there yet, are we?"

I flipped out my GPS and switched it on.

"Actually we're only …"

"Whoa Captain!" Rice said, as he jerked me backwards by my collar.

I looked up from the screen, about to severely dispute his actions, when I saw where I was headed. Suddenly, and without warning, the ground had split, forming what looked like the fault line of a *major* earthquake. Pebbles and bits of dirt I had knocked loose trickled off the edge and fell into the abyss.

"Thanks, Corporal," I said, taking a few more steps back.

"How in the world are we supposed to get across that thing?" Jackson asked.

"Not across," I said, looking back at the GPS, "Down. According to this we are only a hundred meters from the Scrolls approximate location."

"That doesn't necessarily mean it's down there," Roberts said.

"You said yourself that it wouldn't be anywhere that wasn't shielded," I said, "Do you see any place like that around here?"

He shook his head, "I suppose you're right, chap."

I turned back to the edge, my stomach growing weak at the thought of climbing down it.

"How do we get to the bottom?" I asked.

"I've got rappelling gear," Rice said.

"How long are the lines?" Smith asked.

"Two-hundred meters." he said.

"We just need to know how far down it is," Jackson said.

As soon as he got the words out, I heard O'Brian speak up.

"It's exactly two-hundred and twenty one meters to the bottom, lads," he said, leaning over the gorge's edge, with his rifle pointed down, "Scope's got a rangefinder on it."

"We'll just have to scale the last twenty," I said.

Rice nodded, then began securing the lines to a large tree near the edge. It only took him a minute to get the system fully rigged.

"Rice," I said.

"Sir?"

"I want you go first and find a ledge for us to dock on. Gatling, I want you to go second."

"Why me?" Gatling asked.

"'Cause if there is any time lost on your way down the rest of us can make it up. The longer we're waiting here, the more likely we are to be attacked."

Gatling frowned, but then smiled, "I'll be sure and take my time."

Rice gave the line a tug, then disappeared over the edge of the canyon. I carefully leaned over to see how it was going. He was sliding down the line with practiced ease, and in minutes, he had reached the bottom.

"I found a ledge," Rice radioed, "But I'm not sure it's big enough for all of us."

"We'll have to make do," I said.

"Alright, you're next." I said, motioning towards Gatling.

He swallowed, and then cautiously approached the edge. Gripping the line tight in both hands, he peered over, "Oh gosh, I don't think this is such a good idea. I'll just stay up here."

He started backing away, but Collins stopped him.

"If you don't start down that canyon I'm gonna start chunking these at you."

She held up a few small darts.

"They're usually tipped with poison, but they'll hurt without it."

Gatling smiled, "You wouldn't."

A few seconds later Gatling was hopping around in circles, a small dart stuck in his leg.

He pulled it out and glared at Collins, "Why you!"

She held up another dart and smiled. Gatling gritted his teeth and started down the line, cursing and mumbling the entire time. His eyes were clenched shut, his knuckles white, but slowly he made his way to the bottom.

"I'll go next." Yakutsk said.

He grabbed the line and slid down.

After twenty or so minutes, it was only me and Collins left.

"Ladies, first." I said.

She grabbed the line and disappeared over the edge, taking only a minute before she was safely down. I looked over the edge and swallowed dryly. The canyon appeared much higher than before.

Heights aren't my thing, I thought to myself. Slowly, I allowed my grip on the cable to slacken, and I began to slide. Halfway down, I stopped. The wind was picking up, blowing dust into my eyes. I wiped them on my shoulder and glanced down. Below, the squad was eagerly waiting, shielding their brows and staring up at me. With a deep breath, I started back down, but just as I began to rappel, the line went limp. I clawed at the rock for maybe a half second before gravity had its way. The air rushed past me, sending my stomach into my throat. Inside, I was panicking. Even if my parachute did activate, which they were notorious for failing, it would leave me injured, and in this crosswind, up to a mile from the rest of the squad. I saw the canyon face flying past in blur, and, at that point, saw my lifeline. A small tree was jutting out from the wall of the canyon, like a lighthouse on a stormy coast. Almost instinctively, my hand shot out and grabbed hold of the sapling. The jolting stop nearly ripped my arm from its socket, but I held on for dear life. Dirt being loosened at the base of the tree tumbled past me and to the rocky bottom.

"Hang on, Captain," someone shouted from below.

I couldn't help but get irritated at the irony in this. Just as I felt myself slipping, a grappling hook sailed through the air and wrapped itself twice around the tree. I quickly grabbed on and slid down, gripping the line tight enough to choke it. When my feet finally touched solid ground, I collapsed.

"What happened?" Rice asked.

"Did the line break?" Roberts asked.

"No," Collins said, holding up the line's neatly severed end, "It was cut."

"Why did the coward not attack when he had the chance?" Yakutsk asked.

I took a deep breath, trying to shake off my brush with death.

"It was probably a worker," I said, regaining my composure, "At any rate they know we're here. Take a second to catch your breath, and we've got to keep moving."

I pushed myself away from the edge, wanting to distance myself from it as much as possible, until my back scraped against rock. I pressed my hands along the stone, relishing the solid ground, then leaned harder against the canyon face. Just as I took a deep breath and closed my eyes, it gave way.

Chapter 5

I tried to grip the edges of the tunnel, but it was no use. They were slick and covered with algae, much like rocks in a river. Light shined weakly from where I'd fell through, but suddenly it was as if someone switched it off. I could tell the tunnel had made a sharp turn, and after only seconds more of slipping downward, I felt the bottom disappear from under me. I hurtled into the now familiar feeling of free-fall, but this time, I couldn't see where I was falling to. I braced myself to smack into solid rock and landed with a splash. Icy cold water enveloped me, chilling my skin, shocking my senses, and dragging me down, into its cloudy depths. I was dazed. I had the urge to stay within the cool confines of the watery realm forever. Yet as I sank ever deeper, my mind began to catch up with my senses, and reality took hold. I thrust upwards, moving my arms and legs in frantic circles, trying desperately, against the weight of my gear, to break free of the water's deadly grasp. My lungs ached. I had the impulse to breathe, even though I was still fully submerged. Finally, the surface broke, reuniting me with precious air. I inhaled it with vigor, never more grateful for oxygen. Staying afloat, however, was still a struggle. I kicked franticly and began swimming in a direction that I could only hope would lead me to dry land. After swimming for a surprisingly short time, my hands struck something solid. I clawed at the smooth rock, trying to find a place to grab hold. Finally, my fingers sank into a crevice. With all the strength I could muster, I hauled myself out of the water. Dripping sounds reverberated all around me, splattering against rock and splashing into the lake. I felt along my left wrist for my suit's light, terrified of where I might be. My fingers finally fumbled across the small button, and with a shaking flick, I switched it on. The bright LED beam radiated from my wrist-light, illuminating the entire area and revealing it to be a small cavern. Large stalactites hung from its ceiling, their saturated tips the source of the constant dripping. About ten meters up the far wall, I saw the tunnel from which I'd fell. A strand of algae hung from its mouth, it too, dropping countless beads of water into the cavern lake. I stood and swept the light 360 degrees. The place was roughly a circle, with a diameter of around eight meters, and, most disappointingly, appeared to have no exits. I adjusted my pack, and walked to the nearest wall. What I intended to do when I got there escaped me, but on my way, something caught my eye. On the rock opposite of the tunnel, was a symbol. It was drawn in red clay and was no bigger than my hand, yet what it depicted was clear. I pressed the receiver on my helmet's radio. The first one to respond was Agent Collins.

"Where are you?" she asked.

"Did you not see the tunnel?" I said.

"Yes, but we couldn't imagine you'd actually fell down the thing."

"Guess again," I said.

"How are we going to get you out?"

"I think it's a question of how you all are going to get down here with me."

"What are you talking about?" she asked.

"I think I'm right where we need to be," I said, tracing my hand across the drawing...a drawing of a scroll.

After ten minutes of sitting with my back slouched against the wall, I saw a rope fall through the tunnel's mouth and unravel its way to the bottom. Roberts was right behind it, clutching the line for dear life. Upon reaching the tunnels edge, however, he stopped.

"Oh bloody hell," he said, shinning his light down.

"Toss me your gear," I said, scrambling to my feet, "It's almost impossible to swim with it."

He shed his pack and rifle, then tossed them down to me. After a deep breath and some curse words, he jumped from the ledge. No sooner did he splash into the lake, did Jackson jump as well. One by one they made their way down the tunnel, into the water, and finally, to the bank.

"I hope your right," Collins said, "'Cause if you're not, getting out of here is going to be horrible."

"Look," I said, pointing at the depiction of a scroll, "It must mean we're close."

"I think it means more than that." Gatling said, inspecting the symbol, "I think it means that the Scroll is literally this way. Look at these."

He ran his fingers along a small crevice that traced a table-sized circle around the drawing.

"Let's see if we can get it open." I said.

Stillworth, Yakutsk, and I placed our palms against the smooth stone and began to push. After some forceful encouragement, the rock began to move. We pushed it forward almost a meter before the circular block fell to the ground, revealing yet another down-sloping tunnel.

"How far down do you think that last tunnel put us?" I asked.

"I'd say about twenty meters," O'Brian said, "That ought to put us about level with the canyon floor."

"That means that this second tunnel is underground," I said grimly.

I could tell that everyone had reservations about going somewhere where we'd be so trapped, but there was no other choice. With weapons ready, we ducked into the shaft.

The stale air almost gagged me, making me quickly forget how grateful I'd been to breathe. Pools of water splashed beneath our feet and dripped from overhead, echoing throughout the tunnel in a way that I found very unnerving. My light flickered across the walls, illuminating a line of drawings that depicted all sorts of battle scenes. Up ahead, the tunnel made a blind turn. I shouldered my rifle and crept along the outside wall, slowly increasing my field of vision until I saw the shadow of a Scorpion. I stopped. My pulse was pounding, my breath short. There was no way my light could have gone unnoticed, yet the shadow never so much as stirred. I slowly eased around the corner, my finger already beginning to squeeze on the trigger, when I saw why. The shadow, while indeed that of a Scorpion, belonged to a creature long dead. A crude pole was holding him upright, and his scales had been charred black. The unfortunate Scorpion had in some way broken the rules, and as punishment, had been burned alive by his own kind. As the rest of the squad lit up the room with their lights, our location became terrifyingly clear. Within the confines of this small room, was a Scorpion torture ground. Strewn throughout were the bodies of almost every creature on Xavier, from the Brute tribe to humans. Their rotting mouths still appeared to be screaming for mercy, something the Scorpions don't usually give.

"I've seen some gruesome stuff lads, but this tops it all." O'Brian said, though I barely heard him.

I was focused on the remains of a particular soldier whose life had been ended in this dreadful place. His feet were strung from the rock ceiling; his body was covered in lacerations, but most horrifying of all, I recognized him. I was staring at the corpse of Lieutenant Mason, a man I had seen alive and breathing not three days before.

"We've got to move," I said, "They haven't been gone long."

I brushed past several more of the tortured carcasses, trying my best to not look into their eyes. The exit to the room was both obvious and welcome, and with no pause or hesitation, we left.

"Sir, I think it's sloping back up," Smith said.

We had been walking through the second tunnel for over twenty minutes with no sign of its end, or anything it might lead to. However, Smith was right about the gradually increasing slope.

"Is it just me, or can anyone else see light up ahead?" Roberts asked.

I stopped. If daylight was ahead, it would be a relief, but if Scorpion torches were the source, we were in a terrible situation.

"Get your lights off," I whispered.

One by one, the beams shut off until we were left in complete darkness, apart from a faint glow that settled up ahead.

"That's sunshine, lads" O 'Brian said.

I let my rifle slump and blew a sigh of relief. As we walked on, the glow grew brighter and brighter, until the tunnel emptied into daylight. I squinted my eyes, trying to force them to adjust. When they finally did, I realized that we were at the bottom of the gorge.

"Well, this is what you call 'square one'," Rice said.

"Maybe not," said Stillworth.

He was pointing about fifty yards ahead at the opposite side of the canyon wall. Carved into the rock and tangent with the ground, set another tunnel. I sighed, but reluctance would get us nowhere.

Just as I took off towards it, Smith stopped me.

"What the devil is that?" he said, looking up and shading his eyes against the sun.

I traced my eyes up the canyon until I was looking at what appeared to be stairs, cut into the reddish stone. Adjacent to them were long, flat lines of rock that were set into the canyon wall, much like benches. Together, they circled around a crater-like impression, with the canyon floor being its base.

"I don't know," I said.

"Well the main structure is exactly what it looks to be," Gatling said, "It's an impact crater, Crater Tysh to be exact. It's believed that the collision caused an earthquake that formed this canyon."

"That's fine, chap," Roberts said, "But who carved it into a flippin' stadium."

Gatling shook his head.

I was just about to turn away, just about to let the puzzle be solved some other time, when I saw movement along the crater's ridge. Mottled specks of green and tan poured down the canyon, leaping over rocks and charging down the carved stairs.

"Get back in the tunnel," I said, hoping they wouldn't see us, but fearing it was too late.

We hustled back into the crowded cavern, retreating just deep enough to stay concealed, but still have a good view of the exit.

"Yakutsk," I said, "I want you to watch our backs. We can hold this entrance indefinitely, but if we're attacked from behind, we are screwed."

I pressed my back against the tunnel's edge and slowly peered outside.

"How many?" Stillworth asked.

"Hundreds."

"What do we do?" O'Brian asked.

I started to reply, but the sound of throaty clicks, just outside the tunnel, stopped me. We pressed ourselves against the wall, trying our best to disappear into the shadows. The clicking purr continued, growing louder after each pause. Suddenly the tunnel went dark, the light blocked by the silhouette of a warrior Scorpion. I could see the outline of a spear in his hand. Feathers, bones, strips of leather, and crude tattoos, all symbols of rank, lined his scaled body. His raptor-like head slowly turned, until he was looking directly inside the tunnel. Just as he began to screech, Rice fired. A hefty load of buckshot slammed into the Scorpion's head, splattering his brain across the rock.

"Get ready," I said grimly.

We sat with weapons trained, waiting for them to charge into the tunnel by the hundreds, but after all of five minutes, nothing happened.

"You smell that, chaps?" Roberts said, sniffing the air.

Before I could answer, I felt a burning in my nose. Thick, black fumes floated through the tunnel from the direction we'd come. The noxious smoke grew thicker and thicker, burning my eyes, clogging my throat, and threatening to choke me out. I knew they were trying to flush us out. I knew that leaving the tunnel meant death. However, inhaling much more of whatever noxious thing they'd burned would bring the same result. I cursed inwardly, in disbelief that our defense had toppled so easily.

"On three we charge out," I said, between coughs, "One, two, three!"

I burst through the smoke shrouded entrance and into the hordes of waiting Scorpions. Instantly, they caved in around us, forcing us into close quarter combat. A greenish tan hunter charged me, a large knife clutched in his hand. Before he could plunge its blade into my chest, I swung the butt of my rifle at his head. The hefty stock caught the Scorpion above the eye, knocking him to the ground. Not giving him a chance to rise, I drove my bayonet deep into his side, pinning him to the arena floor. Before I could pull the blade free, an arrow sank deep into my leg, causing me to stumble forward. A dark green warrior rushed me, bringing the shaft of his spear crashing over the top of my head. I felt my limbs go weak, and despite how hard I fought to remain standing, I crumpled to the ground. No longer controlling my body, I could only lie there. After only seconds, I was consumed by the cool, dark wave of unconsciousness.

Chapter 6

My eyes slowly flittered open, but I saw only the ground before they closed again. I groaned and turned over, almost subconsciously. Slowly, they blinked back open. This time, I saw an overwhelming brightness. The penetrating beams of sunlight tormented my aching head, but also brought me into realization. Slowly, painfully, and in a dazed form of panic, I rose to my knees. Around me on three sides was nothing but stone, much like a small cave. Covering the one opening was a gate made of thick, knotted timbers. I noticed that my combat suit was gone, leaving me with only camouflaged cargos and a white tee shirt. The second thing I noticed was the searing pain in my left shoulder. I heard groaning, and only then did I realize that the rest of the squad was in the same predicament.

"Oh my head," Roberts moaned, slowly pushing his back against the wall.

"Where are we?" Jackson asked.

I shook my head, still staring at the gate. Suddenly, a bellowing roar vibrated through the wall on our right side, loud enough to send streams of dust trickling down from the ceiling.

"Brute," O'Brian said calmly.

He was the only one who did not seem startled by the dreadful cry.

"I spent three months stationed on the walls of sector 178953, sniping Brutes that got too close. That roar is all too familiar, lads."

"What's a Brute doing in the Scorpion territory?" I asked.

"I think he might be in the same shape we are," Roberts said, "Take a look outside."

The intense sunlight still sent waves of pain through my head, but I forced myself to stare out the gate. On the other side of the canyon were the same cave and bar enclosures. Trapped within their rocky confines were creatures ranging from the small, insect-like Spiders to massive Brutes, all fighting viciously to escape.

"I've seen this before." Yakutsk said.

"What do you mean?" I asked.

"Two years before I was sent to Xavier, my unit was charged with breaking up a multi-million ruble fight club at the heart of Kazan. It was run by drug lords, who made fortunes off taking wagers on who would triumph in their modern day coliseum. They had everything from Siberian tigers to men so deformed and enraged they looked like monsters, kept in cages facing the arena just like us."

"I'll tell you one thing," Jackson said, "If I get an opportunity to make use of it, I'm gonna give 'em a surprise."

He lifted back his sleeve and pulled a golf-ball sized spitfire grenade from a hidden pocket.

"I keep it there for emergencies," he said, "Worthless critters didn't see it apparently"

My spirits lifted slightly, though I don't know why. The chances of a single grenade getting us out of here alive were laughable. Suddenly, a strange trumpet bellowed and I heard gates to our left winch open. From them stumbled three men. Their eyes darted franticly, and two of them were near the point of weeping. If they saw us, they never acknowledged it as they ran past our enclosure close enough for us to reach out and touch. Another trumpet sounded, and two spears were thrown from the stands and into the center of the bloodstained arena. The stone tipped weapons thudded onto the dusty ground, clattering against each other as they did. The three men stared at them dumbfounded, not yet understanding their cruel predicament. One of them suddenly caught on, his eyes filling with shock. Without hesitation, he bolted forward and jerked one of the spears up off the ground. His companions were right behind him, but one, a younger man with white-blonde hair, was swifter. The blonde man dove upon the second spear, clutching it tight to his chest and rolling to avoid the clawing attempts of the third prisoner. At this, I heard the Scorpions watching the spectacle break into, loud, rapid clicks that unmistakably served as laughter. The third man, a tall Hispanic with a lion tattoo on his shoulder, was horrified, left standing in the dusty arena with nothing to defend himself with save his bare hands. Another trumpet sounded, but this one was continuous. The crowd of Scorpions stood, some of them moving aside to form a pathway that stretched all the way to the canyon's top. At the end of the pathway, a large throne was carved into the rock. It was lined with gold embellishments and draped with fur. A canopy, some ten foot tall and made of died leather, shadowed the seat. Its occupant, up until this point, had been shrouded in the darkness of this shade, but as he rose, I couldn't help but gasp in shock. I had never seen nor heard of a Scorpion as large as the one I was witnessing. As he made his way down the path, I realized that he stood at least two foot taller than any other member of the tribe. His waist was garnished with a belt of human skulls, and his arms were draped in tight nets of gold links. His entire body was covered with elaborate tattoos and gold piercings, and atop his sandy yellow head was a crown made of feathers and bones. I saw a small, worker Scorpion hand him a massive weapon. It had a polished staff and a scythe-like head, from which dangled feathers and strands of bones. The king Scorpion took the weapon then began strolling down the canyon stairs. As he passed, all of the other Scorpions bowed before him, scraping at the dusty rock and clicking rapidly. After five or so minutes of this slow and glorified entrance, the Scorpion was in the arena, not twenty yards from and facing the three terrified men. One of the prisoners, the blonde one who had fought for the second spear, turned and ran, a whimpered cry escaping his lips. The scorpion moved like lightning, flipping a stone knife from his belt and hurling it towards the back of the fleeing combatant. The forearm sized blade screamed through the air, turning end over end like a saw, before burying itself up to the hilt in the man's neck. The unfortunate prisoner crumpled to the ground without a quiver, his own blood adding to the crimson soaked sand. The man with the first spear, a short barrel-chested fellow with a shaved head and narrow eyes, hoisted his weapon and charged, screaming obscenities and curses at his foe. The king Scorpion stood his ground, not wavering in the least until the spearhead was mere feet from his chest. At this point, he spun sideways, dodging the thrust and sending his large tail crashing into the man's knees. I heard bones break and saw the man fall to the ground. He cried out in pain, then rolled over on his back. Towering over him and blocking the sun from his eyes, was the

Scorpion. The massive creature placed his clawed foot on the man's shoulder, pinning him to the ground. With a single strike that showed no sign of exertion, the Scorpion decapitated him. The crowd of spectators erupted into excited shrieks and shrills as their king hoisted the head into the air. At this point, something peculiar on the king Scorpion's neck caught my eye. It was jutting out like a piercing, but was beneath the skin. Every few seconds, it would flash in a streak of brilliant, blue light.

"What do you suppose that is?" Roberts whispered.

Before I could reply, the Scorpion threw the head into the crowd and turned upon his final victim. The unarmed man cowered, retreating backwards until he was pressed against the bars of our enclosure. The Scorpion advanced on him, his weapon hanging limply at his side. I could hear the man whimpering as he tried in vain to back up further. The Scorpion pressed forward until he was inches from his prey and staring down at him. I saw the man's hand tremble slightly, but then stop. Out of nowhere, he lurched forward and spat up into the king's face…a move that for the final seconds of his life, he would regret. The Scorpion trembled in rage, and a deep growl escaped his throat. He lifted his weapon in the air, then tossed it aside. The unfortunate captive had time for one final sob before the Scorpion was on him. The enraged king brought his right arm down in a blur, dragging his razor claws down the man's neck and torso. Before the blood had time to fall he had hit him again, sweeping his left hand across his victim's face in a blow that sent shreds of tattered skin flying to the ground. Again he struck, this time in an upward sweep that sunk his claws beneath the man's ribcage and hoisted him into the air. He held him there for a second, watching him convulse, before slamming his body into the rock wall some four times. At the fourth, he let him slump. The Scorpion stared at his bloody handiwork, his chest heaving in rage. Without warning, the Scorpion swung his hand in an upward sweep. His claws caught the man in the throat, and in an arcing heave, he sent the dead body sailing across the arena and into the stands.

The crowd watched in awe, too revering to applaud his feats. The king turned and began walking back up the carved stairs. Again, his followers scraped and bowed at his feet, almost tripping over one another in order to make room for his stroll back to the throne.

I saw two workers scamper across the arena and drag the bodies into a small opening at the canyon's west side. After ample time for the dust and mood to settle, the trumpets sounded again. However, this time, it was our gate that opened. My heart went to my throat, and I felt my knees go weak. I heard O'Brian behind me, mumbling a prayer. Two worker Scorpions entered our enclosure, but the only one of us they paid any attention was Yakutsk. They grabbed him by the shoulders, but to my surprise, he didn't seem dismayed. He let the two lead him out, not even bothering to struggle. Just as they exited the gate, I saw Jackson slip his grenade into Yakutsk's back pocket. Yakutsk made no gesture of acknowledgement, but I knew that he was aware of it. Once he was in the arena, our gate closed back. One of the Scorpions removed a large knife from his belt, and the second drew a hatchet. They bowed and placed the weapons into Yakutsk's hands. Again, I was surprised. Any respect that they had denied the previous three men, they were now showing Yakutsk. I realized that even his fight was to be fair, as the king's finger traced across the crowd and settled upon a light-green hunter. The Scorpion was sitting atop a large pillar and was clutching a bow and satchel full of arrows, his apparent duty being to eliminate any who refused to fight. He shuffled slightly, unsure of the king's command, but when the claw pointing at him never wavered, he moved, dropping his bow and scrambling down into the arena. Yakutsk clutched his weapons, his face grim. The Scorpion, still showing signs of hesitation, pulled a curved blade from his belt and charged. Yakutsk flew forward as well, screaming out in Russian. The two headed straight for one another, yet in the instant before their collision, Yakutsk sidestepped and brought his hatchet down into the Scorpion's head. The young hunter dropped and slid forward across the sand, leaving a trail of dark, almost black blood behind him. Yakutsk stepped forward and retrieved his weapon, wiping the blade clean across the Scorpion's back before returning to the arena's center. The crowd was stunned. None of them made a sound, and even the king remained still. After a moment of this silence, the king raised his hand and pointed to one of the warriors at his side. The thin, tan Scorpion bowed and sped down the stairs, jumping at least ten steps at a time before landing in the arena with a thud, causing a small cloud of dust to rise from his feet. In his hand, he was clutching a wooden club with two large canines embedded in the wood. He faced Yakutsk, a deep snarl emitting through clenched fangs. Suddenly, he darted forward, snaking side to side in a manner that stirred up clouds of sand, camouflaging him perfectly. Yakutsk's eyes traced his movement, trying franticly to keep sight of his attacker. Just before reaching his target, the Scorpion bolted to the side, sending a spray of dust into Yakutsk's face. Yakutsk stumbled backwards, and the Scorpion hit him, driving the spike of his club deep into his calf in a blow that took his feet from under him. Before Yakutsk could rise, the Scorpion was on top of him, pinning him to the ground. The warrior swung his hand down in an attempt to tear out his adversary's throat, but Yakutsk blocked his wrist with the shaft of the hatchet. The Scorpion was surprised, but his hesitation did not last. He brought his club down towards Yakutsk's head in a downward arc, but again his attack was blocked. Yakutsk's muscles strained and he groaned audibly as he struggled to keep the spikes that were hovering above him from pressing down into his eyes. Yakutsk dug the knife into the Scorpion's wrist, and with a heave, sent the creature sprawling off to the side, disarming him in the process. In seconds, they were both on their feet and facing each other. The Scorpion drug his tail across the ground, sending yet another wave of sand flying into Yakutsk's eyes, before charging forward in an effort to get in close. Yakutsk swung the hatchet at the Warrior's raptor-like head, however, the creature ducked beneath the blow. Jolting up like a spring, the Scorpion raked his claws up Yakutsk's abdomen, yet the Spetsnaz was not fazed. He drove the blade of his knife deep into his foe's ribs and swung his ax at his head. While mortally injured, the fierce Scorpion was still fighting. He caught the shaft of the hatchet in his hands, before spinning full circle in a double hit that grazed claw against cheek and brought his heavy tail crashing into Yakutsk's legs. Yakutsk sprawled back into the wall, but before the Scorpion could continue the attack, he lurched forward, hurling his ax like a baseball. The weapon somersaulted through the air before driving itself deep into the Scorpion's neck. The shocked reptile stumbled back, his throat dripping with blood. Not giving him a second to recover, Yakutsk kicked his foe to the ground. The Scorpion clawed and writhed at the sand, trying desperately to spray up dust, however, it was no use. The battle was over. Yakutsk planted his boot into the creature's head, then wrenched his blade free. With a grunt of exertion he drove it back into the wound, slicing through the dying Scorpion's vertebrae, killing him instantly. Again the crowd was shocked. Some began shrieking in dismay. I saw a massive, dark green Scorpion, outsized by only his leader, step forward, intending to enter the arena. However, he didn't take two steps before the king stopped him, pushing him back with his hand. The king Scorpion rose, his green eyes locked on Yakutsk. Slowly, and without breaking his stare, the towering reptile walked down into the arena. Yakutsk hardened his face. He tensed his muscles and put up a threatening front, but I could tell that he was both exhausted and terrified. Like a missile, the Scorpion flew across the ground and drove the point of his weapon into Yakutsk's shoulder. Yakutsk cried out, then whirled around in an attempted stab at the Scorpion's stomach. Unfortunately, it was like the king could anticipate his moves before he made them. The Scorpion sidestepped nimbly and spun his tail into Yakutsk's chest, sending him skidding across the sand. Yakutsk coughed up blood, his lungs apparently pierced by broken ribs. The Scorpion strutted over to him, taking great pride in how quickly he'd finished the fight. Inwardly, I was begging for Yakutsk to keep fighting, wanting like nothing else for him to draw blood on his conceited foe. Yet as the Scorpion raised his weapon high above his head, it appeared as if this would not happen. Yakutsk groaned and rolled over, still coughing up spurts of blood. Just as the Scorpion brought the tip of the scythe-like weapon crashing down, Yakutsk rose. He dodged the blow then, with a heave, brought the edge of his knife dragging across the Scorpion's chest. Dark blood, mingled with scales dropped to the ground. The Scorpion was shocked, and even though this wound was nothing but a scratch, his pride had been slain. He drove the blade of his weapon up into Yakutsk, lifting him up off the ground until their eyes were level. Yakutsk gurgled. His face shook, and his color drained, but suddenly, he smiled. His hand lifted from behind his back, a grenade pin dangling from his fingertips. The kings eyes filled with shock and a blazing sphere of fire engulfed them both, reducing the scene to nothing but wisps of dust and blood. The crowd was in disbelief. After a second of horrified silence, they began to shriek and tumble their way down the arena, heading straight for our enclosure.

Chapter 7

Just as the first of our would be killers touched foot to arena sand, another explosion sounded, this one born of a missile. Dozens of Scorpions went flying into the air, and before their scorched remains could hit the ground, another warhead impacted, this one collapsing the canyon wall and sending piles of rock tumbling down.

"Get back!" I said, fleeing to the far end of our enclosure.

Missile after missile rent the ground, sending the tribe scattering in every direction. After five minutes of the relentless bombing, there was silence. We sat crowded against the cavern's end, unsure whether it was safe to move.

"Look," Stillworth said, pointing at the gate.

A large chunk of rock had crashed into it, splintering the wood and making escape a possibility. We went at the crushed timbers with force, tearing and clawing with our bare hands until there was a hole large enough for us to exit from. Jackson stepped forward, but I stopped him.

"Wait a second," I said, "We have no idea what else has managed to escape out there."

"What do you suggest we do?" O'Brian asked.

"I say wait. Give it ten minutes. By that time, anything that was freed by the explosions should be well out of here."

Jackson frowned, but backed away.

"Ten minutes," he said, "And I'm out'f here."

I nodded.

"Say, Captain," Roberts said, "What do you suppose that blue light on the big yellow one's shoulder was?

"I don't know," I said, "But I sure didn't like the looks of it."

After waiting for ten minutes, a decision that was accepted by all after the roar of a Brute echoed through the canyon, we left, crawling one by one through the small hole in the gate. The scene outside was turmoil. Bodies were strewn everywhere, and the stadium was all but destroyed.

"We need to find our gear." I said, "Especially the radios. We may be here for a very long time if we don't."

"I thought that we were supposed to be under constant surveillance," Stillworth said.

"Not if they thought we were dead," said Gatling.

"What are you talking about?" Stillworth said, "You're a doctor. You know well we have monitors that transfer information back to HQ every second. The only way they would think us dead, is if we were."

"Unless someone cut the monitor chips out," Gatling said calmly, "The wounds on our shoulders are no coincidence, Corporal."

"He's right," I said, "We've got to find our gear."

"Did anyone see where the workers brought the weapons into the arena from?" O'Brian asked.

"They came in from the left," Roberts said, "Why?"

"They might have been interested in storing our arsenal for use in future battles." O'Brian said.

"Maybe," I said.

I scanned my eyes across the left side of the canyon, searching for a suitable spot to place an armory.

"Look," Smith said.

He was pointing to an enclosure that was identical to all the others except that it was larger and lacked a gate.

"Looks promising," I said, and started walking forward.

"Wait," Collins said, strolling up from our right.

In her hand was a shiny metal cylinder with scrolls carved all across it. Instantly, we recognized what she was holding.

"Let's get it open chaps and see what's inside." Roberts said.

"We can't do that." I said.

Roberts frowned, but I could tell that he knew this before he ever mentioned opening the case.

"Where did you find it?" I asked.

"It was attached to the top of the throne, or what was left of it."

"Good work," I said, "Let's get our gear and get out of here."

Sure enough, the gateless cavern was indeed an armory and a large one. The walls, floor, and even ceiling were lined with weapons, ranging from massive axes, to slim daggers and poisoned darts.

"Start searching," I said.

I riffed through the pile of blades, clubs, bows, and occasionally guns, but none of them proved to be ours. I was beginning to give up, when O'Brian found them.

"All here lads…and lass," he said, "Combat suits, weapons and packs."

"Divvy 'em," I said, reaching for the radio, "I'm going to get ahold of Stacks. The sooner we get out of here the better."

I tuned the frequency and pressed the receiver. After minutes of nothing but static, a voice finally came on.

"Dawn?"

"Yes, sir."

"We thought you were all dead."

"Close to it," I said, "Look, I can explain later. We are at the north end of Sector 11954 at the bottom of…"

"What's the name of this place?" I asked Gatling.

"Crater Tysh." he said.

"We're at the bottom of Crater Tysh." I told Stacks.

"You're kidding," he said, "That place just got bombed to dust."

"We know. Look, we need to get out of here. Is there any way you can arrange for a transport."

He paused.

"Are you the only one listening, Captain?"

I discreetly walked to end of the cavern.

"I am now," I said.

"First thing," he said, "Did you find the Scroll?"

"Yes," I said, "We're just waiting to get out of here."

"Good work, Captain, but that might be a problem."

"Why?" I asked.

Again he paused, "The bombing you were in the middle of was an attempt to exterminate a good bunch of the tribe while we had them in one spot. We sent three P4 drones to carry out the assignment, but as soon as the job was done, all three of them went

46

offline. Someone's attacked us Dawn, someone with weapons far beyond knives and spears, and until we can find the source, our fleet is grounded."

I couldn't believe what I was hearing.

"We can't just stay here, sir."

For a few seconds there was nothing but static.

"Ugh hmm, there is a European Alliance DX3 that could be rerouted to pick you boys up, but at the moment, we are considering the EA a potential threat."

"The EA a threat?" I said.

"We don't know," he said, "All we know is that three of our best aircraft don't just fall out of the sky."

I exhaled deeply.

"Sir, all things considered, I would still feel a lot safer inside an EA aircraft than I feel down here."

He sighed.

"I'll get ahold of Prime Minister Chambers right away. If things go as planned, the craft should arrive in twenty minutes. Whatever you do, don't mention a thing about the Scroll to whoever's piloting it."

"Yes, sir," I said.

I breathed a sigh of relief and walked back to the armory.

"Stacks has arranged for an EA craft to transport us to the Brute territory," I said.

"Did he mention who the pilot was?" Roberts asked, seeming thrilled with the prospect of seeing one of his RAF comrades.

"No," I said, "But the craft was French."

Roberts frowned, but didn't seem too disheartened. I grabbed my gear and after putting my combat suit back on, slumped back against the wall. Surprisingly, Agent Collins sat down right beside me, her long red hair practically touching my shoulders. I found myself shuffling nervously, something I hadn't done in years.

"Perfume," I said, "You know these things can smell stuff like that from a mile away."

"Not when it's purposefully fragranced like local wildflowers," she said smiling.

"Oh," I said, slightly embarrassed, "Did I mention that was a good job you did finding the Scroll?"

"You did," she said, "But you can say it again."

I smiled. For a moment, I wanted to allow feelings for her. For a moment, I forgot where I was. I sighed and casually turned away, sitting for the rest of the time in silence.

After twenty-five minutes, a small, grey craft, with rotors on either wing and one small one at the back, hovered down into the canyon.

"There's our ride, Chaps." Roberts said.

I quickly glanced to make sure that the area was clear, then began jogging towards the roaring ship. As I got there, the doors slid open. I threw my pack inside, throwing myself in right behind it. I was more than eager to get out of this place.

"Bonjour," said the pilot, a thin man in a French flight suit.

"Merci," Collins said, "Nous sommes très reconnaissants pour le transport."

"Impressive," he said, "And you are most welcome, but for the sake of our monolingual friends I will converse in English."

"Thanks," I said.

"My pleasure, sir," he said as the craft lifted off, "May I ask your assignment?"

I was about to say that it was classified, but before I could Collins cut in.

"I am supposed to eliminate a specific Brute that poses the threat of leading an uprising against Secured Sector 76512, one of the only joint nations sectors remember. These men are charged with getting me there."

He nodded. I glanced over at Collins and raised my eyebrows.

"It's a lot better than making him curious," she whispered, "This way the only story he spreads, is false."

I nodded, compelled to agree with her, even though I had always considered honesty the best approach.

"Prime Minister Chambers gave me the order to drop your force off at Sector 76515. We should be there in approximately an hour. In this time, feel free to rest. You all look as if you need it."

I nodded, agreeing entirely, then laid back against the craft's inside wall. It only took minutes for the consistent humming of the rotors to put me to sleep.

The gentle thud of landing woke me. I glanced at my watch,

purely out of habit. It had been an hour and ten minutes since I had dozed off, meaning that we had undoubtedly arrived at Sector 76515.

"I wish that I could help you further my friends," the pilot said, "However, all I can do is wish you luck."

"Thanks," I said, "You've done a lot."

He flipped a switch and the craft's doors slid open. With hesitation, I stepped out of its protection and onto the grassy plains of the Brute tribe.

Chapter 8

"We'll camp here for today," I said, after walking not twenty yards from where we were dropped.

"Here? I mean now?" Jackson said, "It's still four hours 'till the sun sets."

"We've had a *very* long day." I said, "I don't think jumping right into the next task is a good idea. Come daybreak we'll move out, but for now, we stay here."

I shrugged off my pack and placed it down beside a small shrub.

"For now," Gatling said, "We've got to take care of these injuries."

Before I had time to even consider a protest, he had sprayed my cuts with a thick, yellow liquid.

"What is that stuff?" I asked, but he didn't answer.

Almost immediately, the wounds began to scab over.

"Huh," I said.

I took a deep breath of the cool air and lay back on the ground.

"Should we post sentries, sir?" Smith asked.

I sighed. The area we were in was not considered a zone of high risk. It was in a sector that was unpopulated by the tribe and rarely even visited. Yet it was still an unsecured sector and, as bad as I hated to rob from our rest, carelessness could not be risked.

"Yeah, I think we should," I said, "Arrange the shifts, Sergeant."

He nodded and took off. At that time, Roberts walked over and sat down beside me.

"Ah, feels good to rest, doesn't it cha-Captain?"

I laughed a little.

"Roberts, do you call all of your superiors in the RAF 'chap'?"

He grinned roguishly.

"The ones who allow it I do."

I smiled and stared up at the bulging white clouds; a slight breeze was slowly dragging them across the sky.

"Do you ever find it unnerving how similar this place is to earth?" I asked.

"You mean other than its occupants?" he said.

"They look different," I said, "but in ways, they don't act it."

"Sometimes it's disturbing." he said, "Sometimes the similarities between the two play tricks with my mind. Then again at other times I see them as the handiwork of God, the perfect design for the living."

I frowned.

"Sure doesn't seem perfect to me."

He sighed, then changed the subject.

"How different do you think fighting the Brutes will be compared to the Scorpion tribe."

"A lot," I said.

In fact, this was an understatement. Brutes are the counterbalanced opposite of Scorpions. They are huge, standing almost nine feet tall and weighing around half a ton. They stand on two muscular legs that come to a hoofed foot. They have a bull's head, complete with massive horns, but their mouths were like what you might picture on a leach, with toothed mandibles extending all the way around it in a full circle. They have huge arms, about as big around as an outdated telephone pole and large, heavy hands, a lot like a bear's paw, but with fingers. Their skin is smooth and black with thick veins coursing through it. Unlike Scorpions, they're not much for concealment, preferring instead the art of open battle. Their weaponry is similar to an ancient knight's, consisting of massive broadswords, flails and axes, and complete with chain mail armor and a helmet that interlocks around their horns. I relayed this description to Roberts, but it didn't seem to concern him.

"Honestly, they sound like my mother-in-law." he said.

"You're married?" I asked.

"If you want to call it that. I haven't seen Emily for four years. How about you?"

I shook my head, "Nope, never had the time."

"That's a shame," he said.

"Hmm, maybe, maybe not."

After that I simply lay there, watching the sun slowly creep downwards until it disappeared below the hilly horizon.

A slight noise startled me awake. I grabbed a pistol from beneath my pack and rose. It sounded again, but this time I was able to identify it as human. I walked to the edge of our encampment and saw Sergeant Smith, leaning against a tree and clutching a worn picture in his hands. Any trace of the hard-nosed, militaristic traits that defined him had vanished. I thought I saw a tear in his eye, but it was too dark to tell.

"What's going on?" I asked.

"Personal matters, sir," he said straightening up slightly.

"You wanna talk about it?"

He sighed and looked up at the starry sky.

"Six years ago today, my ten and thirteen year old sons were executed by Rebel Commandos because they refused to give up information they didn't even know."

He hung his head back down again. I was truly sorry for him; The Great War had hit everyone hard. Radical terrorists, rebels and, regrettably, the formal militaries, had been causing turmoil for the past twenty years, plaguing an already dying world with war and destruction.

"We have to fix this planet," I said, "Make it safe, so people will be able to get away from all of earth's miseries and start over."

He lifted his head up and took a deep breath, "What makes you think that the people of Xavier won't have the same fate?"

"I don't know," I said, "Hopefully, if they don't learn their history, they won't repeat it."

Smith frowned, "Isn't that the other way around, sir?"

I shook my head, "No, I don't think so. Hopefully, the future inhabitants of Xavier know nothing about their violent past."

Smith nodded.

"Better get some sleep, Sergeant," I said, "We've got a lot of work to do tomorrow."

"Yes, sir."

I eased back over to where I'd been sleeping and sprawled out on the ground. My dreams that night were scrambled and frightening, so much so that morning came as a blessing.

I slowly rose, listening to my joints pop and crack, voicing their complaints of the hard ground. I turned my face towards the soft orange light that was creeping above the horizon. Overnight, the ground had been blanketed in a thick frost, reminding me of how miserably cold it had been. Suddenly, the thought of fire flooded into my mind. I strolled over to a pile of branches that someone had gathered. The wood was green to begin with and had also been dampened by this morning's frost. After a few dozen matches, a burnt thumb, much frustration, and finally a bit of gunpowder, I got a decent fire going. Wonderful heat rose up from the flames, slowly warming the life back into my numb muscles. I filled a tin coffee pot with water from my canteen and placed it in the middle of the blazes. Once the water was good and hot I stirred in a pack of instant coffee and took the pot from the fire. Using my glove as a pot holder, I gingerly poured my mug full of the steaming liquid.

"Oh, a cup or two of that is just what I need." Collins said.

She crouched beside me and started combing the tangles out of her hair. I filled a cup full of coffee and handed it to her.

"Thanks." she said smiling.

I tried to ignore it, once again, but I couldn't. Ashley Collins was stunning. I had noticed before, but this time it was different. Something about today, the soft sunlight glinting off her hair, the melting frost reflecting in her deep green eyes...the eyes of a killer. I slowly shook my head, as if to physically clear my thoughts. Any relations between soldiers was strictly forbidden and, in some cases, punishable by death. Besides, those gorgeous eyes truly were the same ones that watched countless people die at her hand.

"Is something the matter?" she asked.

I shook my head, "Nope, just fine."

She flashed me a smile and went back to sipping her coffee.

The next couple minutes were a little uneasy. I was mentally scolding myself for being attracted to her, and although I was pretty sure she didn't know why, I could tell she sensed the tension. So much so, that I was glad when Gatling showed up. He sat down and poured a cup of coffee without even acknowledging me or Collins.

"Ugh, what did you do to this stuff?" he asked, pulling a wry face.

He sat his cup down, put in a couple packets of sugar and powdered milk and quickly stirred it until the black liquid transformed into a creamy brown.

"There," he said, "At least now it doesn't taste like bitterweed."

I shook my head in comic disapproval, "Always complaining."

My stomach growled loudly. As if on cue Gatling winked, then disappeared into a small patch of woods to our right. He returned a few minutes later, two stout, rabbit-like creatures draped across his back.

"Where did you find those?" I asked, barely able to hide the excitement in my voice.

He tossed them down on the ground and started poking the hot coals back into flames.

"I set a couple snares," he said, "The animals around here are just as hungry as we are and plenty willing to stick their head through a loop to get at some food."

He drew a small knife from his jacket and quickly readied his catch for the fire.

The smell of coffee may have not woke up the rest, but the mouth-watering aroma of cooking meat had them up in a flash. We all waited around the fire, conversing the plans for the day, while Gatling served portions of the juicy meat.

"What did you say this thing was called?" Jackson asked Gatling.

"A wajala," he replied, "They live in swamps, so I was pretty surprised to have caught one. Didn't seem like their kind of habitat until I noticed there was a pond nearby."

I swallowed my mouthful of meat, "There was a pond?"

"Yep."

I looked around. Most of the ground looked like it hadn't seen rain in weeks

"What do you suppose keeps it full?" I asked.

"An underground reservoir maybe," Gatling said, "But most likely a stream."

"Good," I said, "We can replenish our water supply."

"I think we'll wind up following it as well," Gatling said, "If I'm not mistaking, it'll be flowing in the direction we need to head."

54

"We get to take the scenic route, chaps," Roberts said.

I frowned, "Let's just hope it isn't too scenic."

Just as Gatling had guessed, the pond was fed by a small stream that flowed across the plains. I knelt down and dipped my canteen into it, savoring the chill of the cool water.

"Where are we going?" Rice asked.

"Thirty klicks northeast to sector 76518," I said, "And Gatling was right. We should be able to follow the river for most of the way."

I rose and straightened my gear. Memories were suddenly, and without reason, flooding back, and the beauty of our surroundings began to lose its tranquility.

"We need to get moving," I said.

Chapter 9

The march went exactly as I expected, easy and fast. A few hundred yards along, the stream had been damned up by creatures almost identical in behavior as beavers. Only a small trickle managed to get past their effective construction. Smooth, grey stones lined the bed of the dried-up river. Besides this, stubby grass covered the terrain for as far as I could see, which was a very long ways. The landscape reminded me of the United States Midwest. Hills were as rare as trees and trees were practically non-existent. It didn't bother me though. If we kept our eyes open, nothing could sneak within a mile of us. Every hundred yards, we would stop and scan the area with binoculars. It was at one of these precautionary stops that Smith saw movement.

"What do you think it is?" Roberts asked.

Smith never took his eyes away from the spotting scope as he replied, "I'm not sure, but it's big."

"How far away?" I asked.

"Two miles and closing." Smith said.

I took a deep breath and tried to concentrate. If it was a Brute, it wouldn't be able to see us from this distance. Their eyesight is good, but far incapable of spotting a camouflaged figure two miles away. That didn't change the fact that there was nowhere to hide and that it was between us and where we needed to get.

"Any conformation?" I asked.

"It's a Brute sure enough," Smith said.

I shook my head and cursed. Engaging it would be easy, but I had really hoped to avoid conflict this early along. The further we got before ticking off these monsters the better.

"Let me see the scope," I said.

Smith handed it over. Even from this distance, the Brute was massive. It was strolling through the ankle-high grass, a terrifying sword hung across its back.

"O'Brian," I said, putting the scope aside.

"Yes?"

"Do you think you could hit him from here?"

He sighed and shook his head.

"To be honest, no. If I had a heavier rifle, intended only for extreme ranges, it would be easy, but I've only got a lighter more tactical sniper. Four kilometers is just too far. Sorry Cap'n."

"We'll just have to go to plan B," I said, "About how close would you have to get to make the shot?"

"Two kilometers and he won't know what hit 'em." O'Brian said with a grin.

"Okay," I said, "That's what we're gonna do. Stillworth, you and me are going to follow him in case things don't work out. The rest of you stay low."

We took off at a low crouch. I would have felt much more concealed doing a belly-crawl, but by the time we crawled a mile, the Brute would have died of old age. O'Brian was in the lead. He seemed quite comfortable at stalking a target and was snaking through the grass with practiced ease. It took about thirty minutes to get within range, but the Brute had moved very little. O'Brian lay prone and extended his rifle's carbon bipods.

"I've got a shot." he said, his eye pressed to the scope of his rifle.

"Take him." I said.

The creature was almost exactly two kilometers away, and a light breeze blew from the south. O'Brian took a deep breath and started slowly applying pressure to the trigger. An instant later the rifle bucked, sending a 500 grain bullet spinning towards the Brute's head. Unfortunately, just as O'Brian had applied the final ounce of pressure to the trigger, the creature had swayed sideways. The bullet that would have been the death of him whistled harmlessly by, leaving a red tracer line still floating in the air. Even from a mile away I could tell that the enormous beast had locked its eyes directly on us. He charged forward at a *very* alarming speed, pulling out a machete-shaped sword in mid-stride.

"You've got plenty of time," I said, "Just stay calm and shoot again."

O'Brian jacked the bolt and ejected the spent cartridge, but in the process of shoving the next round into the chamber, chaos struck.

"The bolt's jammed!" he said.

I cursed under my breath, then rose to my feet and opened fire. Stillworth was already pumping rounds from his M7A3, but if he or I either one had managed to hit him, he sure wasn't showing it. Within a minute, the Brute had closed within a quarter mile. If he was able to get within a hundred yards without sustaining critical injuries, there was no guarantee that we could stop him in time. Running was useless. He was charging forward at around twenty miles an hour. I thought I saw blood spew from its right shoulder, but the Brute didn't even seem to flinch. I sent three more rounds downrange, inwardly begging for him to go down.

Just as the Brute closed within eighty yards, a flash of green slammed into his side. The thirteen foot tall giant was sent tumbling to the ground, a spray of dirt and grass rising up from his impact. The attacker, a light green Scorpion, was on her feet far before her adversary. She scurried back a few yards and sent an arrow thudding into the Brute's stomach. The monster bellowed, and I lowered my rifle, opting to let the two fight it out, rather than risk turning both of their aggression against us. The Scorpion circled her prey and notched another arrow. Just as the Brute started to rise, she sent the shaft sailing towards him. This time, her arrow struck a heftier portion of the Brute's armor. The stone tip clanged into iron plating, shattering it into fragments and giving the Brute all the time that he needed. In an instant, he was up and swinging his sword in a deadly blur. The Scorpion ducked beneath the first swing, drawing her knives and rolling sideways in the same motion. She was not as fortunate on the second strike. The heavy blade came down with unbelievable speed and force, lopping off the Scorpion's tail with ease. Despite her gruesome injury, the determined Scorpion continued her attack. She rolled behind the Brute, then sprang up, driving both of her knives up into his back. The Brute gave an agonized cry, then whirled around to face his attacker. The Scorpion however had switched sides again. She drew a hatchet from her belt and drove it into the back of his head. The Brute stumbled forward a few steps, the hatchet still wedged in his brain. Any creature between Heaven and Hell would have died without a quiver from the injuries he'd sustained, but so great was the life inside him that the dying Brute was able to muster the strength for one final strike. As he was falling to the ground, he threw his sword. It closed the short distance to the Scorpion in an instant. All six foot of the foot wide blade sank into the Scorpion's chest, killing her instantly. I wiped the thick beads of sweat from my brow and tried to calm my shaking hands.

"Radio the rest of the squad and tell them to get over here," I told Stillworth.

He nodded.

O'Brian shook his head, "I'm sorry Cap'n. I-I don't know what happened."

"It's okay, O'Brian. A *lot* can happen with a shot that long. I knew that when I told you to fire."

O'Brian didn't look convinced. He shoved a knife into the chamber of his still jammed rifle and popped out the shell, still cursing under his breath.

"What's going on?" Collins asked, running up beside me.

"Well," I said, "we witnessed a Brute and Scorpion fight, for one."

Gatling's face drooped.

"You're kidding me," he said, "I used to spend hours trying to catch a battle between the two tribes."

"I figured they'd be warring constantly," I said.

He shook his head, "No, hardly at all. It's kind of strange really. They'll kill one another any time their paths cross, but as far as we know there's never been a tribal war in over a thousand years."

"One way or another, it's a good thing the Scorpion came along,' I said, "We had our hands full, that's for sure."

"So who won?" Gatling asked.

"Why don't you go see for yourself," I said.

Upon reaching the bloodied battleground, the first thing I noticed was the rank of the Brute. For what I could remember, the engraved gauntlets on his wrists meant he was a Noble, which was impressive. Brute rankings were similar to a feudal system, but with more barbaric attributes. The bigger and stronger the Brute the more land he was given, equaling more money and thus equaling better training and weaponry. Nobles were directly under Overlords. Below Nobles were Battlers, then Infantry, then Serfs.

"Must've been some fight," Rice said.

"Would you look at the sword that thing carried," O'Brian said.

Actually I didn't want to. After seeing how easily the Brute had wielded it, I was trying not to fully take in its size. I turned my eyes towards the blade anyway though. Just like I knew it would, my heart started pounding again. I had roughly known the size of the sword by how it compared to the beast wielding it. Still though, there was a big difference between seeing a six foot blade from a hundred yards away and staring at one protruding from a dead Scorpion. The entire sword was fire blackened, just like most all of the Brute's weapons, and the back edge was serrated in a way that reminded me of a chainsaw blade. I knelt down and carefully ran my finger across the straight edge. It was, not surprisingly, sharp enough to shave. The handle was so big that I could put both my hands around it and my fingers wouldn't touch each other. Pictures of battles, weapons, and what I assumed was their gods had been etched into the dark wood. All in all, it must have weighed around a hundred pounds. I walked over to the Brute and thanked God he hadn't reached us. His horns, jutting from holes cut in his interlocking helmet, were about as long as my arm. His entire body was covered in black chain mail and plate armor, but what skin I could see was bruised and scared. The only thing on earth I could compare his mouth to was that of a leach. A tube of muscle about as big around as a saucer extended out from his face about eight inches, and flexible canines formed a full circle around its end. His fingernails were ingrown and broken. Deep red blood oozed from his head and stained the ground.

"What on earth do they eat with that thing?" Rice asked, kneeling next to his tubular mouth.

"They let their food putrefy, then suck it straight to their stomachs," Gatling said, "Scientists guess that before they evolved into a sentient, they were scavengers."

I stared back into his deep brown eyes that, even in death, still seemed to resonate hatred. "Let's get out of here before they come looking for him," I said.

"Hold on," Gatling said, "I just need to do one more thing."

He knelt down and shoved a syringe into the dead Brute's arm. Gatling slowly pulled back the stopper and the syringe filled up with blood.

"What's that for?" Roberts asked.

60

"Research."

Gatling put the sample into his pack, "Okay, I'm ready now."

"Alright," I said, "Jackson, Roberts and O'Brian, you three take the front. Stillworth, you watch our back. The rest of you keep an eye on our flanks."

We took off at a good pace, but were slowed incredibly by having to stop every hundred yards and scan around with binoculars. I flipped out my GPS. We were a mere half-mile away from the eastern border of the Brute's territory. Once we neared within three hundred yards I shut the GPS off and sighed.

"Sir, you need to see this," Smith said, handing me a pair of binoculars. I raised them to my eyes, instantly spotting a line of figures on the horizon. At first I thought they were Brutes, but then realized most were too small. Suddenly, I realized what I was looking at. I checked my GPS to be sure, my stomach churning, and was, unfortunately, right. Along the border of areas they denote as particularly important, Brutes were known for placing a fence of impaled bodies, ranging from Marsh to human. It stood as a warning for anyone who might think of trespassing. I raised my binoculars again. Spiders, Scorpions, Wolves and anything else you could imagine were all held upright by crude poles. A shiver went down my back. I had seen several human carcasses that had been impaled and could only hope that they hadn't been alive to experience it. I explained to the squad what it was, though most of them already knew, then we reluctantly headed towards the barrier. I kept my eyes on the ground once we got close. I didn't mind seeing the dead bodies of the aliens, but I didn't want to look at the humans. A splotch of blood dropped onto my boot. Without realizing it I looked up. Protruding from the end of a rough pole was a young doctor. He couldn't have been dead more than a day, and the story of what had happened was written all over his face. The look of utmost agony, combined with the lack of wounds, led to only one terrifying conclusion. He had been alive during his torment. I struggled trying to keep my lunch down and quickly stumbled forward. My eyes teared up with a burning hatred as I stared out over the gnarly plains of the Brute territory.

Chapter 10

"Why have we barely seen a single Brute so far?" Roberts asked.

"Are you complaining?" I asked.

"No, just curious."

"Actually," Gatling said, "Brutes prefer to live in the hilly portion of their territory."

I looked around. The flat terrain we had started in was slowly morphing into a land of rolling, green hills.

"Shouldn't last much longer then," I said grimly.

"What are we headed for anyway?" Rice asked.

I pulled my GPS from m pack and flipped it on.

"Satellite imagery shows two structures," I said, "But I don't know what they are."

"What Sector is it again?" Gatling asked.

"76518," I said.

Gatling stopped walking, his face pale.

"Are the structures at its southwest corner?" he asked.

I checked again.

"Yes they are."

"You've got to be kidding me," Gatling said, "Those two buildings are the highest fortified positions on Xavier. Going in there is suicide."

"Tell me about 'em," I said.

"One of them is the castle Nightshade. At least that's what we call it. It's populated by at least eight thousand Brutes. Getting inside would be impossible. Since we've been here, that place has survived six organized attacks by rival clans."

"Why haven't we destroyed it?" I asked.

"I don't know, but my guess is because it's doing such a good job of killing Brutes."

"Makes sense," I said, "Do you think the Scroll will be in there?"

"No, actually I think it would be in the second building," he said, "It's a temple of sorts, the very heart of the Brute's religious expansion. We call it the Temple Luna. It would be fitting that a sacred object like the Scroll be kept inside it."

"I've heard about this place," Roberts said, "There's supposedly a demon that lives at its top."

Stillworth snorted.

"It's not completely untrue," Collins said, "His codename is The Demon. That's where the myth came from."

"Who's called The Demon?" I asked, already growing tired of the conversation.

"That story I told the pilot wasn't completely false," Collins said, "It was more or less a real mission I had been assigned last year. I was scheduled to assassinate a spiritual leader that lived at the temples top. Intel gathered that he had usurped power from the king and had the intentions of leading a rebellion against us. There were lots of stories and I'm not sure how many are true, but if half of them are, then his name is fitting."

"Was the mission successful?" I asked.

"It was never carried out," she said, "The probability of success was considered too low."

I frowned, "Great. Can you tell me why?"

"That place is crawling with priests, and every one of them is an Overlord or higher. Getting to the top of the temple would have been horrible in its own right, much less dealing with that monster."

"Would you have been allowed air support?" I asked.

"No," she said, "It would have most likely scared the target into hiding."

"That could be the difference we need," I said, taking the radio from my pack. I walked away from the others and pressed the receiver. Almost instantly, Stacks picked up.

"What's going on, Dawn?"

"If things go as planned," I said, "We will be infiltrating the Temple Luna by sometime tonight. I was wondering if you could arrange for air support."

"Can't do it, Captain," he said, "The fleet is still grounded."

"What about weapons equipped satellites?" I asked.

He sighed.

"Captain, I'm about to, once again, tell you something I probably shouldn't. Two hours ago, WESleys from all three super-nations were shot down from a source we cannot trace. These attacks, as well as the ones on the P4s, are being blamed upon an outside terrorist group. Whoever they are, they're good. I'm not sure if *we* could have taken those satellites out without detection. Until we find out who's done this, we can't risk aerial attacks on any of the tribes."

"What does attacking the tribes have to do with anything?" I asked, "Don't they stand just as good a chance being shot down floating up there?"

"All seven of the satellites were initiating strikes when they were shot down. We think the purpose of the terrorism is to keep us from launching attacks."

"What do you expect us to do?" I asked, "This Luna place isn't going to be easy."

"If it were easy, Captain, you and the soldiers with you would not have been chosen."

With that he hung up.

"There's more to it," I heard Collins say.

I turned to see her standing just a few feet away.

"Huh?" I said.

"Terrorists didn't shoot down those satellites."

"You heard all that?" I asked.

"I heard enough," she said, "The point is that no group outside the super-nations would have the technology to take them out in the first place, much less without detection. There's something we're not being told."

"Maybe," I said, "but, one way or another, we're not going to receive any air support."

She bit her lip and brushed her hair back behind her ear. I caught myself staring at her and quickly looked away.

"Captain," she said,

"What?"

"I didn't make it this far in the CIA by not being able to read people."

I smiled, but on the inside I was coming unraveled. I decided to make an attempt to throw her off, even though I knew it was unlikely to work. "Well then, Agent Collins, won't you give it your best shot," I said with a smile.

She smiled, "If I gave it my best shot, I could figure you out better than your mother. I think I'll go with an assumption that even a girl in high school could make and say that you're attracted to me."

I couldn't play it off any longer. After glancing around to make sure no one was listening, I told her the truth.

"Maybe you're right," I said, "But sadly it does not matter. Some other time and some other place things might be different, but here and now, it's too dangerous."

She smiled and stood.

"Someday that may not be the case,"

With that, she turned and walked away, leaving me in bewilderment. What had she meant by *someday*? At that point I wished that I was able to read her as well as she could read me. I sighed and put the radio back up. The squad, including Collins, was waiting for me about twenty yards away. I trudged over to them and broke the news.

I could tell they were all about to crack. None of them were happy about having to go into the temple without support, but before they could voice their resent, Roberts broke in.

"Captain, you need to see this."

Within minutes, we were at the top of a hill, peering down onto an entire village of Brutes. At least a hundred clay huts lined the valley, and a small stream trickled across the ground, weaving its way through the center of their encampment.

"I happened to see smoke while we were waiting for you," Roberts said.

"Good thing," I said.

"What do we do, lads?" O'Brian asked.

I shook my head, "We can't engage them."

"Any chance we could sneak past them without alerting them?" Jackson asked.

Collins bit her lip, "There's quite a few of them down there and if even one spots us, all bets are off."

"We've got to try," I said, "We're way too close to the temple to be giving away our positions now. If we keep low and quite, we might be able to get past them."

"After you," Roberts said.

I put my rifle out in front of me and pulled myself over the hilltop. The valley below us was covered with Brutes engaged in various activities. Some were chopping wood; others were beating on heated metal. It was obvious that the entire village consisted of Serfs. A Brute of higher class would not live in such primitive dwellings. I looked to my left to check on the rest of the group. They were all crawling through the short grass, their weapons clutched tightly in their hands, though I hoped they would not have to use them. I turned my focus back towards the village. We were getting closer. Before long, we would be right alongside their huts. I put my head down and kept crawling. A few minutes later, an agitated bellow made me look up. Two small Brutes were throwing a carved stick back and forth. One of them appeared to be much better at the game than the other and was getting agitated with his companion's poor throws. It suddenly struck me how human these creatures seemed. Children playing games, families tending to various chores, when they weren't out impaling things, you might consider Brutes *civilized*. Suddenly the Brute who was poor at the game made a throw that would be *very* costly. The carved stick floated through the air, landing right in front of me. Its intended receiver let out a frustrated cry and ran to retrieve his stick.

Chapter 11

I froze, froze and prayed he wouldn't see us. Even though the young Brute was small by normal standards, he was still a foot taller than me. He ran and picked up his stick, so close that I felt the breeze off his movement. He was about to turn away. He was about to make a decision that could save both our lives, but then he stopped. He turned and stared right at us, his face twisting into puzzlement. Just as he was about to bellow out an alarm, Roberts's knife silenced him forever.

"It's a shame." He whispered, retrieving his blade from the Brute's windpipe.

"Come on," I said, "We've got to get out of here before they realize he's missing."

We took off at a low crouch, no time for crawling now. It only took a minute before I started hearing calls that were undoubtedly intended for the dead adolescent. Just seconds later, I heard a distressed bellow coming from where he'd been slain. I picked up the pace a little more, even though we were practically in the clear. We had just about passed the village, and it would take them a while to figure out what had happened, if they figure it out at all. Like Roberts, I almost felt sorry for the poor fellow. It's sad when anything that young dies, especially if it didn't have to. I looked back at the village. Three large Brutes were standing over his carcass, a mixture of confusion and anger evident in their actions. A smaller female Brute was kneeling down next to his body, crying out with long shrill sobs, and I guessed he was probably one of her young. Suddenly, one of the male Brutes pointed his ax in the direction we'd taken.

"They're on us, Captain," Smith said.

"How do they know which way we went?" Gatling asked.

Collins pointed behind us. There were subtle impressions in the ground that we had crawled over.

"If we make it over the next hill in time they may not follow," Gatling said.

It was all we had to go on. We took off running at a crouch. Apparently, the Brutes hadn't seen us yet; they were too interested in the path we had left. The next hill was about a half-mile away: an easy run if we didn't have to worry about being seen. I checked back over my shoulder. The Brutes were having a hard time tracking us, and I could tell that some were beginning to doubt that the small trail in the grass even had anything to do with their young's death. The hill was now just about three hundred yards away. I pushed myself harder. Upon looking back, however, I relaxed. The Brutes were following the trail the wrong way. They were heading up the hill we had come down. I took a sigh of relief, just as I crossed over the hilltop.

"Fifty-fifty shot," Jackson said, lying back against the down sloping ground.

"Maybe," I said, "if they'd been better trackers it could have gone far worse."

"How much further do we have to go?" O'Brian asked.
I checked my GPS.

"Six kilometers."

My radio began humming, causing me to jump. I pulled it from my pack and switched it on.

"This is Captain Dawn, over,"

"Dawn, this is General Stacks. I found something that might be useful."

"Good, we need something positive."

"Every night at midnight, most of the temple's guardians go into the castle to perform a ritual for the masses. If you attack at this time, you should only have to deal with ten or so percent the Brutes you normally would."

"Thanks," I said, "anything else?"

"Have you heard about The Demon?" he asked.

"You mean the myth or the real one?"

"The real one."

"Yeah I've heard about him," I said, "Any chance he'll be gone?"

"I doubt it,"

"Oh well," I said, "he'll die just like any other."

"I hope you're right," he said, "At any rate, it may be a while before you hear from me again. We're trying to keep radio frequencies at a minimum."

Before I could question him further, the radio went silent. I put it aside and relayed the news to the rest of the squad.

"We'll keep moving until we're within sight of the temple," I said, "Then we'll hole up and wait 'till midnight."

Exactly fifty-five minutes later, I was on my stomach, peering through binoculars at the Temple Luna. Its massive size and construction resembled artistic illustrations of the Tower of Babble. It had a large, circular base that spiraled upward, decreasing in diameter as it got higher, until coming to a summit that seemed to graze the clouds. All up and down the temple, I could see small figures moving along its outside walls and though I couldn't exactly see the entrances from which they came and went, I could tell there was a network of passages that led in and out. To its left was a massive, octagonal building made of grey stone. Large towers extended from its corners and a wall some fifty-foot high surrounded it. Brutes were swarming the place, walking in and out of the castle and standing guard on the ramparts.

"Any ideas how to get in?" I asked, putting the binoculars aside.

"I think it would be a good idea for only one of us to try and sneak in while the rest provide cover from the outside," Collins said.

I nodded, "That sounds good."

"Who'll be the one on the inside?" Smith asked.

I looked at Collins, "You trained to infiltrate this place right?" She nodded.

"Do you think you can do it?"

She sighed, then nodded again. I could tell this was an assignment she dreaded, and I hated to send her in there alone. However, she was the most qualified for the task.

"Alright then," I said, "Now we just wait 'till midnight."

"With your permission, I'd like to have a look at the castle," Collins said, "It's close to the temple, and it might give us some trouble. We'd be a lot more prepared if we knew what we were up against."

I frowned, "Kind of risky don't you think?"

"Maybe, but I still think it's worth it. I won't do anything extreme, just look around."

I didn't like the idea, but she was right. If there was anything about that place that might hinder us, we needed to know about it.

"Alright, but be careful. If you get into any trouble, radio us."

Collins nodded and quickly took off towards the castle. I pulled the radio from my pack and set it close in case she needed us. Once again, I didn't like the idea of sending her in by herself, but it was obvious that sending anyone with her would only be a hindrance. I sighed. It would be the same story tonight except on a much more dangerous note. I picked up my binoculars and took another inspection of the Temple Luna. Maybe it was just me, but there seemed to be a haze of gloom surrounding it. I put them back down having already seen enough. I was dreading tonight, yet strangely, it couldn't come soon enough.

"Jackson," I said.

"Yes, sah?"

"Listen for the radio. If it goes off, answer it, then wake me immediately."

"Absolutely," he said.

I positioned my pack as a pillow and soon fell asleep.

I woke at twenty-three hundred hours and rubbed my eyes. The sun had long set, leaving the area in darkness. Even starlight was obscured by a thick blanket of clouds. I fumbled through my pack until I found my flashlight, then switched it on, flooding the camp with its light. The first thing I noticed was that Collins had returned. She was snuggled up against her pack, trying to stay warm. If we had built a fire, we would have been spotted for sure, but as our luck would have it, the night had turned out to be bitter cold. As much as I hated to wake her, I needed to know what she'd found. I edged over and gave her a slight nudge. Collins' eyes opened at once, and her hand shot beneath her pack. Before she was able to retrieve her pistol, I pinned her wrist to the ground. She began to retaliate, but then stopped and smiled.

"Sorry, Captain. You startled me."

"I need to know what you found out about the castle." I said, letting go of her hand.

"Oh, I found out a lot of stuff," she said, "I'm not sure how much of it will be helpful though."

"Like what?"

"Well, for one thing, The Brutes are far more religious than we thought. I personally witnessed a mother cheerfully cut her own child's throat in sacrifice to some god of theirs. Intruding upon that temple will be an abomination of the highest degree, and I guarantee they would gladly give the lives of every creature on this planet to keep trespassers from breaking the so called 'purity' of the temple Luna"

I gave a concerned nod, "Anything else?"

She shook her head. I paused and glanced at my watch. It was twenty-three thirty.

"Get your gear together," I said, "We leave in ten minutes."

The glowing hands on my watch slowly rotated around, my pounding heart keeping rhythm with every tick. The instant the minute hand struck forty the pounding stopped. I nodded at Collins. She pulled a jet-black ski mask over her face and slipped into the shadows. The rest of the squad watched her nervously, their weapons at the ready.

"How long do we give her?" Stillworth asked.

"Ten minutes." I said.

I resumed staring at my watch. At ten 'till we would radio her and make sure she made it to the outside of the temple. If everything has gone to plan at this point, we would give her another twenty minutes to scope the place out before the rest of us create a diversion. Once the Brutes had been distracted, Collins would infiltrate the temple and retrieve the Scroll. It worked well in theory, but to physically carry it out was entirely different. I glanced back down at my watch. In two minutes, we would check in on Collins. I looked back up just in time to see the flashing muzzle of her gun. Her light came on, illuminating at least a dozen blood-lustful Brutes. As the rest of us flew into action, grim reality sank in. For Collins, those two minutes may never pass.

Chapter 12

When life is threatened, one of two things can happen. Either every ounce of your strength and courage gives out and your limbs become weak and useless, or every ounce of strength and courage you have, kicks in and combines with pure adrenaline, making you almost superhuman. As I rushed towards the melee, speed and strength I didn't think possible coursed through my body. A Brute at Collin's back was charging forward, intent on blindsiding her, but I was determined to get there first.

Unfortunately, I had no idea what I intended to do if I did. My rifle was securely strapped to my back. The rest of my weapons lay in a nice little pile where I'd left them. A small, spring-loaded knife was my only available defense, and it wouldn't offer much. No matter how fast I pushed myself though, I was not going to get there in time. Just as the determined Brute closed within ten paces of Collins' back, a three round burst of two-hundred grain copper-plated rounds from Stillworth's rifle smashed into his skull, sending bone fragment splintering everywhere, including my exposed face. The Brute dropped a few feet from her, stone dead. The sharp pain and warm blood dripping from below my eye jolted me back into a logical reality and not a second too soon. I stopped my blind charge and slid forward feet first in the slick ground, ducking below a large crossbow bolt that spiraled past my head. By the time I picked out the Brute that fired it, he had reloaded, this time taking aim at Collins. Swifter than a gunslinger, I jerked the silver stiletto from my boot. The instant its spring-loaded blade was open I chunked it end over end. I was no knife thrower and had always thought that throwing away a perfectly good weapon was foolish, so the chances of the blade finding its target were almost nonexistent. That's why when I saw its shiny handle sticking out of the stunned Brute's throat, I muttered a hasty thanks to the angels that must have directed its flight. That alone, however, was not going to take him down. Before he could recover I un-strapped my rifle and sent four rounds into his chest. A few steps later and I was back-to-back with Collins, the power and accuracy of my rifle, combined with the continuous swarm of shells spitting from her dual Deathdealer Uzis, brought destruction to any Brute that got close. Support fire from the rest of the squad picked off the archers and stragglers. For a minute, it looked as if we were going to get out unscathed, but a small army of Brutes was pouring out of the castle, like ants from an anthill.

"We've got to get out of here!" Collins shouted.

I glanced around, we were surrounded on all four sides, but the obvious route was to get back with the rest of the squad.

"Left flank!" I shouted.

Collins swerved, shoving both of her still firing Deathdealers into the face of an oncoming Brute. The second he dropped to the ground, I hurtled over him. My feet were flying forward, my eyes locked straight ahead, but suddenly something jumped in my way. My boots dug into the ground as I fought to keep from running into him. His cold, unmerciful eyes locked with mine, sending chills of terror down my spine. His right hand was gripping an oak staff about five feet long, at the end of which was a spiked sphere, about the size of a basketball. Every muscle in his body suddenly tensed, causing his oversized veins to bulge out of his skin. His leach-like mouth opened into a bone-chilling battle cry, so full of hatred it could have come from the devil himself. He dug his hooves into the ground for traction and charged. I had plenty of time to take him down. I could have put seven, maybe eight rounds into him before he reached me. That is, if the first pull of the trigger had resulted in something more than a click. I froze up. His eyes had not broken their gaze upon mine. He didn't even seem to notice the full clip of pistol rounds that had riddled his left side. I heard Collin's empty clips hit the ground and knew she could not possibly reload in time. I knew death would come someday, but I had hoped to delay it a while longer than this. I tensed my muscles and locked my eyes into his. If he was going to kill me, I was going to go down fighting. I gripped my rifle around the barrel and rushed forward. The Brute seemed caught off guard. His charge slowed a little, but only for a second. His fingers flexed around the wood handle of his mace, and he hurtled forward like a wild animal. White foam hung from his mouth, and his bloodshot eyes seemed to narrow on me. When we closed within five feet, he swung his deadly weapon. The veins in his black arms bulged even further, as the spiked ball came down at a devastating angle, one that would have crushed through my left shoulder and down into my ribcage. At the last second, I lifted my rifle with both hands to block the attack. The spiked head crashed into the barrel crumpling me to the ground and nearly breaking my hands. Ignoring the numbness in my wrists, I rolled to the left and picked myself back up. The entire midsection of the rifle had been bashed in, leaving it not only unloaded, but destroyed. I lifted it over my head, like a batter awaiting a pitch, and charged again. The Brute stood his ground, his mace hanging loosely at his side. When I got close, he swung again, this time bringing the weapon in a downward arc. I sidestepped, and the spiked ball slammed into a rock, sending a shower of sparks streaming into the dark night. Before he could recover from his miss, I swung my crushed rifle at the back of his head. With every ounce of strength I possessed, I brought the butt crashing into his helmeted skull. Shockingly, his head exploded into a mess of blood and brains. For a second, the decapitated body remained standing, but then tumbled to the ground. I stared down at it in disbelief. When I looked up, O'Brian was jacking another shell into his rifle.

"Let's go!" I yelled to Collins.

"What about the Scroll?" she asked.

I gazed back at the temple. Even in the dark, you could see its ominous outline stretching into the sky. I cursed. To leave now would be pointless.

"Come on," I said, "We'll both go."

Worry spread over her face. I looked down and saw her clutching a gruesome gash on her left leg. A small stream of blood flowed from between her fingers, all the way down to her foot.

"Find Gatling," I said, and turned towards the temple.

"I can make it!" she said.

I shook my head, "You'd only slow me down."

"You don't even have a weapon!" she said.

Feeling foolish, I turned back around. As I did, Collins tossed me one of her Deathdealers along with a bandolier of clips and a karambit knife. I caught the gear in midair, then shoved the weapons in my belt and threw the bandolier around my shoulders.

"Get to Gatling," I said as I turned away.

The wet ground splotched under my boots, splashing cold water against my ankles with each step. The closer I got to the temple, the more I could feel my courage falter. Small fires burned from within it, casting flickering shadows throughout its interior. Somehow, I knew that they were prepared for me. I hoped that the rumors of the temple were exaggerated. Otherwise, getting inside was hopeless. When I neared within thirty meters of the Temple Luna, I dropped to my stomach and began crawling towards the glowing entrance. Suddenly, a young Brute bolted from the main doorway, running towards a water-filled shrine that sat a mere five meters to my right. Even in the darkness, I could see that his hands had been cut to shreds, like someone had taken a grater to his palms. He stopped at the bowl shaped shrine, then dipped them into the cool water, staining it a filmy red. He had not yet received his symbols of rank or weapon, a trainee you might say. It was even possible that whatever ritual that had gored his hands had been part of his initiation. Whatever the reason, I could not have him spotting me. I clenched my teeth and pulled the wickedly curved karambit from its sheath. Slowly rising to a low crouch, I began to inch my way towards the young Brute's back. I could hear the anguish in his breathing as he splashed his hands in the shrine's water. My heart stopped every time he made a sudden twitch or movement. Once within reaching distance, I bolted up, silently slipping the blade around the front of his neck. Before he could make a sound, I dug the knife into his throat and wrenched it around, severing both his windpipe and jugular in a single motion. The unfortunate Brute died without a shudder, slumping into a pile at the shrine's base. With great exertion, I managed to drag the body into a position where it could not be seen from the temple entrance. My hands were shaking from the sudden surge of adrenaline and I decided to take a second to steady my nerves. I slumped back against the base of the shrine and inhaled deeply. From where I'd came, the sounds of the battle had subsided, and though I wasn't sure why the fighting had stopped, some form of instinct told me it was not because the squad had been killed. After wiping the karambit clean on the wet grass, I rounded the corner of the shrine and resumed crawling towards the temple's entrance. Ornate steps, carved out of stone, led up to the massive doorway.

Upon reaching them, I rose to a crouch and scrambled up to the left side of the entry, then flattened myself against the wall. A horrifying chorus of sounds was echoing from inside the temple, causing my hands to resume trembling. Overruling my sense of preservation, I slowly crept towards the entrance until I was close enough to peer inside. The light hit my dilated pupils, making it impossible to see anything in detail. I did, however, make out a very large figure heading for the doorway. I recoiled back from the entrance and flattened myself the best I could against the wall, trying to melt into its shadow. The thunderous clanging of armored hooves against stone grew louder and louder, until a horned shadow stretched out from the doorway. A few footsteps later and the light from the temple was blocked completely. I stood petrified. My breathing had ceased; I didn't dare blink. Even my heart seemed to slow its pounding beat to a mere thump. So close I could have reached out and touched him, was an Overlord Brute. He stood about nine feet tall, not counting his horns, which in themselves were longer than my arms. A solid black breastplate adorned with gold imagery was on his chest, and a matching helmet, covered with spikes, protected his head. Thick chain mail that had been plated in gold covered his arms and legs. Gripped between his gauntleted hands was a ferociously curved sword, some six-foot long. The horrendous figure suddenly turned, his golf ball sized eyes scanning the grounds outside the temple. It was my guess that he was searching for the young Brute I had slain. He stood at the temple entrance for what seemed like eternity, before slowly making his way toward the shrine. I wasted no time. Once he was down the steps, I bolted inside the temple. Instantly, I was gagged by the stench of rotting flesh. The entire lower floor was covered in the decomposing remains of human beings, most of them appearing to be sacrifices. I trained my eyes straight ahead and rushed towards a spiraling staircase at the room's far end.

After flying up the torch lit stairs for almost a minute, I came to the entrance of the second room. Only a small flicker of candlelight came from the doorway, and I could feel a cool breeze blowing from within. The soft tinkling of chimes reverberated throughout the chamber, sending an unnerving chill down my neck. I took a step forward to get a better view, but instead of my foot landing upon solid stone, I stepped upon a spot slick with blood. Before I could react, my feet flew from under me. I landed on the staircase with a heart-wrenching thud. The chimes suddenly stopped. What few candles that had been lighting the room went out. My hands trembling, I flicked on my wrist-light. The bright beam revealed a small, but purely evil looking Brute standing right in front of me. He was clothed in a robe that had been stained crimson. Even his horns were caked with dried blood. I choked back a startled wail and began fumbling in the dark for the Deathdealer I'd dropped. The Brute, however, seemed unconcerned by this action. He stood perfectly still, staring down on me with a look of embarrassed pity. After what seemed like hours, my fingers landed on the handle. I flung the weapon off the ground, shoving it in the Brutes face in the same motion. I jerked down on the trigger, but all that followed was a click. The Brute had not even so much as flinched. Without removing his stare, he slowly lifted his hand from behind his cloak, revealing the pistol's clip. I ignored my shock and swiftly drew the karambit. I drove the point towards his chest, but the Brute caught my wrist with ease, his expression still unchanged. He tightened his grip immensely, digging his nails into my wrist and threatening to break it entirely. After a couple of anguishing seconds, I was forced to drop the knife. I gritted my teeth and threw a hard left at his face. To my surprise, he didn't bother blocking it. He merely let it hit him, not even blinking when it did. With a flick of his wrist, he flung me against the wall. I landed with a crash against the cold rock, the wind completely forced from my lungs. I stood up, gasping for air, and faced the doorway, but the Brute was gone. Before my confusion had much of a chance to take hold, a crashing blow to my shoulders sent me sprawling back to the ground. Groaning through the pain, I picked myself up and turned around. I was beginning to speculate that this Brute held the position of some form of sorcerer, and whether his antics were merely well practiced tricks, or somehow for real, did not matter; he was good at them. The horrendous creature stared at me from across the room, waiting on my next pathetic attempt to harm him. My next attack, however, would not be on his body, but his mind. I hastily grabbed a large, glass idol off the ground and hoisted it above my head. For the first time, I saw fear in the Brute's eyes. Before he could stop me, I smashed the idol against the ground, splintering it into a thousand pieces. His eyes filled with hatred, and he flung himself at me. This time, it was my turn to stand unflinching. Just before the Brute tackled me to the ground, I reached down and retrieved a shard of glass from the floor. Bolting up, I drove the glass deep into his eye. The Brute howled in agony, stumbling backwards and clutching his ruined eye. Before he could recover, I retrieved my clip from his bloody cloak and jammed it back into the Deathdealer. A short burst of fire later and the battle was finished. I scooped the karambit off the floor and rushed towards the second set of stairs. There was no doubt the Scroll was on the top level, and by then, every Brute on Xavier knew where I was.

Chapter 13

The white stone walls flew past me in a blur. I was running so fast, if I'd happened to meet a Brute on the staircase, I would have crashed into him. The next room was up ahead, and I could see light shimmering across the walls. Once I got close, I went back into procedure. This time, however, there would be no glitches. Flattening myself against the wall, I slowly peered around the colossal doorway. The room was slightly smaller than the last one and well lit, but it rose up for what seemed to be the extent of the temple. At least a dozen idols made of various materials encircled the floor. Kneeling beside one of these idols was a Brute. His hands were pressed against the floor, and his head was pressed against the dead body of his young. I forced all thoughts of pity from my mind and pressed the Deathdealer in-between his horns. Before he could turn, I tapped the trigger. The Brute died instantly, slumping down on top of his young's body as if he was protecting it. I shoved the pistol back into my belt, eager to keep going, but upon looking around the room, realized there were no exits. I searched franticly for some kind of hidden passageway, but with no luck. Panic was setting in; I could feel my heart racing. Something at the corner of the room caught my eye. Protruding from the floor was a metal lever, its top adorned with a silver handle. A wave of hope flooded through me. I wrapped both of my hands around the lever and tugged, and tugged…and tugged. No matter how hard I pulled, the lever would not budge. I envisioned the creatures it was made for, then gave up. With going back down out of the question and going up seemingly impossible, I was stuck in place. I could faintly hear the sound of Brutes on the lower levels and could tell they were getting closer. Overwhelmed with desperation, I began searching for what the lever was attached to. It didn't take me long to find a set of thick chains ascending up the temple. At the top of them sat what looked like an elevator system. Without hesitation I grabbed hold of the chains and started climbing.

After much exertion I reached the top and carefully swung myself into the elevator. It looked a lot like a giant bird cage, suspended in midair by a massive, stone counterweight. I gripped the bars and peered over the edge. Just as I did three Brutes crashed into the room. One of them was the broadsword wielder I had encountered earlier. The other two were slightly smaller and brandished double ended spears. Even from where I sat, I could see the confusion on their face. They searched the room thoroughly, even turning over the body of the Brute I'd slain, as if I might be hiding beneath him. I prostrated myself against the elevator's cold floor and prayed they wouldn't see me. One flick of the lever is all it would take to lower me right into their hands. One of them suddenly turned his head upward, his large, brown eyes looking directly at me. I froze, terrified to even blink. After a few grueling seconds, he turned away. The trio of Brutes, growing weary of searching an empty room, sheathed their weapons and left. I waited a couple minutes, then stood. The ground was at least five stories down, meaning I was almost halfway to the top. I turned to exit the elevator, but realized it lead to nothing. The birdcage like enclosure merely dangled there, with no room or passageway connecting to its exit. Before I could even begin to come up with a plan, the elevator lurched into motion. I was thrown against the door, and, had it not been closed, I would have tumbled out. The elevator soared up at an incredible speed. Room after room flew past me in a blur. While my problem was solved, and I was heading in exactly the direction I needed to be, not knowing *what* set the elevator into motion horrified me. After going up for about five minutes, the elevator jerked to a stop, its base landing flush with a stone ledge. I creaked open the barred door, as quietly as I could, then stepped out. A quick glance up told me I'd reached the temple's top. In front of me was a large, red curtain, covered with interwoven symbols. A light draft swayed its tattered end back and forth, making it appear alive. I faced this cloth, this lone barrier between me and what was undoubtedly the realm of a Brute so vicious, he was called The Demon. I slowly pulled the clip from Collins' Deathdealer and replaced it with a fresh one. My heart felt like it had stopped. My breath was caught short. I grabbed hold of the dyed fabric and, with a swift tug, jerked it down. My eyes darted back and forth, searching the dark chamber for any sign of threat. A shadow caught my eye, but it was motionless. I strained my vision, trying to make out details of the dark outline. Suddenly, coming from the silhouette's top was a brilliant flash of blue. I heard strained breathing, and the figure rose. He stood almost eleven foot tall and was adorned in polished black armor covered with silver spikes. A cape of solid white fur hung from his massive shoulders, and his horns were silver-plated. A sword hung from his waist and in his hand was a massive staff made of silver and studded with onyx, whose end was topped with a jagged meteor as large as my head. Again, a small patch of his neck flashed blue, lighting up his helmeted face. I took a step backward, intending to flee back down the temple as fast as I could, but something caught my eye. Behind him, encircled by a ring of candles, was the second Scroll. For an instant I wavered, then bolted, not backward, but forward. I brushed by the massive creature and dove straight for the shiny cylinder. The second my hands wrapped around I jerked up. With a metallic click, the Scroll broke free from the pedestal it was fastened to. I turned back just in time to see the Brute charging forward, his symbolic weapon whizzing towards me with blinding speed. In one fluid motion, I dropped to the floor and rolled. The meteor head of his staff smashed into the stone pedestal, breaking it into dust. I scrambled to the doorway, then whirled my pistol back around. I jerked back on the trigger, emptying the twenty-round clip of pistol bullets into his decorative breastplate in mere seconds. Yet whatever exotic material it was made from had no trouble stopping the low energy projectiles. Just as I turned to dive into the elevator, something caught my eye. Dangling from the crushed pedestal was the last thing I expected to see in a building built by *any* of the tribes...wires. Crushed wires, microchips and other bizarre electronics hung in a destroyed jumble, feeding up from the pedestal's base. However amiss this was, now was not the time for curiosity. I dove for the open elevator, but in midair, something stopped me...abruptly. The end of his staff crashed into my side, driving me into the wall. I crumpled to the ground, inches from the end of the ledge. With the butt of his weapon, the monstrous creature shoved me off. I saw his neck flash once more, before gravity dragged me into darkness.

I hit the temple's base hard, though not near as hard as the last time I'd dealt with falling. I knew that the combat suit I was currently wearing was equipped with a larger parachute, but I couldn't believe the difference it made. Rather than landing with bone snapping force, I was merely knocked breathless. I scrambled to my feet, the sacrifices of the first floor seeming to stare at me mockingly. With speed built of pure terror, I cut myself free of the parachute and rushed from the temples entrance. The outside air washed over me, and I inhaled it gratefully. There was movement to my right, and no sooner did it register, the Deathdealer was in my hand.

"Don't shoot!" Jackson said.

I lowered the weapon.

"Are the rest here?" I asked.

"Yes," Collins said, stepping forward, "Did you get the Scroll?"

"Yeah. We need to get out of here," I said.

I turned to run, but upon hearing a dreadful cry echoing through the walls of the temple's lower levels, I realized it was too late. I turned back around to face The Demon, charging out the doorway and past the shrine, and could only wonder how he'd managed to make it down so quickly. Both blade and staff were clutched in his hands, and his eyes were locked on me. I heard a rifle buck and saw a patch of his armor explode into blood, but he didn't seem fazed. He closed the distance between himself and me in a matter of seconds. He swung both blade and staff with such blinding speed that all I could do was cower to the ground and hope that he could not strike that low. I felt the edge of his sword sear into my thigh, quickly dismissing this chance. Again, O'Brian's sniper bucked, followed by spurts of fire from the rest. His staff dropped from his grip, but the enraged Brute did not go down. His gauntleted hand swooped down and picked me up by my shoulder. His grip was crushing, but even so, I could tell that it was weakened by death's icy fingers. He stumbled forward, his eyes fading, but still boring into mine. Before he could bring his sword across in one final blow, a load of buckshot tore through his helmet and into his head. The creature fell, dropping me as he did. I scrambled to my feet, not entirely convinced that the monster was dead.

"Whew," Rice said, his hand shaking, "That was one tough

critter."

"Too tough," I said, watching the small spot on his neck flash rapidly, then go dark. Suddenly, I was struck with the bizarreness that there were no other Brutes around.

"What happened?" I asked.

Collins shrugged, apparently catching the drift of my question. "I really don't know. A craft flew over about the time you went into the temple. For some reason it scared the sense out of the Brutes. Every one of them tucked tail for the castle."

"What kind of craft?" I asked.

"I don't know," she said, "It was triangle shaped, kind of like a Starfire, but it moved differently."

I was curious as to what it could have been and why the Brutes were so scared of it, but with the few seconds of safety we had, I was far more interested in determining the source of the light we had seen on both the king Scorpion and The Demon. As it turns out, Gatling was way ahead of me. He lifted the helmet from the Brute's mangled face, then dug a screamingly sharp scalpel into the raised portion of his neck. With the flick of his blade, he popped out a bloody object.

"It's an electronic," Gatling said, holding the device between his gloved fingers, "But nothing like anything I've ever seen."

"But why?" I asked, "And more importantly from where?"

"I don't know," Gatling said, "It would have to be analyzed at an electronics lab."

"Sir, may I suggest that we bug out of here," Smith said, "Those Brutes aren't gonna stay in there forever."

"Hold up," Gatling said, looking at the gash on my leg.

"It'll wait," I said, "Smith's right. We'll put some distance between ourselves and this place, then hole up at the first spot we find."

Though it didn't matter, I wasn't sure whether my leg would hold out or not. Torn by pain and eerie confusion, I turned in the direction opposite of the Temple Luna and began walking.

It was well over an hour before I was comfortable with our surroundings. By this time my leg was on fire, but the sight of a suitable resting spot eased the pain. After trekking to the top of a large hill, I collapsed. Gatling was there in a second, hovering over me and spraying the laceration with a variety of ointments, each one burning more than the last. The almost instant healing effect, however, was a blessing. I sighed and lay back against the grassy hill. From what I could see in the moonless night, the extra march had been well worth the position we now occupied. With the height advantage we had, nothing would be able to sneak up on or easily attack us. I closed my eyes, intending upon getting some sleep, but sensed someone next to me. I opened them and saw Collins, sitting on her knees and staring down at me. Again, I felt attracted towards her in a way I could have never imagined, but this time it was different. This time, my mind had changed.

"So um, I just wanted to thank you for saving my life back there. It was like they knew we were coming. I walked right into a trap."

"That's alright," I said, "With what I've seen today it wouldn't surprise me if they did."

I reached in my pack and pulled out her karambit and Deathdealer.

"Here," I said, "These belong to you."

She took the gun, but refused the knife.

"Keep it. It seems to fit you."

I nodded and put it back in its sheath. Collins started to rise, but I stopped her.

"I need to talk to you," I said.

She flashed a smile, but I could tell it was a nervous one.

"Later. Right now you need to talk with a certain general about how we're gonna get out of here."

I was apprehensive about waking a five star general at two in the morning, but she was right. I took the radio from my pack and dialed General Stacks' personal radio. After a good minute of static, he picked up.

"This had better be good, Captain."

"We've got the second, uh…'object of interest' in our possession. We just need a way out of here and preferably an escort that could take it and a couple other items back securely."

The general sighed, "I'm afraid the mission is going to be terminated. President Young is considering packing up and leaving all together. The simple solution would be to request a craft to escort you and your squad to the next location and set you down right on top of the 'item of interest', but I'm afraid that would push him over the edge."

I couldn't believe what I was hearing.

"General, I've already had a man die for the sake of this mission. I don't need to tell you of this, but there is something very important contained within those things. The way these creatures defend them there has to be."

The radio crackled with static for a few seconds, "I'll see what I can do."

There was a clicking sound on his end, then the radio went silent, leaving me in dread.

Chapter 14

"Do you think it would be okay to build a fire?" Gatling asked.

"I suppose," I said, "Just make it small."

"Got it," Gatling said.

Despite all that had gone on, I really wasn't tired, just hungry. I rose, expecting the pain in my leg to flare violently, but, surprisingly, it didn't. After gently testing it to be sure, I flicked on my light and headed for a small bush I had seen on our way to the hilltop. It had been loaded with yellow berries and beside it, I had seen a plant with tubers coming up from the ground, much like potatoes. It took a little longer to find them than I had expected, but when my light flashed across the loads of golden fruit, ready to burst, I knew it had been worth it. I took off my hat and filled it full of the berries, then pulled a handful of the red tubers. The flickering of firelight slowly illuminated the hilltop and told me that Gatling had succeeded. Delighted with the prospect of warmth, I shoved the roots in my pack and jogged back to the camp.

"Find anything?" Gatling asked, while stoking up the fire.

"Keep it on the small side, remember," I said.

He nodded and stopped fueling the hungry blazes.

"And yeah, I found some berries and some tubers,"

"Let's see," he said.

I handed him the hat full of berries first.

"Cherriums," he said, eating a few of them. "What else?"

I tossed the tubers down beside him.

"Maybe we can cook these," I said.

The instant he saw the first deep red root roll across the ground, his eyes grew wide.

"You didn't eat one of these did you!"

"What? No. Aren't they gricham roots?"

Gatling kicked them away with his boot.

"Did you put your fingers in your mouth? Anything! Those things are lethal."

"I ate some berries after I touched them, I think." I said.

He started rummaging through his pack and produced a small syringe. Without pause, he jammed it into my arm. I winced and watched him apply a second shot to himself.

"What's going on?" I asked.

Gatling took a deep breath and nodded, "You'll be okay, but these berries aren't fit to eat now. Those tubers are deathreds. The indigenous have used them for hundreds of years as a pesticide, suicide aid, you name it. We've recently been using the juice off of them ourselves as a bioweapon. Ask Collins, there's a good chance that's what she dips those darts of hers in. You need to take off your gloves and burn them. I'd even wash my hands in alcohol if I were you."

I was taken aback, "Are they really that toxic?"

Gatling looked at me seriously, "If you had taken a bite out of one of them you would have been dead before you got back to camp."

I took a deep breath. Sometimes, when things seemed to be going alright for once, it was easy to forget how deadly everything on this planet is. I reluctantly tossed my gloves into the fire, then let Gatling douse my hands with a bit of alcohol.

"Those berries looked good," Jackson said, standing up and turning away from the fire, "I'm gonna go back and get some that won't kill us all."

I forced a smile, never taking my eyes off the fire. Incidents like this made me seriously question the safety of this planet even if it was secured and colonized. I picked up a small stick and poked the glowing embers in the fire. Sparks slowly lifted into the cool air, before flickering into darkness. I sighed and flipped the stick into the flames. They devoured the dry branch hungrily, sending a wave of heat as their token of appreciation. I heard footsteps behind me, but didn't bother turning around. I was held in a delicate trance caused by the brush with death and the flickering fire, or maybe it was too little sleep. Collins came over and sat down across from me.

"Do you think they would really terminate the mission?" she asked.

I shrugged, "The way Stacks was talking, they might terminate the entire Xavier Project."

I could tell this made her angry, but she tried not to make it obvious.

"Do you realize if they gave up on colonizing this planet most everyone here would have nothing."

She paused for a second, staring into the fire, "I would have nothing."

She took a deep breath and tossed a small stick into the flames.

"It's not like we can just go back to earth. We left that place for good, there's no going back."

She was right; it didn't make sense. We needed this planet. Earth was practically gone, its resources depleted, its population overflowed. Why were we just giving up?

"All hope's not lost yet." I said, "From what I could tell Stacks was on our side, and next to Young, he's the most top brass we could ask for."

She smiled.

"What would you do?" she asked.

"If what?"

"What would you do if you had to go back."

I shook my head, "Something very different than I did with my first chance."

Surprisingly, this seemed to make sense to her.

"It's bad when you have to completely leave the planet in order to start over," she said.

I smiled, "No kidding."

"It's kind of hard to start over though, when you've left people behind," she said.

My interest piqued, or maybe it was concern.

"Who's that?" I asked, hoping I wasn't pressing too far.

"Really," she said, "The only person I was ever close to was my little sister."

I knew it was foolish, but I was relieved.

"What's her name?" I asked.

"Charity," she said, "Charity Collins. I pray every night that name will be drawn."

"Drawn?" I said.

"You don't know? When the time comes for this place to be colonized, they'll select the lucky few through a drawing."

"If the time comes," I said, and immediately realized I

shouldn't have.

"What about you?" she asked, "Any name you hope to be drawn?"

I shook my head, "No, I don't guess there is."

She smiled briefly. Was she relieved too? I hoped so, but was doubtful.

"Lookey what I got," Jackson said, walking beside us and holding a furless, cat-sized deer-like animal known as a dimroo. Frankly, I was disappointed he'd shown up at this particular time, but I wasn't disappointed about having the meat.

"I didn't hear a shot," I said, "How did you get it?"

"I used a rock," he said, "Pegged the poor sucker right in the back of the head."

I glanced down at the animals fist-sized head.

"You hit that with a rock?" I said, "That's incredible."

He shrugged, "Should've been a pitcher, huh?"

"I guess so," I said, "Let's get this to Gatling."

In fifteen minute's time, the air was filled with the mouth-watering aroma of roasting meat. Gatling was engaged turning the wooden spit on which the morsel was skewered. The flames licked at the delicious looking meat, turning it a charcoaled brown.

"That sure looks good," I said, "I just wish there was more of it."

"Don't worry," he said, "It looks like half of them won't be eating."

He motioned to Rice, Roberts, and O'Brian, all sound asleep.

"When's it gonna be ready?" I asked.

"Right, about, now."

Gatling tried to remove the skewer from the fire with a graceful flick, but only succeeded in burning himself. It made me wonder a little about his surgical skills.

"Here," I said, taking the meat off the fire.

Gatling then took over, divvying out the small meal to everyone who wasn't asleep. After we'd eaten, he pulled out a small spotting scope and trained it towards the sky.

"Can you see earth's sun from here?" I asked.

"Not with this scope," he said chuckling, "Besides, there is only a two day window every fifteen years in which earth's sun can be seen from Xavier."

I was disappointed. I'd hoped in some way that looking back on the home I left would in some way help me move on. I lay down and stared up at the inky black sky. Again, and this time more powerful than ever, I was hit with the fear that the Xavier Project would be terminated. There would be no doubt I would have to return to earth, everyone would. The problem was what I'd be forced to do when I got there. The Great War would still be raging, and I would have to go fight and most likely die for a cause that I hated. The war's objective was simple. All three super-nations were forced to fight over limited resources in order for their country to survive. As another upside in the eyes of world leaders, the war led to mass population reduction for an overflowing planet. From a statistics standpoint, The Great War was the best solution, the survival of the fittest resolution on a worldwide scale. From a moral standpoint it was wrong. By working on the Xavier Project I was able to not only escape the bloodbath, but also help to stop it. Now, all of those efforts could be in vain. Suddenly, the radio sounded. I hastily picked it up and answered. As I expected, it was General Stacks.

"Good news, son, the mission's go. I've arranged for a chopper to pick you and your squad up at dawn and escort you to your destination. Any questions?"

I smiled, "No, sir!"

"Good then," he said "I want you to send the first two Scrolls back with the pilot."

"I've got something else I'd like to send back with him as well," I said, flipping the strange electronic over in my pocket.

"Go ahead. This boy's more trustworthy than my own mother."

"One more thing, General." I said "Do you think you could get me another rifle. The one I had was kind of, um, destroyed."

"Not a problem," he said, "In fact I think I know someone who would be more than happy to arrange you a little gift."

"Thanks, General."

"You're welcome, Dawn. Good luck to you."

With that, the radio went silent. I set it aside, my heart still pounding with relief. The mission was still on. There was hope.

Chapter 15

Dawn came along with a vicious thunderstorm. Lightening riddled the air, followed by earsplitting thunder. The howling wind drove sheets of rain and hail into my face. I held my hat down to keep it from being blown away and stared up at the tormented sky. Two lights shined through the torrents of rain, growing closer and closer until I could make out the form of a helicopter. The craft slowly landed, its rotors sending water spraying all directions. I hastily ran to the open door of the chopper, throwing my pack in first, then jumping in myself. The rest of the squad was right behind me. I had to dodge a barrage of packs being thrown into the cabin. The second everyone was inside, the engine revved up, and the helicopter lifted back into the sky. I wiped the water from my eyes and rung out my hat. The pilot looked back at us. I could barely see his face through the helmet and visor he had on, but could tell he was the same pilot who'd flown me to Fort Celtic.

"Welcome back, Captain," he said, "I see you brought some friends this time."

I nodded. I was about to introduce the squad when a deafening clap of thunder rocked the air.

"Is it even safe to fly in this weather?" I asked.

Lieutenant Richards acted like he was offended, "Captain, I've flown this bird through tornadoes, electric storms, over countless battlegrounds. Flying through this little shower is going to be a breeze."

A bolt of lightning streaked through the air, followed by another massive clap of thunder. I rested my back against the wall of the chopper and sighed.

"Oh," Lieutenant Richards said, "Colonel McBride sent something for you,"

He motioned to a cardboard package at the back of the chopper.

"Thanks," I said.

The karambit made quick work of the box and in a matter of seconds I had it open. I carefully pulled from the bubble-wrap a brand new assault rifle. It had a black synthetic stock with bits of camo lining around its edges. A grenade launcher was attached to it, along with a flashlight, laser sight, red-dot scope and a collapsible bayonet. At the bottom of the box were a couple of extra magazines, several cartons of ammo and a bandolier of grenades for the grenade launcher. Beneath these was a note from the Colonel.

Captain Dawn,
I hope you put it to good use, and try not to ruin this one. How do you destroy an assault rifle anyway?
Your superior and friend,
Colonel Logan McBride.

I put the note down and went back to the rifle. It was hefty, but had a thickly padded sling around it to help in carrying it. I noticed lots of dials on the red dot scope, one was labeled zoom, another night vision, another was to adjust the shape and color of the reticule.

"Hey! Why didn't the good old colonel send us all one those?" Roberts asked, "Seems kind of unfair if ya ask me."

I put the gun around my shoulder and shoved the rest of the items in my pack.

"Seems perfectly fair to me," I said, " I'm the only one who even knows Loga-I mean Colonel McBride."

Roberts pretended to be hurt, but I could tell he was putting on. I stared out the window of the chopper at the ground flying by below us. Trees were bent double by the wind, some of them to the point of breaking, and what used to be a small stream had flooded, soaking the flatlands in over a foot of water. I saw lightning strike a dead tree, causing a fire that was almost immediately smothered by the pounding rain.

"Could this thing get struck?" I asked the pilot.

"Sure could," he said, giving us a mischievous smile.

I frowned, then watched as another bolt rent the sky.

"So what exactly are your orders, Lieutenant?" Collins asked.

"General said to set you right down on top of the scroll, then extract you once you've retrieved it."

"Won't the tribe ambush us?" I asked.

"Not the Spiders," he said, "They're more of the defensive sort.

That'll make getting the Scroll miserable, but at least you don't have to worry about being attacked.

"How long do you think it will take us to get there?" I asked.

"Oh, about three hours I'd say."

"Well, it sure beats walking," Gatling said.

Richards laughed, "Yeah, I guess it does. Especially in weather like this."

"I'm just glad they decided to send us an escort in the first place," Rice said.

The pilot frowned, "You realize things would have been a lot worse for you guys than you think if they'd canceled the mission."

"How's that?" I asked.

"If they didn't send a chopper to continue the mission, do you think they would have sent one to get you out?"

I frowned, "I didn't think about that."

I decided to see if the pilot knew anything about the strange craft the squad had seen.

"Have any new aircraft been put into action while we were gone?"

The pilot pondered for a second. "No, not since you've been gone."

I had Collins tell him about the craft she had seen. It was obvious that he was skeptical.

"We certainly don't have anything like that," he said, "Are you sure of what you saw?"

"Positive," Collins said.

He shook his head in disbelief, "Well, I've no explanation for it. Maybe we're testing some kind of new craft that I don't know about. It wouldn't surprise me. I mean, I've only been on the planet for a year now"

"A year?" I said, "I've been here for three. What was happening on earth when you left?"

I waited with anxious anticipation. Since I had left, I'd only heard bits and scraps of what was happening on my home world. Communications between Earth and Xavier were nonexistent, and to catch up on two years of happenings was something I considered priceless.

"Same story, different day, Captain. That's about all I can tell you. I spent my last year on earth inside a military prison."

I was disappointed.

"Why?" I asked.

He sighed, "Once the Great War started, I was drafted into the air force to fly an attack helicopter. They had me escorting bombers for the first year, but after that, there was a need for fighter pilots to take out fortified locations so the troops could move through. They had me shooting up every village and small town I came across. After a year of killing women and children, I couldn't go any further. So I went AWOL. They drug me right back though, and, after being court marshaled, I was forced to do a year in military prison. Once I got out I joined the Xavier project to keep from going back."

"Any family on Earth?" I asked.

Again he sighed, but this time with more remorse.

"Before the war, I lived in Seattle, had a wife, a son and flew a security chopper for the governor. Once I was drafted though, that all changed. It had been three years since I'd seen them, the day I got the letter. It said that a nuke had gone off in Seattle and that ninety-seven percent of the population was dead. I never found out whether or not my family was one of the survivors."

"I'm sorry," I said.

"Things happen." he said, "You've got to go on and not let it ruin you. Besides, there's a three percent chance that they're alive and waiting for me, and until I find out otherwise, that's what I'm going to believe."

I nodded and started to say something else, but before I could, something thudded into the side of the helicopter. I turned and looked out the window. Below us, a small band of Brutes armed with crossbows was firing up at us. Another bolt flew through the air and bounced off the choppers armor before falling back to the ground.

"Are you going to engage them?" I asked.

"No," he said, "Just gonna fly a little higher. It's not like they're going to penetrate our armor, but if a bolt managed to make it into the rotors, it would be disastrous."

"Why not light 'em up?" Rice asked.

"General Stacks ordered all artillery and aircraft not to engage in combat unless absolutely necessary."

"Do you know why?" I asked.

He shrugged, "Beats me."

"Are you authorized to provide air cover while we retrieve the scroll?" Roberts asked.

"You mean blow the place to shreds if you guys get in a pinch?" Lieutenant Richards asked.

Roberts smiled.

"Yeah, I can do that. General Stacks gave me permission to do whatever necessary to ensure success."

"I'm sure glad we don't have to go tramping through the entire Spider territory," Roberts said, "Those creatures have more traps than they have warts, and they're pretty warty, chaps."

The pilot shook his head and smiled.

"I hate to end the conversation, but we're about to reach a zone where my navigation system won't work, I'm going to be flying blind and need to concentrate."

I sat back and watched the ground fly past as the helicopter tore through the turbulent sky.

I had been very entertained by watching out the window and the time passed quickly. In fact, I was startled when the pilot told me we were entering the Spider tribe's territory. I scanned the ground, expecting to see traps lying everywhere, but then realized that they would be so well disguised that I wouldn't have been able to see them if I was right on top of them. Suddenly, the chopper was rocked by a deafening report, much louder than thunder.

"What's going on," the pilot said, "My equipment's shot."

"Maybe it's another dead zone," I said.

He shook his head worriedly, "Dead zones only disable the radar. My entire computer system is dead. We don't have missile guiding, missile sensors, anything."

Before I could reply, I saw an aircraft in the distance. It was jet black and shaped like a sharp triangle. Red and yellow lights flashed from beneath it, and blue flames burst from its thrusters as it shot towards us.

"Shoot it down!" I yelled.

The pilot expertly aimed without any electronic aid. His finger jerked the trigger and two missiles went flying out from beneath the chopper. They sped towards their target with deadly precision, but just as they were nearing close, they detonated. The mysterious aircraft flew through the debris unharmed. The pilot sent another missile flying towards it, but with the same result.

"What's happening?" I asked.

The pilot shook his head, "I don't know! It's detonating them somehow."

The aircraft suddenly stopped and hovered in mid-air. A cannonball like object surged out from its missile compartment. Electricity mingled with fire shot from the projectile's back end as it whistled towards the nose of our chopper. The pilot turned so sharply it threw me against the cabin's side, but it was too late. The strange missile smashed into the tail rotors with a thundering explosion. Three different alarms went off, forming an earsplitting chorus, and the helicopter began to spin out of control. Again, I was thrown violently against the wall. I saw Lieutenant Richards tearing at his seat belt, but couldn't understand why.

"Get me out of this thing! This seat's about to eject. I don't stand a chance down there by myself!"

I tore my knife from its sheath and grabbed the belt, but before I could cut the thick fabric, the seat shot from the helicopter, taking Lieutenant Richards with it and knocking me backwards. I landed hard against the chopper floor, a painfully large bump welling on my forehead where the seat had hit me.

"Grab hold of something, quick!" Roberts said.

I crawled over to a rail jutting from the side of the chopper and clutched it tight. The helicopter bucked and shook violently as it spun out of control. The ground appeared to be flying towards us, and at any second, we would crash into an ocean of trees. I looked away and braced myself, just in time to feel the helicopter slam into the ground.

Chapter 16

I slid violently across the chopper and smashed into the cockpit. The rotors continued to spin, sending up torrents of dirt and debris until the ground tore them off entirely. I could see flames rising up in the back end. Choking through the smoke, I tried to open the cockpit door, but with no success. Jackson was stumbling towards me to help, and, with our combined strength, we were able to force it open. I jumped out onto the ground, landing in a small puddle.

"Make sure everyone gets out!" I yelled to Jackson.

One by one, the squad jumped from the chopper. Once they were out, I hurried them away from the helicopter in case it exploded. We stood for about five minutes, watching the chopper burn and spit dark billows of smoke into the atmosphere.

"Is everyone okay?" I asked.

"We're alive," O'Brian said, "If that's what you mean."

The fire reached the helicopter's fuel compartment, and the chopper exploded, sending fiery debris in every direction.

"It was the same craft I saw," Collins said, "Same type at least."

"Where are we?" Jackson asked.

I pulled out my GPS, but it wouldn't come on.

"It's shot," I said, staring at the dark screen.

Stillworth cursed and shook his head.

"Try the radio," Roberts said.

I pulled it from my pack, not even the least bit optimistic, and switched it on.

"Fried," I said, "Just like every electronic in the chopper."

Stillworth shook his head and spat. All around, I heard the incessant chirping and screeching of alien insects. The place was a jungle of vines, trees, shrubs and waist high grass. I never imagined that a region could have denser foliage than the Scorpion territory, but this forest was certainly a contender. The only place that wasn't this dense was where the chopper had crashed and flattened the vegetation to the ground. Small fires smoldered all around, sending trails of smoke into the overcast sky. I looked over and saw Stillworth, pacing back and forth like an animal in a cage.

"Dammit!" he said, and threw a rock into the underbrush.

"We've got to stay calm," I said, "Acting like pups who've never been in a tight spot before isn't going to get us anywhere." Stillworth turned around, his face growing redder, and walked towards me.

"I'm about to…"

I grabbed him by the collar, "And I'm about put you in your place…Corporal."

He exhaled dramatically, but didn't say anything.

"Listen close," I said, "Does anyone here have experience with the Spider tribe?"

Nothing but silence and headshakes followed.

"You mean no one here has ever been stationed in their territory?"

"I, um, spent some time exploring it a few years back," Gatling said, "But it was only for a couple weeks."

"Good," I said, "Tell us everything you know about them."

"Well, uh, they're defensive. They won't attack unless there's no other option, or if you're invading one of their nests."

"So we don't have to worry about them?" Rice said.

"Well, no. I mean, yes. You do have to worry about them, a lot actually. They set traps everywhere. One wrong move and you're dead."

"What kind of traps?" I asked.

"I've only seen one, personally. It was a pit, covered over with grass, and at the bottom was a tangle of like, uh, web."

"Web?" I said.

"Yeah, that's where the tribe gets its name. They excrete a clear, web-like substance that has five times more tensile strength than spider silk, and it's about ten thousand times thicker. It's what most of their traps are made of."

"What else?" I asked.

"Well," Gatling said, "I know that they sometimes coat berry bushes, patches of grass, carcasses and anything else that trespassers might eat, with poison. They also dump the stuff in waterholes."

"How much rations did we get out?" I asked, "It sounds like we won't be getting any fresh food for a while."

98

"There's ten MREs, and uh, five bottles of water," Gatling said.

"That's not much," I said.

"How do we even know where we're goin'?" Jackson asked.

I pulled my GPS back out, hoping, without reason, that it had somehow fixed itself. Unsurprisingly, when I pressed the power, it remained dark.

"We don't," I said.

Jackson shook his head and sat down.

"You know, I'm usually a positive person, but this is screwed up man," he said.

"Just stay calm," I said.

At that, O'Brian stepped forward.

"I am calm, lad, but that's only going to help for a little longer and even then not much. We need a plan of action."

"Do you have one?" Jackson asked, looking directly at me.

I was caught off guard. My mind was reeling, trying desperately to come up with some solution, some strategy, but I had nothing.

Just as they were about to give up on me, Smith stepped in front.

"We wait here until we're contacted," he said, "It's not like an American Alliance aircraft is going to be shot down without drawing the attention of every military investigator on the planet. In the mean time, we set up a defense. Rice, I want you and O'Brian to stand guard. I don't care in the least whether or not Spiders are known for attacking. I want you two to act like every monster on this planet is fixing to rain down on you. The rest of us need to pile brush, scraps of rubber and anything else that smokes on top of that burning chopper. I'm no expert on this kind of thing, but if whatever attacked us managed to fry all the craft's electronics, there might not be a way for them to track our exact location."

They dissipated to their assigned tasks, just having a course of action spurring their optimism. Smith turned to me.

"I-I'm sorry, sir," Smith said.

"It's fine," I said, "You did far better than I was doing."

"Doesn't matter," he said, "I broke the chain of command."

"Out here, sometimes, the chain of command doesn't mean anything." I said.

Smith paused.

"Sometimes," he said, "It's the only thing that keeps men alive."

In twenty minutes, the burning carcass of the helicopter had been piled with brush and debris, turning it into a blazing inferno that spewed columns of smoke into the sky.

"I hope you're right about the Spiders," Jackson said, "'Cause every last one of 'em is gonna know where we are."

"They won't attack," Gatling said, "It's not their nature."

"What if the DoubleA doesn't find us?" Stillworth asked.

"They will," I said.

"And what if they don't?" Stillworth insisted.

"Then we go to plan B." I said.

"What might that be?" he said.

"I don't know yet. Hopefully we won't have to come up with one."

He started to say something, then walked away.

"Pain sometimes, huh?" Collins said, sitting down beside me.

"Just a hardnose," I said.

I looked over to see if Gatling was still there, but realized he had gone back to the fire.

"So, you said you needed to talk to me?" she said.

I sighed.

"I do, but not now."

She frowned and stood up. I felt bad for lying to her, for what I'd said was indeed a lie. I didn't need to talk to her. I needed to ignore her, and whatever ill thought out intentions I'd held earlier, had vanished.

"I'm going to go help Rice," I said, eager to get away.

"Help him with what?" Roberts asked, walking up beside us, "All the chaps' doing is sitting there, protecting us from an enemy that never attacks."

"I don't know," I said, "I need to do something."

I walked past the blazing chopper and to the side of the crashsite that Rice was in charge of guarding. He was pushed back against the base of a large tree, his shotgun in his hands and his eyes searching the forest constantly.

"You seem accustomed to this, Corporal," I said, sitting down next to him.

"Huh?" he said.

"Sentry duty," I said, "Doesn't seem like the most common task of a Green Beret, but you seem to be used to it."

He smiled.

"I quit the Berets after five years of service and became a bodyguard. Sitting for hours outside the homes of political figures and billionaire CEOs makes you pretty accustomed to watching for threats."

"Did you enjoy the job?' I asked.

He shrugged, "It was alright. It suited me better I think, too well probably."

"How's that?" I asked.

"Do you remember the attempted assassination on Kelly Ogburn? She was the governor of Florida at the time.

"Yeah," I said, "Someone took a bullet for her."

"Well, that was me."

"Really?" I asked.

"Sure thing," he said, "The round was a 45 ACP. It entered my lower abdomen and exited out my back, not a quarter-inch from my spine."

"You're lucky," I said.

He laughed. "I wouldn't call it that. I spent three months in a coma. When I woke up, things had changed. The not so Great War had started and so had the draft. Funny thing huh, that you would wish that you could stay just a little bit injured, just enough to avoid being drug into a fight that isn't yours. As bad as I wanted to avoid it though, I knew my time was coming, and rather than sit and wait to be put wherever they wanted me, I rejoined the Berets. First chance I got, I signed up for the Xavier Project."

I nodded.

"What about you, Captain? What did you do on Earth?"

I shook my head. "Nothing I'm proud of."

He didn't question further, and, for that, I was thankful.

"How long do we give 'em anyway?" he asked, "How long until we resort to plan B."

I sighed. It was an issue I hadn't really given thought, but one that needed addressed.

"Until sunset," I said, "Come then we'll make a camp, change sentries, and figure out what to do from there."

Twelve hours passed, with no sign of outside contact. As soon as the light of day began to fade, I gave up.

"Smith," I said.

"Sir?"

"Get the squad together. We've got to compose a plan."

"Yes, sir."

I leaned back against the remains of a tree, its trunk split into pieces by the impact of the helicopter. By now, the fire had burned down to a small blaze, just large enough to provide light and warmth. Besides being scorched by the flames, the skeleton of the chopper was still in relatively good shape. I was both amazed and thankful that the craft had not exploded on impact. I was about to venture my thoughts into what would have happened had it done so, what it would have been like to die in a fiery blaze, when the squad showed up.

"Are they all here?" I asked Smith.

"All of them, sir. Are you sure it's safe to leave the place unguarded."

"It'll be alright for now."

I scanned over them, just to verify. The firelight flickered off their faces as they stared at me expectantly.

"Let me start by saying that I firmly believe the American Alliance would find us eventually, but by then it may be too late. Our supplies are not going to last more than a day."

"So what do we do?" Jackson asked.

"We continue the mission," I said, "It's our only option."

"Sir," Smith said, "With all due respect, we don't even know where we are, or where we're supposed to be going. I don't see how that is an option."

"We'll find out where we are and where we're going." I said.

"How many secured sectors of the Spider territory are there on the south border?" I asked Gatling.

"Three, maybe four," he said, "Why?"

"We passed one about sixty klicks west of here. It had an airport."

"Fort McClartey," Stillworth said, "I saw it too."

"That would put us in either, Sector 285782 or 285783." Gatling said.

"That's great," Roberts said, "But how do we know where we're going?"

"All of the other Scrolls have been in arguably the most well defended spot in the entire territory," I said, "Why wouldn't the third Scroll be the same?"

"There's a spot like that not thirty miles from here," Gatling said, "It's called the Supernest."

"Tell me about it," I said.

"I spent about six months studying it. It was the reason for my exploring this territory in the first place. You see, all of the Spiders live in these gigantic underground nests, almost like oversized anthills, but this nest was different. It was larger, and it never produced satellite nests, it just grew bigger. Most of the nests displayed a loyalty towards the others, but this one would attack them, killing most then forcing the others into the Supernest."

"How well defended?" I asked.

"Better than any nest on Xavier."

"Sounds like our place," I said grimly.

Chapter 17

Morning came much too soon, bringing with it, though, wonderful sunlight. Overnight, the fire from the helicopter had died to a mere flicker, leaving us to suffer through the cold night air without our sleeping gear, one of the many things we'd lost in the crash. Overall though, we had been lucky. Every one of us had kept hold of our weapons, and, most importantly, I'd managed to avoid losing the Scrolls.

"Any coffee?" I asked Gatling.

He looked up from the small blaze he was feeding and shook his head.

I frowned, "What direction is that nest in?"

"North," Gatling said, pointing a piece of burnt wood in that direction.

I gazed off into the woods. A slight breeze was blowing, causing the countless leaves to sway back and forth. Rays of sun glinted off fresh drops of dew, and various flowers were in the process of opening their petals to the sun. Besides the beauty, the woods looked menacing. Every bush, every patch of leaf covered ground looked like the perfect spot to hide a trap, and I knew that each step we took into the thick brush would have to be calculated. One false move could mean death.

"Is everyone else up?" I asked, not taking my gaze from the forest.

"I think so," Gatling said.

"Good. We need to get moving."

They must have overheard me, because, almost at once, the squad walked over to us, gear in hand.

"Remember," I said, "Be careful of every step, and be ready for anything. There's no telling what they've placed out there."

I turned to the forest, and, for a second, I hesitated. I didn't want to be the first one to walk into the unknown, but that's the role of a Combat Commander. I checked that my rifle was loaded, then took off.

For an hour we fought our way through the brambles, with no sign of a Spider, or any of their traps. The warmth that sunlight had brought was quickly turning into a curse, rather than a blessing. It amazed me how quickly the temperature could change on this planet, but as beads of sweat formed on my neck and arms, the bitter cold of last night was only a memory. I heard running water to our left, tempting me terribly.

"If the water's running," O'Brian said, "Then they couldn't poison it, right?"

Gatling shook his head, "No, that's not necessarily true. Sometimes they just throw a few diseased bodies upstream."

I pulled my canteen from my pack and shook it slightly. Only a swallow remained. Reluctantly, I put it back. Suddenly, Roberts stopped, his nose tilted to the air.

"Do you smell that, chaps?" he asked.

I took a deep breath of the warm air. Floating into my senses was the most tantalizing, tempting, wonderful thing I'd ever smelled. The scent, unlike anything I could possibly describe or compare to, overwhelmed me.

"What is that?" Rice said in an almost entranced voice.

Roberts began tracing back towards the direction it came from, something that was surprisingly simple to do. Never before had I smelled something so easy to follow, so *irresistible* to follow, and before I could gauge the consequences, I had altered my course. I didn't bother to turn back to see if the others were following as well, but I had a feeling they were. The scent soaked the air, and I inhaled it as deeply as I could. It was hard to tell, but it felt as if I was getting lightheaded. I fought hard to turn back around, but the sickeningly sweet scent was too overpowering, too addicting. I brushed aside a bush, and the aroma's source came into view. Through watery eyes, I gazed at the bright pink flower. It was slightly larger than a dinner plate, and with the slightest shift, I could see lightly colored fumes rising off it. Had I not looked down at its base, I would have kept on walking. I would have knelt down next to it and inhaled the drug-like fumes as deeply as I could, had I not seen the bodies. Beneath the flower, there were three dimroos. Their eyes were bulging out, and their tongues hung limply from their mouths. Their furless skin, normally grey, had changed to an almost purple hue.

105

"Get away from that thing," Gatling said, his nose covered over with his shirt.

With great effort, I forced myself to turn away.

"What is it?" I asked.

"Mactabilis Pertraho," Gatling said, "It means *deadly allure*. That scent they give off is a powerful narcotic. It's also a toxin. What I can't believe is that we've seen one in the first place; they're probably the rarest thing on Xavier."

"Not if they're planted," I said, looking at the mound of fresh dirt at its base.

I turned away from the flower, scolding myself for falling into their trap so easily.

"Hold up," Gatling said.

He pulled a scalpel from his pack and pressed it into the flower's stigma. A thick, bluish slime oozed out of it and onto his blade. He stretched the substance about a foot, but still it didn't break.

"This stuff is where the scent comes from," Gatling said, "Next to those tubers you nearly ate, it's the most poisonous thing on the planet."

With some effort, he managed to break the strand. Slowly and carefully, he wrapped it around the knife blade, much like spaghetti on a fork.

"Looks like chewing gum," Roberts said.

Gatling frowned, then carefully placed the slime-covered blade inside a plastic bag.

"Come on," he said, "If we stick around here much longer we'll wind up like those dimroos there."

I turned and walked away. Every step I took away from the noxious flower seemed to clear my head a little more.

"That makes two Spider traps you've seen," I told Gatling.

"Yeah," he said, "I just hope I don't get to see any more."

"I hope we do," Roberts said, "I hope we see every last one of the bloody things."

Gatling gave him a puzzled look.

Roberts smiled, "It's the ones you don't see that are a real bugger."

Stillworth laughed a little, "Maybe you're not as stupid as I thought."

Roberts was about to retaliate, but I stopped him with a glare. "Stay focused," I said.

The minute after that, I went against the very order I'd just given. I found myself staring at Collins. For someone who had spent three days in the wilderness of Xavier, she could not have looked more beautiful. I was changing my mind once again. I wanted to tell her everything, and for once, I didn't want to be alone. Her allure was overwhelming me, just like the flower. I couldn't help but be humored at their similarities, because, just like the flower, giving in could be deadly. Besides, I didn't even know if she was interested. I picked up signals sure, but it had been some ten years since I'd had to try and understand women; out of practice was an understatement. I took my eyes off her and back to where I was placing my feet. If I wanted to stay alive, that's where they should stay. Something landed on my neck, and before I could brush it away, it stung. My skin seemed to explode into pain, like a hundred wasp stings combined into one.

"Are you allergic?" Gatling asked, a needle already in his hands.

"Allergic to what?' I asked, rubbing my neck incessantly.

"To bee and wasp stings," he said.

"Does it matter?" I said, almost sobbingly, "That's bad enough to kill someone alone."

"It matters," Gatling said, "It's the difference between an agonizing whelp and anaphylactic shock."

"No," I said, "I'm not allergic."

He put the syringe away.

"You don't think that was some kind of trap do you?" Roberts said, "Trained wasps or whatnot."

"No. Just an incendia hornet," Gatling said, "They attack without training. Don't worry though, Captain, as bad as it hurts, their stings have no long term effects."

"It feels like someone's holding a lighter to my neck," I said.

Gatling nodded, "That's where they get their name. Incendia is Latin for fire."

"Why does everything on this planet have to be so unpleasant?" I asked.

Gatling frowned, "Wait 'till you see the Supernest."

By sixteen hundred hours, I had a feeling we were about to. For the entire time thus far, we had marched through their territory without seeing a single Spider. Now though, we were currently watching the fourth one in the past twenty minutes. She was about five feet tall, colored light green, and her body was built much like a combination of a wasp and a praying mantis. She had two long arms that extended from her upper thorax and were tipped with large, scythe-like claws. Her head was small and topped with three eyes. She had ant-like jaws, and inside her mouth, I could see a stinger. It was the second one, in fact. At the bottom of her bulging abdomen, and slightly concealed behind her semi-transparent wings, was another, this one almost as large as a dagger.

"A warrior," Gatling whispered as she scuttled into the forest and out of view.

"What's that mean," I asked, still afraid to rise up from my stomach.

"It means that she's about a foot taller than the drones and workers, and it means she guards the nest's perimeter."

"We're close then," I said.

"I'd say within a hundred yards," Gatling added.

Convinced that she was gone, I rose.

"We'll find the nest, then back off and wait until tomorrow. I'm not about to go into that thing at night."

"Actually," Gatling said, "As frightening as it sounds, that might be the best time *to* go."

"Why?" I asked.

"Spiders aren't nocturnal," Gatling said, "They sleep at night just like we do, and, with this time of year being in the middle of the nest's dormancy, we might be able to get in and out unnoticed if we go in tonight."

I shook my head, not believing what I was about to do.

"Alright," I said, "If we can get a plan together, we'll go an hour after sundown. The first part doesn't change though. We still need a visual on the nest."

After walking only thirty meters north, the forest broke, or rather it had been cleared. Every bit of foliage, from small saplings to massive trees, had been cut to the ground by the industrious Spider tribe. Even the grass had been trampled and destroyed, leaving the ground nothing but dust. At the center of this square mile zone and encompassing most of it, was what looked like the largest ant hill that could be imagined. It was made from clumps of dirt and rock, some larger than boulders, all piling together to form a massive cone. Spiders were moving up and down it constantly, disappearing in and crawling out of the entrance one after the other.

"There's no way we can get in there," I said, putting my binoculars aside, "We don't even know where we'd be going."

"There's a chance we do," Gatling said, "We're assuming that this Scroll is going to be like the other two, right?"

"We have to," I said, "It's all we've got."

"Then the Scroll should be guarded by their leader," Gatling said.

"Do the Spiders have a leader?" I asked.

"Each nest has a queen," Gatling said, "In normal nests she lives at the very bottom, but as different as this one is, there is no telling."

"We'll have to assume it's the same," I said, "Another assumption."

"Is there any way to get to her without going through the main nest?" O'Brian asked.

"There is," Gatling said, "In all the nests I've heard of, there is a small tunnel that leads straight to the bottom. Workers use it to carry the good stuff down to her."

"The good stuff?" Jackson said.

Gatling nodded, "The entire colony is herbivorous except for the queen. Everything caught in the traps is brought to her."

"So if we see a Spider carrying a body, we'll know where they're going," Stillworth said.

"And where we're going," I said.

"With permission, I would like to circle around and see if I can locate the second entrance," Collins said.

I hated to let her go by herself again, but knowing exactly where the secondary tunnel was, would be indispensable.

"Alright," I said.

Without a seconds pause, she rose and began walking east. I watched her for the entire time, telling myself I was keeping an eye out for her, but I knew there were other reasons as well. Suddenly, there was movement from behind her and to her right. Out of the woods, materialized a Spider. His eyes immediately trained on Collins, but he didn't make a sound. The darker colored male, a drone, advanced on her. I raised my rifle, intending to shoot him where he stood, but stopped. If I opened fire, every Spider in the nest would rain down on us. Without thinking, I rushed forward. The karambit sprang into my hands as I closed to within ten meters, but I was afraid I was too late. The insect was right behind her, his massive stinger extending further and further from his abdomen. Just as I reached him, he jumped. His wings fluttered slightly and he landed on her shoulder, driving her into the ground. Just as he tensed, preparing to dig his stinger into her back, I hit him. The blade of the karambit drove deep into his eye, and before he could shriek, I wrenched it out. The Spider died instantly, pieces of brain matter and exoskeleton protruding from the gash.

"You alright?" I asked, helping her to her feet.

"Yeah," she said, "Just shaken."

"Good," I said, pulling her into the woods, "Remember when I said I needed to talk to you sometime; now's that sometime."

I led her behind a large tree, then looked her in the eyes. "What is it, Captain?" she asked.

"I've nearly lost you twice now. Twice now, I've thought that the only woman I've ever felt anything for was going to die before I could even tell her what she meant to me, and I don't care the military and their fraternization policies, and don't care about the danger, I'm telling you now."

I stood there, still staring in her eyes. My heart was pounding, but overall I felt relieved. After a period of time that felt like hours, she smiled.

"I don't think I could have a relationship that isn't dangerous. It wouldn't be fitting."

Before I could reply, she was kissing me. Her lips entangled with mine, sending chills down my spine, and fire into my chest. The scent of her hair, the touch of her skin, was overpowering. I found myself never wanting to let go, but we had to get back.

"You remember when you told me that if it were another time, or place, things would be different?" she asked, pulling away.

"I remember," I said, brushing a strand of hair behind her ear.

"This is the only time and place we're gonna get," she said,

"It'll have to work."

I smiled.

"I guess this means we're on a first name basis now, huh?" she said, smiling.

I was starting to feel dizzy. All of this was so sudden.

"Yeah, but we've got to be *very* careful about this. I don't need to tell you the dangers in us getting caught."

She smiled, "Like I said, I like danger."

"I don't," I said.

"Yes, you do," she said, "You just don't want to admit it."

"Come on," I said, "We've got an entrance to find."

Chapter 18

After circling the nest about halfway around, we spotted a small tunnel dug into the hill's base.

"That's our spot," Collins said.

I saw a Spider, much like the one who'd attacked her, carrying the body of a dog sized rodent, know as a chimchalli, into the tunnel.

"Can I ask you something?" I said.

She smiled. "I suppose."

"I never imagined it would be this simple to attract a CIA agent. I thought you people were supposed to be more reclusive than this."

"We are," she said, "But it gets old. The only person I've ever been close to is Charity, and I haven't seen her in six years. I need someone to make this world a little more bearable."

"Come on," I said, slowly rising to my feet, "We'd better get back."

By the time we were back with the others, the sun had already sank, leaving the sky in pink twilight.

"How far into the night do the drones carry food to the queen?" I asked Gatling.

"All night," he said, "As far as I know, she doesn't sleep. Satellites have picked up activity in secondary tunnels at all hours."

"That's good and bad," Smith said, "We might have to deal with the drones, but at least the rest of the nest won't be alarmed by a little commotion."

I frowned, "I'm afraid it might be a little more than they're used to. Gatling, I want you to stay here."

"Um, with your permission I'd like to go. I spent a year studying this nest, and I can't pass on the opportunity to get inside of it."

I frowned, "You realize that once you're inside, there's no turning back."

He nodded.

"Alright," I said, "But you'd better keep up."

I turned and walked towards where I'd left my pack.

"Get ready," I said, "In an hour we move out."

After picking up my gear, I noticed O'Brian. He was sitting at the clearing's edge, watching the nest intently. His rifle was laid across his lap, and his finger was on the trigger.

"What's going on?" I asked, walking up next to him.

"I'm not looking forward to this, lad." he said, "I'm scared of spiders."

I chuckled.

"Does it never end?" he asked, turning away from the nest, "Will there ever be a time when we're safe?"

I sighed, "I like to think there will be."

He nodded, "I do too."

"You said you were from the IRA, right?" I asked.

"Yes."

"I thought they were disbanded three-hundred years ago."

He smiled, "You didn't keep up with current events much back on earth did you, Captain?"

I shook my head, "Too depressing."

"I'll agree with that, but for the short of things, we were put back into place to combat the European Alliance. The Irish never did like the idea of being overrun, lad and that's exactly what EA was doing. Eventually though, we agreed to join the EA military in the Great War, under the conditions that our country retained its independence."

I sighed and looked back at the nest, "Xavier doesn't care much for being overrun either."

"Makes ya feel like the bad guy sometimes, huh?" he said.

"It certainly does," I said.

An hour later, we were belly-crawling across the ravaged ground towards the secondary entrance. Xavier's blood red moon, Advenacruor, was casting its eerie light down on us, though I wished it wasn't. All of us had donned night vision, and the only thing the red light was doing was making it easier for the Spiders to see us. Suddenly, Jackson lifted his hand, signaling us to stop.

"Two hostiles," he whispered, "Check that, one hostile

dragging a body."

As soon as I saw the drone, dragging his kill across the dusty ground, I recognized the body to be that of Lieutenant Richards. I felt my anger flaring up, and the blood rushed to my face.

"Easy, sir." Smith whispered, "There's nothing you can do for him."

We waited until the Spider disappeared into the tunnel, then followed. Upon reaching its edge, I felt my stomach turn. The hole was barely big enough for us to fit through, and, from the looks of it, went almost straight down. After mentally swearing up and down, I slipped into the tunnel that I prayed would not be my grave. I pulled myself forward, though gravity did most of the work. Bits of rock and loose dirt tumbled down the tunnel in front of me, and, against my good sense, I shut my eyes. It seemed as if all of Xavier was closing in on me. If a horde of Spiders came rushing up this tunnel, turning around would have been impossible. My heart began to pound, and I felt like any minute I would break. The walls looked as if they were caving in, and though I knew they weren't, this sent my mind into a frenzy. Finally, the tunnel broke, leading into a massive chamber. Without clearing it first, I pulled myself out of the tunnel and stood. The walls on all four sides were covered with translucent globs, pinned in place with wads of thick web.

"Larva," Gatling whispered, "The queen's got to be close."

I located at least four exits to the chamber, each one being larger than a garage door.

"Which way," I whispered.

"I'd say straight," Gatling said.

I walked towards the exit right in front of us, but just as I did, a terrible screech reprobated across the room.

"Target, six a clock!" Stillworth said.

At the secondary tunnel's entrance stood a drone. His mouth opened wide and a let out another screech of alarm. He bolted forward, but before he took three steps, Stillworth had gunned him down.

"Stillworth, Smith, cover the entrance!" I yelled.

I spun back around, only to see dozens more drones spilling into the chamber from all sides. I flung my rifle to my shoulder and began spraying bullets into the crowd of Spiders, but for every one that went down, three more replaced it.

"Frag out!" Rice yelled.

He chunked a grenade into the melee of drones. The second it landed, it exploded, sending a shower of insect gore into my face. Startled by the earsplitting explosion, the horde stopped advancing, but only for a second.

"Captain," Stillworth said, "I've got a line of hostiles coming down the tunnel and only one more clip."

I heard the clanging of two clips hitting the floor.

"I'm out," Collins said, clutching her empty Deathdealers.

I swerved my rifle to the entrance of the secondary tunnel and triggered its grenade launcher. The baseball-sized projectile exited the barrel with a thump, soaring into the tunnel and crashing into the chest of a charging Spider. The round detonated, collapsing the tunnel, and killing every Spider in it.

"Hold them off," I said, "O'Brian, come with me."

I rushed towards the forward exit of the chamber, but suddenly, a Spider jumped in front of me. His scythe claws were poised to swing, but a bayonet thrust to the thorax dispatched him.

"How many rounds do you have?" I asked O'Brian, pulling my blade free.

"One," he said.

"Save it."

A screech, ten times louder and far deeper pitched, echoed up ahead.

"Come on," I said.

I took off at a run, the larva covered walls flying past in a blur. Without realizing it, I stumbled into a second chamber. It was twice as large as the one we'd left, making it almost the size of a large house. Sitting at its center, and surrounded by larva, was the queen. She was almost identical to the other spiders except in two aspects. One, her abdomen was far larger than the rest of her body, and second, she was almost the size of a semi. Just as she turned towards me, I saw her bulging neck flash blue. She let out a deafening shriek, then charged. I raised my rifle and sent my last eleven rounds into her thorax, but she didn't seem fazed. Just as she swung, I threw myself to the ground. Her massive claw crashed into the wall, crushing larva and splattering me with dirt and slime. Again she screeched, driving her head down towards me. The stinger in her mouth shot out, heading straight for my stomach. Just before it impaled me, I rolled. With a single motion, I drew the karambit and slashed the stinger off, just above its bulging venom gland. The queen cried out, sending a spray of putrid, green blood from her mouth. I knew that O'Brian was waiting on a perfect shot, and I knew I was going to have to provide him with one. She came at me again; her ant-like mouth flexed wide open, preparing to bite me in half. This time though, as she drove her head down, I jumped up, slamming the blade into her neck and pinning her swinging head still. It was only for a second, but that was all O'Brian needed. His rifle went off, sending a 500 grain tracer round blistering into her skull. The queen groaned, then toppled sideways, leaving the line of red tracer-dust still hanging in the air.

"Good work," I said, my hands shaking.

The instant I turned away from her dead body, I saw the Scroll. It was seated atop a small pedestal of rock, next to a massive pile of larva.

"Get it," I said.

O'Brian walked over and pulled the cylinder up, breaking it loose with a click. Outside, the sound of battle had ceased, and I could only hope that it was because the spiders were dead, not the squad. I rushed out of the chamber, karambit in hand. When I rounded the corner, I saw Stillworth, plunging a knife into the thorax of a gurgling drone.

"That's the last of them," he said, wiping his blade on his pants.

"H-how are we going to get out of here?" Gatling asked, almost tripping over a pile of dead drones, "The secondary tunnel is closed up like it never existed."

"You mean we're trapped down here!" O'Brian said.

I crouched against the ground, racking my brain for a solution.

"How does the queen get out," O'Brian asked, "I know she doesn't crawl through the secondary tunnel. Even the primary would be about fifteen times too small."

"She doesn't," Gatling said, "The queen never leaves the nest."

"But her offspring do," I said.

"Your thinking there's another tunnel?" Gatling asked.

"There would have to be," I said, "A warrior would have a terrible time going up the secondary tunnel, much less an

116

adolescent queen."

"But this nest's queen didn't give birth to other queens, or she killed them if she did." Gatling said, "That's why there are no satellite nests."

"You said this nest was like any other nest in the way it was structured right?" I asked.

Gatling nodded.

"Then it doesn't matter whether the queen gave birth to other queens or not, there would still be a tunnel for them to exit from."

"I suppose," he said.

"Where would it be located?" I asked.

He shrugged, "Your guess is as good as mine. I didn't even think it existed until you convinced me."

"We'll have to search for it," I said, "Spread out."

As soon as I turned to explore the chamber to our right, a voice echoed from the left.

"Found it," Collins said, emerging from the west chamber, "I got tired of waiting."

"Come on," I said, "Let's get out of this place."

The second tunnel, as I knew it would be, was much larger than the one we'd came down. However, going back up was much harder. I dug my fingers and boots into the loose soil, dragging myself up inches at a time. The whole while, I kept the karambit clutched in my hand, though I was careful to keep the razor-sharp blade out of the dirt. After ten or so minutes of this, I was finally able to see the exit. With one last heave, I pulled myself out of the tunnel and onto the ground. The second I did, I saw eyes. By the thousands, and on all sides, were Spiders, poised as if they knew *exactly* which tunnel we would be coming from. At once, they charged. Just as the first few reached us, a giant spotlight shone from the sky, bathing us in a blinding white light. I heard the thunderous sound of Gunship blades chopping through the air. The Spiders paused, obviously as surprised as I was. Multiple miniguns from the Gunship started firing, spitting out shells so rapidly they sounded like giant hummingbirds. Brass casings rained down in torrents, bouncing off our weapons, helmets and anything else close. The Spiders shrieked and ran, but there was nowhere to hide. The unmerciful barrage tore them to shreds, sending their remains sailing in all directions. I dove to the ground, clutching my helmet to my head as clods of upturned dirt rained down onto my back. After almost thirty more seconds of continuous fire, the noise ceased. I slowly raised my head, still apprehensive of both Spider and friendly fire. Everywhere, except for the small circle of ground we occupied had been completely upturned by the millions of shells that poured from the Gunship's main cannons, leaving the area for as far as I could see in nothing but piles of mangled bodies and smoking dirt. The giant beam of light grew closer and closer until the football field- sized craft had landed. Its sealed doors opened with a hiss, lowering a large ladder as they did. The pilot emerged from the craft and, after removing his computerized helmet, walked up to me, extending a gloved hand.

"Sergeant Levi Tanner, I presume you're Captain Dawn."

I nodded and shook his hand. He appeared to be in his early forties. He had deeply tanned skin, small brown eyes and a tangled mess of wiry black hair.

"How did you find us?" I asked, turning my gaze to his massive craft.

"We knew where you'd be heading. I've been tracking you overhead since yesterday, actually."

"Some craft," Roberts said, "Did they think you'd be providing support for a bloody army or what?"

"No," he said, "Since the incident with the chopper, the only aircraft authorized to fly are the heavyweights, Gunships, Ravens, Starfires, and a few others. General Stacks wanted to make sure the next time something like that happened we were able to put up a fight."

"What are your orders, Sergeant?" I asked as he directed us towards the entrance of the Gunship.

"I'm supposed to take you all to the edge of the Marsh territory," he said, strapping himself back into the pilot's seat.

I found a row of chairs toward the front of the craft and settled down. The soft cushions enveloped me, reminding me of how little sleep I'd had.

"Why can't you set us right down on top of the objective like the previous escort was supposed to?" Jackson asked.

Sergeant Tanner frowned, "Whenever a craft gets within a five-mile radius of your team's objectives, it usually gets shot down. It was risky for me to pick you guys up in the first place."

"You mean the chopper wasn't the only incident?" I asked.

"He shook his head, "No, not by a long shot."

I needed to get ahold of Stacks. Sending the Scrolls back with Sergeant Tanner would have been optimum, but if he wasn't briefed on what they were and where they were to go, he might never get them back.

"Do you have a radio I can use?" I asked, "Mine was fried in the attack."

He shook his head, "There's plenty of radios back there, but none of them will work."

"Why?" I asked.

"Three hours ago *something* simultaneously took out every satellite orbiting Xavier. Communications and navigations are worthless without them."

He handed me a small package.

"Stacks told me to give this to you," he said, "I suppose it's a map of sorts. Like I said, your GPS is worthless."

"Have you been briefed on our mission whatsoever?" I asked, taking the map.

"Well, no," he said, "Just the basics."

I frowned and decided that I would be hanging on to the Scrolls once more.

"Is there any ammunition aboard the craft?" I asked, "Me and my team are running pretty low."

"This is an invasion transport craft, Captain. In compartment 17, there are more supplies than you could use in a year."

I turned to go and find them, but he stopped me.

"One more thing, Captain. Whatever you guys are looking for, you're not the only ones after them anymore."

"What do you mean?" I asked.

"Yesterday, an Eastern Empire airbase was destroyed by three unidentified aircraft. After that, they decided they had their own interests in your team's objectives. When their demands were refused, the DoubleE declared a protocol two war against us and embarked on their own efforts."

My heart sank. Most of Earth's wars were under protocol one, meaning they were confined to that planet and that Xavier was excluded from any conflicts that might arise. A protocol two war would throw Xavier right into the mix.

"How far along are they?"

He shook his head, "I don't know. All I know is that you are to continue with the mission as scheduled."

"Have there been any conflicts on Xavier yet?" I asked.

He shook his head, "No, and we hope there won't be. If they don't attack, we sure won't."

"A couple of hostile encounters between their team and mine could certainly lead to an attack, though," I said grimly.

He nodded, "It could, but General Stacks told me to tell you to take whatever means necessary."

I sighed and shook my head in disbelief. Xavier was heading down the same path to destruction as Earth.

"Come on," I said, "Let's restock our supplies."

"Particularly some food," Roberts said, "I'm flippin' starved."

It turned out that Sergeant Tanner wasn't exaggerating. Compartment 17 was stuffed with ammunition, MREs, drinking water and even weapons.

"Grab anything you think we could use," I said, "Just don't overdo it."

"What about radios," Collins asked, "There's a chance they might get some satellites back online."

"Take some," I said.

I peered out a small window at the compartment's side. Below, at least four rivers were snaking across the ground, combining and separating, at dozens of points, slowly forming the flooded lands of the Marsh tribe.

Chapter 19

Almost three hours later, we arrived at our designated drop point, Sector 953987. Slowly the craft stopped, hovering about forty feet above the foliage thick ground.

"There's no place big enough for me to land," Sergeant Tanner said, "I'm going to have to lower you guys down."

He pointed to a door at the back of the Gunship. A large pulley wound with thick cable was next to it. I picked up my pack and motioned for the squad to follow.

"Nice to fly with you, Sergeant," I said.

He nodded and pressed one of the hundreds of buttons on the Gunship's control panel, causing the door to slowly open. I made my way across the vast span of the Gunship and to the exit, the rushing air nearly causing me to lose my balance. Slowly and carefully, I grabbed hold of the thick cable and attached it to my belt. Roberts was trying to talk to me, but the Gunship's deafening propellers made hearing anything but a garbled mess, impossible. After a deep breath, I started lowering myself towards the ground. By this point, the Gunship had hovered down to a somewhat comfortable height of around thirty meters, and after all of my encounters with them, I was finally getting used to heights. This comfort, combined with the slick cable made sliding down quick and easy. My boots landed onto the ground with a squelch, and, right away, I could tell that walking through the marsh's territory was going to be problematic. Roberts came down next, followed by the others. Once we were all safely on the ground, the cable raised and the Gunship took off, leaving us in solitude.

I gazed around, taking stock of our very precarious surroundings. The ground was like what you might expect in the everglades before they were stripped of their resources. Foliage, unlike anything I had seen on Earth or Xavier, covered the swampy ground in a thick blanket. Everything from six-foot carnivorous plants to thick tangles of razor sharp thorns covered the area. I stared at the ground and shook my head grimly. I'd heard of how the Marsh tribe hid beneath the muddy water, with only their crocodile-like eyes showing above the muck, but up until now, I didn't realize how impossible it would be to spot them. I took my rifle from my back and caressed it in my arms.

"Get ready for anything," I said, "There's no telling where they are."

It was three hours before we stopped again. The only thing giving us trouble up to this point was thick mud, tangled vines and endless varieties of biting insects. However, when I heard the faint sound of DoubleE soldiers conversing, I feared that was about to change.

"Can you make out anything they're saying?" Jackson asked.

I shook my head, "I can hear them fine, but whatever language they're speaking, I can't understand it."

Collins crawled over, "They're speaking Russian , but they're not saying anything worth repeating."

I lay there, pressing myself against a tree and trying to think what to do. If we attacked, we would most likely be defeated, seeing as we were far outnumbered. If we held back, they would probably beat us to the Scroll.

"Can you make out *anything* helpful?" I asked Collins.

"The best I can tell, they're going to make camp."

"Good," I said, "That helps."

"Are we going to try and pass them?" Roberts asked.

"Negative," I said, "We're going to make camp too."

"Why?" Jackson asked, "Wouldn't it be better to get a head start?"

"Yeah, it would be, but the problem is we would have to stop some time too, and they would catch back up and possibly find us."

"So what do we do?" Smith asked.

"We'll make camp and move when they do."

Smith nodded, and, along with the rest of the squad, started silently preparing a spot around fifty meters to our left. I decided to sit back and strategize a little, but rather than come up with anything useful, I could only seethe about the DoubleE breaking the pact in the first place. Gatling walked over and sat down beside me. I could tell that he could see my frustration, but he simply sat in silence. After a few seconds of stillness, I spoke. "It's all coming down, Gatling." I said

He sighed and nodded.

"All our hopes and plans for a new life are falling down around us."

He simply nodded again; I could tell he didn't have much to say.

Suddenly Collins rushed over, her Deathdealers in hand.

"Captain, I think there's something you should see."

Minutes later, I was on my stomach, peering into the Eastern Empire camp. At least two hundred soldiers occupied the manmade clearing, though I was shocked at how unconcerned they seemed. A large fire burned in the center of the camp, around which were fifty or so drunk Russians; a group of Chinese soldiers were gathered in a circle watching two of their own engage in a brutal fistfight. None of them appeared to have weapons close by, making me reconsider the prospect of attacking them. Apparently, they thought their force was too large to worry about a group of barbaric swamp creatures, but if so, they were wrong.

"Tell me again why you were sneaking around without telling me?" I whispered to Collins

She shrugged, "Habit, I guess."

"So what were you wanting me to see?" I asked.

"Look," she said, pointing towards the center of the camp. Strung up to a large post was an American colonel. I cursed under my breath, shaking my head as I did.

"We've got to get him out."

Collins nodded, "When?"

I shook my head and sighed, "Tonight."

For the next eight hours, I was able to do nothing but sit in silence and wonder why the DoubleE would want an American soldier along on their attempt to find the Scrolls.

"How are we going to get him out?" Roberts asked.

"A diversion maybe?" Rice said.

"That's what I was thinking, but I'm not sure what kind. We don't want to tip them off that we are here." I said.

"Maybe just sneaking in and getting him would be better," Smith said.

"Maybe, it depends on how well they've got him guarded tonight."

Roberts shaded his eyes with his hands and turned towards the alien sun.

"It's sinking fast, chaps. We'd better come up with something."

I nodded and looked around.

"Where's Collins?" I asked, suddenly realizing she was missing.

"Come to think of it, I haven't seen her in about half an hour," Rice said.

As if on cue, she emerged from the thick foliage. I narrowed my eyes at her.

"Collins, next time you go off somewhere tell me."

I could tell she knew I was serious, but it seemed to excite her.

"Alright, alright," she said, "But I did find something useful. There are eight soldiers guarding the camp's perimeter and two guarding the colonel."

"Ten guards, huh? We should have no problem then, chaps." Roberts said, running his knife against his boot.

I bit my lip and forced myself to face reality. I had hoped to avoid killing a single human being while on Xavier, but there was no other way.

"Alright," I said, "Come sunset me, Roberts and Collins will try and get him out of there. The rest of you provide us cover."

They all nodded and started getting ready. I grabbed my gear and watched as the alien sun slowly crept towards the horizon.

Forty minutes later and I was back at the DoubleE perimeter, knife in hand, staring at the back of a young guard. I was so close I could see the beads of sweat on his neck. Every emotion I had was firing off like rockets, sending my head into a tailspin. I had seen scores of deaths and had caused plenty of them myself, but every time it came down to me and another human being, I had to force myself to kill. Every face of every man I'd ever slain haunted my dreams, and I was about to add another. Locking my eyes on the young Asian, I raised my knife and swore to make it swift. I took a small step forward and drove the karambit into his throat. The shock on his face, the energy leaving his eyes, the feeling of his lifeblood on my hands, I knew if I lived a thousand years, these things would still haunt me. For now though, I had to force them aside. Roberts and Collins had already taken down their targets and were advancing towards the colonel. The two guards assigned to him had their backs turned for now, and they were taking advantage of it. Inch by careful inch, they crept up on them. With a nod, they attacked, taking the guards down in a flurry of stabs. Roberts gave one final strike, then wiped his long knife against the grass and shoved it back in its sheath.

"I haven't done that in a while chaps. I was afraid I'd lost my touch."

I was startled at how easily he and Collins killed, but wasn't sure what I expected. I drew my knife and quickly sliced through the ropes that were pinning the colonel to the crude post. He reached up and pulled the dirty gag from his mouth.

"Thank God!" he said, wiping a stream of blood from his forehead.

"Come on," I said, "We've got a camp set up just a few hundred yards from here. We'll relocate there then make tracks."

"Wait," he said.

I bit my lip anxiously, 'What?"

"They've got two more prisoners they plan to execute tied up in that tent over there," he said, pointing to a large red tent near the camp's center, "It's your call, Captain. I'm in no position to make that judgment."

I sighed and shook my head, cursing my conscience. Normally, I might have been able to force myself to leave them behind, but saving them would further justify the men we had slain.

"Collins, get him back up with the rest of the squad. Me and Roberts will go get them."

She nodded and started escorting the colonel out of the camp. Roberts looked towards the large red tent and drew his knife back out.

"Here we go, chap."

I nodded and we took off at a low crouch, making it to the tent with no trouble. With one final glance at the surrounding area, I positioned my back against the red fabric and peered in through the flaps. A tiny fire was burning in the tent's center, casting a dim light on two young men. Overall, they looked like they'd been beaten to the verge of death. Their bindings cut deep into their wrists and ankles and blood soaked through their uniforms. The one on the left slowly raised his head, a small groan escaping his parched lips. He was barely conscious enough to even recognize that we were there, much less who we were. Fear filled his eyes and I could tell he was about to make a ruckus, but Roberts quickly threw a gloved hand around his mouth and held him in place. A few swift slices of my knife and their bonds fell limp around them. The slightly conscious one was starting to regain awareness, but the other was still out cold.

"How are we going to get him out?" Roberts asked.

I shook my head, "See if you can wake him up."

Roberts started gently slapping the unfortunate man's face, but with no luck. Finally, he gave up and shook his head.

"This one's already gone."

"See if you can get the other one responsive," I said.

Roberts bent over the first and started talking to him in a hushed whisper.

"Come on chap, we're here to help you."

Finally, the young soldier moaned and lifted his eyes towards Roberts.

"You're, you're English?"

Roberts smiled, "Through and through. Come on, let's get you out of here."

The soldier slowly stood, balancing himself against Roberts' and my shoulders. I turned and faced the door, just in time to see a fully armed Chinese soldier rush through the tent flaps. Surprise registered on his face, but quickly turned into a shout. The soldier went for his side arm, but a thrust from Robert's knife ended his would be attack.

"Better dash." Roberts said.

I could hear a horde of confused soldier's rushing around and could hear the clatter of their weapons. I clutched my rifle hard, then exited the tent.

Chapter 20

The first soldier to come across my vision was an officer, trying to load a clip into his pistol. The sight of my rifle flicked across his chest and I squeezed the trigger, dropping him instantly. Another soldier ran out of a tent, rifle in hand, but a bullet slammed into his head before he could cause any harm. My eyes swiftly flicked towards the edge of camp where the squad had been waiting. They had quickly organized and were firing into the melee. Unfortunately, I could tell the DoubleEs were organizing as well. A bullet flew by my ear, grazing me so closely I felt the heat sear against my flesh. I knew I was firing. I knew I was mowing down soldiers left and right, and I could hear bullets buzzing by like angry hornets, but it seemed like it was all a hallucination. Russian and Chinese soldiers poured out of tents, most of them unarmed. Utter confusion on their part was the only reason we were still alive, but I could feel the tide turning. My night vision sight focused on a young soldier on our right flank. He was oblivious as to where we were and was searching franticly for the source of fire. I closed one eye and started pressing the trigger, but stopped. From behind the bewildered soldier, a dark shadow loomed. Fresh mud dripped from its slick body as it rose to a height of about seven feet. The creature's elevated eyes shined like spotlights in my night vision. It flexed its giant alligator like hands and spread its toothed jaws into what I swore was a bloodthirsty smile. The unfortunate soldier never saw the being that would end his life. The Marsh creature slammed his claws into the young DoubleE's shoulders and hoisted him into the air. Just as he started to scream, the creature tore his head from his body with a single bite. I quickly took note of its features and burned them into my memory. The monster had thick legs that came to deeply webbed feet. Its stomach was thin, but quickly thickened into a massive barrel chest. Powerful arms extended from its midsection and came to a hand made of overly long fingers tipped with talon claws and bound with deep webbings. The best way I could describe its vicious head was an odd mixture between a crocodile and a komodo dragon.

"Get down," Roberts whispered.

I quickly slumped behind a small tent and watched the chaotic scene unfold. Eastern Empire soldiers were darting franticly, trying desperately to avoid the bloodthirsty Marsh tribe. Every few seconds, a Marsh creature would explode from the mud and savage a nearby soldier, afterwards carrying the limp body to the edge of the camp and dragging it down into the watery depths. The DoubleEs were managing to gun down a few of them, but not many. My finger nervously stroked my rifle's trigger, but I knew it was best to hold back. With each of the monstrous creatures that emerged from the marsh, I felt my heart pound faster. I could only hope that the rest of the squad was fairing okay. Suddenly, Roberts nudged me.

"It looks like we've got an opening, and we'd better take it. We may not get another chance."

I nodded and we stood. Adrenaline surged through my body as we rushed towards the camp's perimeter. Foreign soldiers flew past, but if they noticed us, they were far more concerned with staying away from the Marsh tribe. Before long, we had emerged into the forest surrounding the camp. My hope was to quickly find the squad, but I didn't see them anywhere. Just as I was about to go searching for them, something grabbed me from behind. I whirled around and drew my pistol in one motion, but quickly realized it was Collins.

"Over here," she said, motioning for us to follow as she took off through the thick brush.

I holstered my pistol and followed her. The almost liquid ground squelched and sucked with every step I took, making me think at any second I would sink up to my waist. It was torturously slow making our way through the muck, but fortunately we didn't have far to go. Collins abruptly stopped and pulled us behind a breathtakingly large tree. The trunk's height and girth outdid any of the giant sequoias I'd seen on earth. The squad was hunkered down behind the tree's massive base, watching the chaos unfold. The soldier we had rescued acknowledged the colonel with a weary salute. The officer returned his salute, but a concerned frown spread across his face.

"Where's Private Carter?" he asked.

I could tell the soldier was far too delirious to answer his question, so I stepped in.

"With regrets, sir, I have to report that Private Carter was dead before we got to him."

The colonel shook his head and cursed. The ongoing commotion regained both of our attentions, and I slowly crept around to the tree's base, a pair of night vision binoculars raised to my eyes. The DoubleEs were still locked in battle with hordes of Marsh creatures and were still getting the bitter end of the encounter. The Marsh tribe was ambushing them left and right, rising from behind the soldiers and killing them before they even knew they were being attacked. I was so mesmerized by the melee, I almost didn't hear the faint squelching sounds to our left. I didn't want to risk the movement involved in shifting my binoculars towards the source of the sound, but soon realized I wouldn't need them. The ominous shadow of a Marsh creature slowly rose from the muck, a mere five feet away. I could only make out an outline, but my imagination filled in the rest. Thick globs of fresh mud dripped from its body and landed with a smack. It was so close. So close, it would've had to seen us coming. So close, it had probably been watching us all this time. Yet I remained still, hanging to the laughable hope that we had not been seen. Suddenly, the creature exploded forward, vanquishing this chance. I was afraid I had been the only one to spot the creature, therefore being the only one who was not caught completely off guard, but suddenly, a shotgun blast rent the air. A baseball-sized sphere of buckshot exited the sawed-off barrel of Rice's shotgun, smashing into the creature's head with a smack. Nerve reactions carried him forward for a few feet before he crashed to the ground, sending a spray of mud splattering against my suit. I stared blankly at the dead Marsh creature, lying just inches from my feet. A sickening wave spread through my body and I felt like I was going to throw up. My hand started shaking uncontrollably, so much so that I had to quickly lean my rifle against the tree to keep from dropping ii into the swamp.

"Let's go," I said.

We found a strip of drier ground to our left and took off running through the dense underbrush, the sound of the battle still ringing in our ears.

After pressing forward for almost an hour, we stopped. A large rock, covered with moss and having a plateau-like top, stood at the middle of a subtle break in the thick brush.

"Think we could make camp here?" Smith asked.

I had to think it through. It was highly unlikely that the DoubleEs would be moving before daybreak, if then, and the rock would provide a good height advantage as well as an escape from the swampy ground. I glanced back towards the American prisoners we had rescued, and that finalized my decision. They didn't look like they could walk another step.

"Yeah, I think that would be our best bet."

The stone was slick with swamp moss, but with lots of ledges. After climbing up about ten feet, we reached the top. One by one, the rest of the squad appeared over the edge, with Jackson helping the two soldiers. The instant we were settled in, Gatling tossed me a small aerosol can.

"I should have had everyone spray down with this when we first got off the Gunship, but it slipped my mind."

He clapped his hands in the air then unfolded them, revealing a large insect. It had dragonfly wings with a fly-like body and an oversized needle mouth, and it was almost large enough to cover Gatling's palm.

"A few dozen of those things will suck you dry. Not to mention all the diseases they carry."

I hesitated for a second, but a sharp pain on my arm changed my mind. I sprayed myself liberally with the strong smelling liquid, then tossed it to Smith.

"A fire would help too," Gatling said, "But I don't suppose that's an option."

I shook my head and walked over to the colonel we had rescued.

"Captain Dawn, U.S Army Rangers," I said, saluting the wild-eyed colonel.

He returned the salute and introduced himself.

"Colonel Langley, U.S Army Recon."

I sat down and lowered my tone slightly.

"There's so much to get cleared up, Colonel, I don't even know where to start."

He nodded, "Well, let me start by saying that rankings aside, I recognize you as the commanding officer as long as me and Gunny Blake over there have to tag along. Whatever your mission, I am certainly not in a position to assume command, however, if there are any services me or Robby could offer, we will be more than willing to do so."

I nodded, "For starters, you can answer a few questions, Colonel. First off, do you know the nature of the Eastern Empire's mission, or ours for that matter?

He shook his head. I was hoping he would, but wasn't surprised he didn't.

"Well," I said, "My question to you is why the DoubleEs would want you and your men along with them."

Colonel Langley laughed, "It's not a matter of wanting us along! Me and a few other Recon soldiers were assigned to keep an eye on them and report their every move. Unfortunately, we were attacked by the Marsh tribe. All but myself and the two soldiers in the tent were killed. We were so close to the DoubleE camp, they couldn't help but hear us. Before we could recover from the Marsh tribe's attack, we were surrounded by Russians. We had no choice but to surrender, and I'm surprised they still didn't kill us on the spot. For whatever reason they took us back."

"How many were killed?" I asked.

"Pardon me, Captain; I'm afraid I don't understand the question."

"How many of your men were killed when the Marsh tribe attacked."

"Oh, about five I'd say."

"You mean you don't know for sure?"

Colonel Langley shifted uneasily before replying.

"Well, that's not counting the ones that may have deserted in the heat of battle."

I wasn't satisfied with this answer, but decided not to press him further.

"So how is your mission going?" Langley asked.

"Good enough so far," I said, unconsciously motioning towards my pack.

"Good," he said.

Something in the colonel's eye made me wary. Maybe it was just caused by their imprisonment, but he and the gunnery sergeant both held the same crazed yet suspicious look that I found very unsettling.

"I'll let you get some rest, Colonel," I said, standing, "There's no doubt you're exhausted."

"As tired as I am, Captain, hunger is taking the forefront. Do you suppose we could help ourselves to some of your squad's provisions?"

"Affirmative, Colonel. Take all you like."

I turned and walked away.

"I'll see you tomorrow" I said, "I'm going to see if I can get some sleep."

I spread my sleeping gear out onto the smooth rock surface and lowered myself down. Just as I always did when sleeping under the stars. I turned my eyes towards the sky. The millions of celestial objects filled my mind, enveloping my imagination into their midst. A meteor sailed across the sky, leaving a trail of burning debris in its wake. Everywhere I looked, there were hundreds of stars staring back, making me wonder what sort of worlds they might be hosting. After gazing upwards for over an hour, I closed my eyes and fell asleep.

It was unusual for me to wake in the middle of the night, but on this occasion, I did. Xavier's pale white moon, Albus, was just beginning to appear above the horizon, casting a subtle glow into our campsite. The raucous swamp insects and frogs still had not stopped their disorderly chorus, reasoning me to believe that they never shut up. I reached over to grab a canteen of water from my pack and realized something was terribly wrong. The zipper on my pack was open and its contents covered the ground. I quickly brushed through the scattered objects, instantly realizing that the Scrolls were gone. My eyes darted up. Just as I had guessed, Colonel Langley and Gunnery Sergeant Blake were gone as well.

I shook my head and swore. There was no telling how far they had gotten and certainly no time to waste.

Chapter 21

"What the bloody hell's going on?" Roberts said as I continued to nudge him with my boot.

"Get up, Private."

Roberts came fully awake. Realizing the urgency in my voice, he quickly rose and jerked his combat suit on.

"What's wrong?" he asked.

"Get your gear. We're moving out."

I hastily went and woke the squad, until they were all gathered in a circle.

"Where's our company?" Collins asked.

"The same place the Scrolls they stole are, wherever that is."

She narrowed her eyes.

"How long ago did they leave?" she asked.

Her demeanor had changed in a second to one of a cold hard tracker. I glanced at my watch.

"It couldn't possibly have been more than two hours," I said.

"We shouldn't have any trouble tracking them in this type of ground," she said, "The problem will be catching up. We'd better get going."

Jackson threw his pack around his shoulders and jacked a shell into his sidearm. I was immediately horrified with the idea of shooting down American soldiers, but they were traitors, and taking them prisoner wasn't an option. They had stolen my rifle, so I pulled a pistol from my belt and jerked back its slide. If we caught up with them, the protocol would be kill-on-contact.

Despite their hopeless attempts to cover their tracks, we discovered them almost as soon as we were off the rock. As far as the beam of my light could reach, I saw the two sets of boot-prints extending into the forest.

"Where do they think they're heading?" Stillworth asked.

I pulled the crumpled map of the Marsh Tribe's territory from my pack and turned my light onto it. After studying it for a second, I drew my conclusion.

"Those two are going back to the DoubleEs."

"Why do you suppose they'd do that?" Rice asked.

"I have an idea," I said "But I hope I'm wrong."

Stifling back a yawn and brushing a vine from my path, I continued marching. It was nearing dawn and for the past three hours we had been trudging nonstop through the thick marsh, with no sign of Colonel Langley or Gunny Blake. Just as I'd expected, their tracks had led all the way into the DoubleE camp, but then turned around and headed east. I leaned against a tree trunk and inhaled deeply.

"We'd better catch our breath," I said, "There's no sense in killing ourselves."

Relieved, the squad took off their packs and slumped onto the ground.

"Whew, I don't think I can go anymore." Gatling said.

I sighed. Gatling wasn't the only one who was exhausted.

"We'll hold up here for a while." I said.

I slid the pack from my shoulders and casually tossed it onto the ground. Beads of sweat rolled off my forehead and onto the swamp floor. The thermometer on my watch read a hundred and five degrees. We were nearing closer to Xavier's southern pole, however, unlike Earth, the closer you get to the South Pole of Xavier, the hotter it becomes. Due to Xavier's extreme tilt, the South Pole can reach one-hundred and fifty degrees and never get dark, while the North Pole can get down to negative two hundred and never see the sun. I wiped the perspiration from my brow and stared up at the blazing star. Without warning, far away cries echoed throughout the forest, undoubtedly from Colonel Langley. I swiped the pistol from my belt and rushed towards the noise. Without hesitation, the rest of the squad followed. I swatted away branches and leapt over rocks as I flew forward. My concern for the two soldiers was very little at this point, however, getting the Scrolls was vital. Suddenly, I was sliding in the mud, trying to keep from running into the midst of a battle between Colonel Langley and a horrendous looking Marsh creature. Alone, and apparently out of ammo for his stolen rifle, Langley looked to be fighting a losing battle, but with the help of Roberts' knife, he was holding his own. I wondered where the other soldier was, but my question was answered when I saw his severed body lying against a tree. For an instant, I thought of helping the colonel, but I forced this thought away. He had not only betrayed the very people that had rescued him, but his country as well. I narrowed my eyes grimly, knowing that his end was near. Suddenly, the monster charged. Langley raised his machete above his head and started screaming profanities at his attacker, before rushing forward himself. The colonel was the first to strike, burying the edge of the blade into the Marsh creature's thigh, but he would not be the last. The beast grunted in pain, then hoisted Langley into the air. With a heave, the Marsh creature flung him brutally into a nearby tree. Langley smashed into the wood with a grimacing crunch. He tried to take a breath, but even I could tell by the raspy result that his lungs were punctured. The Marsh creature picked up a rock, bigger than my pack, and started ambling towards the colonel, happy to take his time knowing his victim wasn't going anywhere. Upon reaching him, the massive beast placed the rock in one hand and reared back. I didn't know whether Colonel Langley's last expression was one of fear or un-intimidated anger, as I could not force myself to look at him having stood by and done nothing. I did know, however, that his death was quick. An immensely strong right arm sent the rock crashing into his face. Blood squirted the tree as Colonel Langley's head imploded under the force.

"Take him," I said, nodding to Jackson.

He raised his rifle and gunned the creature down. Fighting my urge to get away from the grotesque scene, I walked over to what was left of Colonel Langley and started searching for the Scrolls. I scoured his garments first, but found nothing. I turned him over. His pack was covered in blood, but undamaged. I slowly unzipped it, but found nothing.

"They're not on this one either," Stillworth said, allowing the body of Langley's companion to slouch back to the ground.

I sighed, searching my wit for any solution other than the one I feared. They would have placed absolute value on those Scrolls or else they wouldn't have risked stealing them in the first place. There was no way they could have lost them. Then something very wrong caught my eye. Off to Colonel Langley's side, a DoubleE issued side arm was laying in the mud, a bullet jammed awkwardly into its magazine.

"Do you remember the colonel or Blake salvaging any weapons while we were getting them out?" I asked Roberts, still clinging to a hope.

He pondered for a second then shook his head.

"As far as I recall, they were unarmed. In fact I'm sure they were because I remember wishing they would pick up a gun and help us out."

"Take a look at this, Captain." Collins said, handing me a large satchel.

My eyes lit up and for an instant, I was relived, having thought we'd found the Scrolls, but upon receiving the satchel, I realized it was far too heavy. It was made of an ultra strong fiber called Maxalite and was a deep black. Across the front was red inscriptions, but I didn't bother having Collins translate them. I loosened the bags thick drawstrings and peered inside. At its bottom was a small electronic with two buttons and a touchscreen. I pulled it out and tossed it to Gatling.

"What is it?" I asked.

"It's an electronic check," Gatling said.

"How much is on it?" I asked.

"Hold on a second," Gatling said, pressing a few buttons on the device's screen.

All of a sudden, he stopped and his eyes grew wide.

"Holy..!" he said, still staring at the screen.

"How much," I reinstated.

He looked up and shook his head, "Two billion dollars."

I sighed, forced to accept my conclusion. Colonel Langley had sold the first three Scrolls to the Eastern Empire.

Collins shook her head, "It must have taken some kind of negotiating to keep the DoubleEs from just killing them and taking the Scrolls."

I shook my head in complete disbelief. All the work that had gone into reaching those Scrolls, all of the blood that had gone into retrieving them, only to have them whisked away by a couple of thieving traitors. I inhaled and turned my eyes toward Xavier's wispy clouds. This time there would be no simple solution, no wit inspired gimmick to get us out. The only way to get back the Scrolls was quick and forceful action.

Gatling started to hand me the check, but I refused.

"Keep up with it," I said, "The rest of you get ready. At dusk we launch a full force hit and run attack on the Eastern Empire camp."

"Shouldn't we check with General Stacks first, sir?" Smith asked.

"The radios are shot," I said.

"Negative," Smith said, "I tested them earlier. They must have launched an emergency satellite."

I cringed at the thought of having to report this, but Smith was right. Grudgingly, I shrugged the radio from my pack and grabbed hold of its receiver, then slowly typed the three-digit number that would connect me with General Stacks' headquarters. After two minutes of nothing but static, I set the radio aside.

"That leaves us no choice," I said.

Jackson quickly stepped forward, "Captain, we don't want to start a full-blown war with the Eastern Empire."

"It's too late for that. I want a full weapons check by every one of you. Meet for briefing in forty minutes."

Small tendrils of steel curled their way off the blade's edge and fell into the soft grass as I ran the karambit across a small whetstone. Once it was able to bite into my thumb with barely a touch, I slid it back into its leather sheath and buckled it to my waist. A quick glance at my watch told me it was time. I slid the bolt on my rifle back once more, just to be sure that there was a full clip of shiny, brass hornets waiting to do their deadly work. Satisfied, I slung the rifle's sling across my shoulder and started trudging towards the center of our crude camp. The fully assembled squad was gathered in a tight circle around our designated rendezvous point.

"Where's O'Brian?" I asked.

Jackson motioned a gloved hand towards the tree line. O'Brian was knelt on his knees with his hands folded together. His lips quickly moved beneath his closed eyes, tracing along with the words he was thinking. After a few seconds, he drew a deep breath, crossed his heart with his hands, and opened his eyelids. I saw him kiss a worn wedding band on his finger before he rose and jogged over to join us.

"Sorry, Captain."

137

"No need O'Brian, I just hope you included us."

He nodded sharply then turned his eyes to the ground. A tight knot began to well up in my stomach, but I fought it back.

"We've been through all the danger one planet could throw at us, and I couldn't be prouder of how you all have pulled through. We've still got a ways to go before we're done, but I can guarantee you if we fight like we have been we will *all* live to call this place home. All of you are warriors; this is what you were born for."

I saw a shift in their character. Fire shined in their narrowed eyes, and suddenly, the only fear I felt was for the poor souls who stood in their way. For the next ten hours, we devised a plan of attack. As soon as the first twinkle of starlight pierced the sky, we struck.

Chapter 22

We moved in unison, every bit as silent and alert as a pack of wolves on the hunt. As soon as we closed within two hundred yards of the Eastern Empire camp, the squad broke into three. O'Brian, Roberts and I formed the left flank of the attack, while Jackson, Smith and Collins formed the right. The rest of the squad was positioned slightly behind and in the middle of the two flanks. Without warning, the woods broke into the massive clearing in which they'd made their camp. I hastily dropped prone and disappeared into the thick, marsh foliage. Only a few small fires were burning in the camp, showing that they had learned well their lesson in stealth. This was concerning, since our entire strategy was based around their arrogance. Fortunately, my fears were buried when O'Brian spotted a heavily fortified tent at the camp's center.

"Just like we figured, Cap'n, dead in the center and armed to the teeth."

I nodded. It was a risky assumption to say that the Scrolls were in that tent. If we were wrong, if it was merely a decoy, then our lives would be worthless. The cold truth was that we were all in on one roll of the dice.

"Alright," I said, "Let's get this show started."

Roberts positioned his hand over his lips and gave three shrill bird whistles. Moments later, the same signal was returned from the other side of the camp. O'Brian drew a deep breath and softly laid his cheek against the butt of his rifle. His sharp, blue eye pressed against the rubber padding of the gun's massive scope, and with a swift flick of his gloved fingers, he shifted the optics into night vision. My eyes locked on his trigger finger and I felt my heart pound faster with every bit of pressure he applied. Suddenly, the large rifle bucked, spewing a quick burst of flames out the barrel's end. Even though I couldn't see a thing, I could tell by the sound of the bullet's impact that one of the main tent's guards was now lacking a head. The camp exploded into action almost immediately. They had been ready, but so far, things were going exactly as planned. As soon as O'Brian confirmed his shot, he repositioned himself about thirty yards east. Roberts and I waited in heart-pounding anticipation as a small group of five or so soldiers stormed in our direction. I muttered a quick prayer, trying to keep my nerves under control. Within what seemed like seconds, the DoubleE soldiers were so close we could hear their footsteps. Roberts and I both were clutching a knife in our left hand and a pistol in our right. A DounleE boot thudded into the ground, so near it splashed mud onto my helmet. That was close enough. I exploded upwards, swinging my arm in a full ark before slamming my blade into the first soldier's forehead. His body went limp, but I managed to hold him upright. Using his torso as a shield and his shoulder as a pistol-rest, I opened fire on his comrades. Strength born of adrenaline allowed me to fling the hefty soldier around like a rag doll as I moved from target to target. With every jerk of the trigger, I was rewarded with a burst of blood and another dead enemy. Between my gunfire and Roberts swinging his knife like a madman, it was only seconds before half-a-dozen soldiers lay dead at our feet.

"Find the radio-man!" I told Roberts, but he was already on the task.

He hastily stripped a radio from a dead soldier's back and handed it to me. Just as I had planned, the radio crackled and a deep Russian voice muttered a few incomprehensible words from the other end. I took a deep breath, hastily mumbling over the line that Collins had spent over an hour teaching me, then pressed the radios receiver. In the best Russian accent and dialect I could muster, I replied.

"Vse khorosho. Bylsol'nyi navodchika. My vzyali yego s soboi nikto ne postradal, no ya dumayu, chto chto-to zdes' nuzhno videt'. Prinesite reserving kopirovaniya na vsyakii sluchai."

The voice from the other end replied, but I could not understand a word.

"Was he convinced?" Roberts asked.

"Let's hope so," I said, "If he is, he should be sending up a unit of men now."

I tossed the DoubleE radio aside and grabbed my own.

"Collins, all clear."

I heard a short burst of static on the radio as she hit the send button in conformation. Phase two had begun.

Infrared showed that at least a dozen soldiers were heading our way. That was perfect. Unfortunately for them, the only thing they would find waiting for them at the edge of the camp was an armful of carefully placed claymore 2100's. We threw one last bunch of foliage over the bodies to ensure they wouldn't be spotted before tearing off to where O'Brian had repositioned himself.

I held a pair of night-vision binoculars locked to my eyes, carefully watching the small unit of soldiers trek towards the trap. As they neared closer, I began to fear that they would become suspicious about the lack of activity. However, the ill-fated step of a Chinese private put this fear to rest. The second the first claymore's motion sensor was triggered, all five of them went off. A wall of pyramid shaped rounds tore through the small group of soldiers, leaving some disemboweled and others missing more than one limb. Not even a solitary cry echoed from the grisly scene. However, the remaining camp was a different story. Upon hearing the thundering report, the camp flew back into a chaos. Tents, backpacks, logs and anything else the DoubleEs could find were quickly thrown in a circle to use as cover. Every last soldier scrambled to take a position behind the makeshift barricade, even the ones guarding the main tent. I hit the send button on the radio three times, our designated signal for phase three. Simultaneous fire opened up from all three positions, raining lead into the entrenched soldiers. I swept my rifle back and forth, the trigger jerked all the way back like the pedal of a racecar. As soon as I was out of rounds, Roberts stepped into my place, employing the same tactic. With all three positions using this method, there was no window of opportunity for the DoubleEs to counterattack. Every chance he got, O'Brian would snipe the ones who dared look up from their cover. Out of the corner of my vision, I saw Collins rushing towards the main tent. The instant before she slipped inside, my heart sank. If that tent was a trap, anything from landmines to an ambush of soldiers could be waiting for her inside. After a few torturing seconds, she emerged, a large briefcase in her arms. I breathed a sigh of relief, before taking Roberts spot and opening fire. A few quick bursts were all I got off before a small yellow flare streaked up into the sky. It burned all the way up like a blazing meteor, before fizzling out just as I reached its highest point. As simultaneous as we had started, the squad ceased fire.

"Let's go," I said, and tore off into the woods.

I had no doubt they were following us. They may have waited for a good while before breaking cover, but they were coming. I was oblivious of where I was running; my face was bombarded with branches, and my feet were constantly landing in holes or smashing into rocks. Still, I flew forward.

After nine hours of this blind rush, I was unable to go another step. I took a ragged breath, then collapsed into a small thicket of marsh grass. The sweet green shoots enveloped me in their primitive comfort, provoking further my urge to sleep. My chest heaved relentlessly for over three minutes, before slowly settling into a more controlled rhythm. I planted my hands into the soft ground and painfully hoisted myself up. O'Brian wiped his sweat-covered forehead with his sleeve, then locked eyes with me.

"I can't go any further, Cap'n."

"Don't worry, we're not." I said.

The thick foliage completely blocked my view of the horizon, however, I could faintly see the filtration of dawn's light. Layer by layer, I removed my sweat drenched clothing until I was down to a dingy, white undershirt. My throat was so dry, it felt like it had been scraped raw on the inside. I slowly unscrewed the cap on my canteen and drained the last bit of water. It was enough to wet my tormented throat, but not nearly enough to replenish all of the fluids I'd lost.

"We've got to contact the others," I said.

"Good luck," Roberts said, "The radios are shot dead."

"They were working earlier," I said.

"Sorry, chap. It was the first thing I tried. They must have taken out the backup satellites."

I pressed the call button on my receiver just for conformation. Nothing but silence followed. A sick feeling swept through my stomach. For the second time, *something* had taken out our communications, and now, we were separated and lost in the middle of the Marsh territory with no way of regrouping.

"I don't suppose we have any food," O'Brian said.

Roberts shook his head. "Gatling carried all the food."

"Find a water source, Roberts" I said, "And make it fast. I don't care what it looks like, the first pool of water you find, fill the canteens and drop a few of these in."

I tossed him a pack of water purifiers.

"O'Brian, take stock of our equipment and run an ammo check. I'm going to try and find something to keep us from starving."

A few more slivers of young wood fell to the ground before I was satisfied with the point I had carved. I tested the balance of the makeshift spear, then trekked into the swamp. Any file you could read with a title similar to *Xavier Swamp Survival 101* would tell you that the most readily available source of food in this region is an amphibious eel-like species called leespers. These fat insectivores wait patiently beneath the surface of mud/water pools for swamp insects to land on the thick slush. This time tested method of filling their bellies is exactly what makes them so easy to catch. I spotted something scuttle across my boot and quickly snatched it up. A nice and fat beetle writhed in my palm, biting futilely at my thumb. Bait in hand, I scanned the ground for a promising pool. About ten yards to my right was a large pit of marshy slosh that looked like it would be chock-full of leespers. I stealthily crept to the edge of the hole, hoping to avoid scaring them into seclusion. The beetle writhed furiously, pure instinct telling him to stay clear of these traps, but with a careful flick, I tossed the hapless insect into the water. His armored legs kicked rapidly as he tried in vain to get to the edge. The point of my spear was positioned a foot or so above the pool surface. My eyes were locked on the beetle and had they not been, I would have missed his disappearance entirely. A snout tip, no bigger than a pencil eraser, surfaced and sucked the unfortunate bug inwards. Just as the leesper submerged, I drove the wooden spear downward. The tip sank deep into the top of the creatures head, pinning him in place. He thrashed violently, sending a mixture of muck and blood flying onto my suit. With a small bit of exertion, I flipped the writhing fish onto the bank. A few more thrashes of its muscular tail and the leesper gave into death, his eyes still staring blankly at the strange stick protruding from his head. I slid my knife from its sheath and quickly went to work on the kill, knowing there was no time to waste.

143

It wasn't long before the leesper was reduced to a pile of fleshless bones. I slipped the long, reddish-white strips into a small bag and headed back to the grass clearing we had stopped in. Upon arriving, I found Roberts and O'Brian standing beside a pile of march ready gear.

"Any luck?" O'Brian asked.

I nodded and tossed him the bag of raw meat.

"Have at it, you're going to need the calories," I said.

He reached his hand into the bag and pulled out a sliver of meat, still dripping with oil. His face curled in disgust. He shook his head disapprovingly and popped the morsel into his mouth. After chewing twice, he swallowed hard, threatening to expel it back out.

"Oh, come on now, ya pansy, it can't be that bad." Roberts said, taking the bag from O'Brian and tossing a slice of meat into his mouth. He chewed amply, then swallowed.

"Tastes like sushi, chaps. Not bad really."

O'Brian and I were able to choke down the remainder of our serving, drinking gulps of water at a time to wash out the stagnant taste of the raw leesper. Roberts seemed to rather enjoy the ordeal, however, cracking jokes at us and offering to finish ours if we couldn't handle it. In spite of these light-hearted moments, the discussion afterwards was serious as death.

"We've got to regroup," I said, "But with no way to communicate I don't see how."

O'Brian stuck a blade of grass in his teeth and chewed it nervously, "Is there any spot that the rest of the squad might think going to?"

I thought hard, staring down at the maps Sergeant Tanner had given me. Finally, I gave up.

"I've got nothing. The only spot of any significance is where the Scroll is."

Roberts perked up.

"Then why don't we just head that way and assume that the rest would do the same. After all, we were all told to continue the mission no matter the circumstance, and the mission is to get those bloody Scrolls, right?"

"That'd be great Roberts, but what chance do they have of

finding it without these?" I said, holding the maps up for him to see.

An almost goofy smile spread across O'Brian's face as he reached in his pack and retrieved three photocopies of the maps.

"Collins made them. She gave them to everyone so far as I know."

"It's still an assumption that that's where they'll be going," I said.

Roberts frowned, "Maybe, but it's our only shot."

Chapter 23

An uneventful march is always ideal, and after three hours of walking through the heart of Marsh territory, without seeing a trace of its dreadful inhabitants, it was looking like that's what we'd receive. I indifferently brushed a biting insect from the back of my neck; It had gotten to the point that their stinging attacks ceased to have any effect.

"I dunno, Captain," Roberts said, "Maybe they're taking a break."

I didn't take my eyes off a curious pillar of steam rising from a puddle, but gave a doubtful frown.

"It's so hot out here," O'Brian said, "Maybe they went somewhere cooler,"

This was laughable if he was talking about the Marsh creatures; they were far to evolved to this climate. However, if the DoubleEs were the "they" in question, it was a possibility. I really didn't know which one Roberts and O'Brian were talking about and nor did it matter. Both the DoubleEs and Marsh tribe were after us, and neither one of them had shown.

"You know," O'Brian said, "It's fairly dry around here compared to some of the other spots we've been through. I wonder if it's *too* dry. For the Marsh creatures I mean."

"Maybe," I said.

I stopped to examine a sizable track in the swamp mud. Deep webbings extended off to the sides and small indentions at the tips of the marks indicated claws. It was undoubtedly that of a Marsh creature, but it was also old.

"I'd say about two days. What do you think, O'Brian?"

After a few seconds with no reply, I turned to see O'Brian standing over a second track, a fresher one.

"I don't know. But I can tell you however old it is, this one's far less."

He was right. Fresh mud clung to the outside edges of the print, and a crushed flower that'd not had time to wilt lay at its bottom.

I sighed, but kept silent. They knew the drill; break-time was over.

The burning sun finally set at around twenty-two hundred hours, giving relief to our scorched bodies. At this point, I was wondering just how much I could take, how many more steps it would be before I simply collapsed. No matter how hard a pace we set, though, there would be no traveling in the dark.

"See anywhere we could make camp?" I asked.

"One spot looks the same as the other," O'Brian said, shining his light around.

"Good," I said, throwing my pack aside and slumping onto the damp ground.

"Look," I said, trying to stay awake, "I know how tired you must be, but I'm going to give it to ya straight. Somebody has to be keeping watch every minute of the night. There's about nine hours until daybreak so we'll divide into three-hour shifts. Roberts, you've got the first."

I heard him grumble, but pretended not to notice.

"I'll take the second shift," I said, "O'Brian, you've got the third."

Roberts perched his back against the base of a large tree, while O'Brian and I gathered moss for bedding. We even made Roberts a spot for when his shift was over, a gesture he acknowledged with an appreciative nod. When I finally lay back against the thick pad of tree moss, it felt like heaven. I took a deep breath then slowly let it out. Overhead, the pale white moon had faded, sometimes disappearing entirely as thick black clouds drifted in front of it. I was overjoyed with the cool night breeze that was pushing them along, but could only hope it didn't mean storms. My eyelids fluttered, and I could feel myself drifting. A wave of comfort enveloped me fully, just before I fell asleep.

Smoke, fire, death everywhere, even on the face of someone I loved dearly, though I couldn't make out who that might be. A simple gesture, a stroke of the hand I believe, or was it a kiss? Then I was running, running to meet my death, until suddenly a voice intervened.

"Captain, for God's sake wake up."

I slowly opened my eyes, allowing my vision to adjust to the

147

stream of white pouring from Roberts' flashlight.

"You must've been having some kind of a dream," Roberts said.

"Nightmare more like," I said, still rubbing the sleep from my eyes.

"At any rate, it's your shift,"

I took the light from Roberts and sleepily trudged to my post, the strange dream all but forgotten.

The night passed slower than honey in the dead of winter. While I'd been asleep, thick black clouds had poured in, blotting out every star in the sky. I was now convinced there would be a storm. The cool breeze that had lulled me to sleep slowly turned into a gusting wind, forcing me to rely on sight more than hearing. I leaned back against the gnarly tree base and stifled a yawn.

At least the swamp bugs shut up, I thought, *a storms almost worth it for that alone.*

Over the wind, I heard the snap of a twig. My finger slowly eased down the rifles stock until it was resting on the trigger. Slowly, I maneuvered around the tree until I was facing the direction of the noise. A slight movement caught my eye, and I raised the rifle to my cheek. I was just about to pull the trigger, but then stopped. Not very many hostiles on Xavier have long red hair.

"Collins?" I said.

"Who do you think it is?" she said, walking over and kneeling down in front of me,

"I've been tracking you three since noon. That was some pace you were keeping. I might have not closed the gap if you hadn't stopped."

"You weren't being very stealthy," I said, half-way joking.

She shrugged, "Wasn't trying to be."

"Did you see any sign of the others?' I asked.

She shook her head, "No, but we both know where they'll be heading."

"That was a good idea to make photocopies," I said.

She shrugged this off too. I suddenly remembered a very important question.

"Did you get the Scrolls?"

"I think so…maybe," she said, a concerned look spreading over her face.

"What's that supposed to mean?"

"I'm sorry, but I'm too exhausted to explain now. I'll tell you everything in the morning. I promise it can wait."

I nodded understandingly, though I would have really liked to have known what she'd meant by "maybe". Collins rose from the ground and gave me a sleepy wink, before resigning to my bedding.

Morning came much quicker than I would have liked, bringing with it a slight drizzle. The refreshing shower felt great on my sunburned skin, but I knew it was only a lead-up to a full-blown storm. An ominous clap of thunder sounded in the distance, foretelling of a miserable march. I gave the laces on my boots a final tug before strolling over to Collins' small pup tent.

"Collins, you in there?"

"Yeah, come in."

I lifted the tents plastic flap and entered into the closet sized tent. There was nothing inside but a tarp, so I crossed my legs and sat on the soft ground.

"Let's cut to the chase," I said, "Did you get the Scrolls back?"

Rather than reply, she grabbed what looked like a small briefcase and slid it in front of me.

I raised my eyebrows questioningly, "What's in there?"

"I'm assuming the Scrolls are," she said.

"Can't you open it?"

"That's the problem, Michael. This thing's what they call a DoubleE death-case."

I start to question her, but she quickly elaborated.

"You see all these knobs and dials," she said, pointing to a series of complicated locks and switches at the edge of the ink black case, "If they're not opened in exactly the right way, the outer shell of this case is gonna blow sky-high."

"Can't we just bring the case along with us and open it when we get back?" I asked.

"We could," she said, "But there are two problems with that. For one, I don't know if the Scrolls are in there or not. It could still just be a decoy. Second, there's a good chance that there's a tracking device inside this thing. The DoubleEs would know every

149

move we make."

I started to say something then paused, "We wouldn't have to worry about being tracked. At least I don't think we would. Any device I know of would communicate via satellite, and as far as we know, there aren't any satellites left."

She nodded, "I guess you tried the radio, too."

"First thing I did."

She shook her head then bit her lip, "There's some crazy stuff going on."

I gave a dry laugh.

"So what if the Scrolls are not in here after all?" she asked.

I shook my head and sighed. I was tired of problems, tired of solving them based purely on speculation. I picked the briefcase up and gave it a good shake. A slight rattle of something hitting the case's sides is all I heard.

"Doesn't mean anything," Collins said, "They could have shoved a few rocks in there just to throw us off. That's what I would have done, if I was trying to make a fake that is."

I roughly set the case aside. A startled look from Collins reminded me that the thing was wired to blow.

"Careful," she said, sliding the briefcase into her pack.

I started to protest her carrying the Scrolls, but then stopped. I trusted her absolutely.

Suddenly, she gave a quick glance to make sure the tent flaps were closed then shot me an alluring wink.

"Did you get the tent off the Gunship?" I asked.

"Yes," she said, scooting a little closer.

"Why?" I asked.

She smiled, "It only weighs five pounds, and it'll keep the rain off."

"I think you had ulterior motives," I said.

"Well," she said, once again sliding a little closer, "Maybe I did."

She laced her fingers together around the back of my neck and gracefully pulled herself into my lap. Her subtle lips locked with mine, sending me into a tailspin. I slowly traced my hands down her body as we kissed, savoring her shapely curves before settling my hands into her back pockets. The passion in our caress swiftly rose. I could tell my body was taking over, overruling my mind. I lifted my hands up to the top of her suit, until my shaking fingers fumbled across the first button on her heaving chest. No sooner did I get it unfastened, there was a knock on the tent's flap.

Collins threw herself off me and hastily buttoned her suit back.

"Yeah?" I said questioningly.

"Uh hmm, um, we kind of need to get going, chaps, don't ya think?"

"Uh, yeah, be there in a minute."

I looked at Collins, then took a deep breath, "I love you, Ashley, but 'this', is not what we need right now."

She simply nodded, a distant look on her face. I brushed a lock hair behind her ear and smiled.

"I guess we'd better go,"

She smiled a little, quickly regaining her composure. I broke my gaze, then lifted the tent's flap and left.

The heat of the humid rain, the heat of our encounter, combined to break me into a cold sweat. I leaned back against the base of a small tree then took a few gulps of water from my canteen. The first thing I'd done upon leaving Collins' tent was to get away. I had trudged well past the edge of our camp before setting down at the tree. Now my thoughts were whirling uncontrollably. *This* shouldn't be happening. My initial approach of ignoring had morphed into a full blown and dangerous relationship. It was treacherous, and I knew it was. I shouldn't even be socializing with her. That alone could get me court-martialed, and that's not to mention the danger in being so distracted. I had completely forgotten about where we were and what we should be doing. Even now, I was burning precious daylight trying to get myself under control. There had to be restrictions. Some other place might not be an option, but some other time was. I jerked my rifle off the ground and headed back to camp.

"Good news, Cap'n," Roberts said as soon as I arrived, "More sushi!"

I looked at the oil dripping carcass of a leesper Roberts was holding in front of me then frowned in disgust.

"A 'thank you for catching breakfast' would have been customary."

I ignored him. He sat down and started peeling off strips of meat. I walked over to the center of camp and started getting my gear together. Small drops of rain were quickly turning into large ones, and magnificent plumes of black storm clouds were being sucked thousands of miles into the atmosphere. A flash of lightning twisted from one of these plumes and into another, followed by a clap of thunder. The sky looked dreadful, but we had to march. There was no way we could hole up here. I rose to my feet and was about to give the call to head out when I heard my radio crackling.

Chapter 24

I stared blankly at the transmitter. The radio crackled again, and I could barely hear a voice. This broke my disbelief. Fumbling with the receiver, I pressed it to my ear.

"This is Captain Dawn, over."

"There's not much time, Cap'n, so I'll make it quick. Your orders are to rendezvous with SEAL Team 11 at the north end of sector 953995 before continuing your mission. The rest of your squad has been contacted and are on their way now. "

There was a pause, for questions I suppose, and I had plenty.

"Why do we need backup?" I asked.

"There's been a few complications. It's likes the entire Marsh tribe has communicated across their te'itory. As far as we can tell every single one of them have gathered towa'ds the Scroll and we don't have a guess why they would care. At any rate, you guys aren't going to be able to get in and out of the'e alone."

I started to ask another question but was interrupted.

"I'm sorry, Cap'n, I wish I had time to fill you in completely, but I don't. We're operating off an eme'gency satellite launch and I've got a lot mo'e messages to get out before they shoot it down. Good luck.

I set the receiver down, starving for more information. I could tell by his accent that the man on the other end was Private Scott, General Stacks' assistant.

Stacks must be some kind of preoccupied to have his secretary relaying that kind of info, I thought.

I wasn't sure whether to be relieved or concerned about having backup on this one. It was relieving to not have to go at it solo, but very worrisome that we needed it in the first place. We had gone through some pretty grim situations getting the first three Scrolls and they decide to send help *now*?

"Get ready," I said, shoving the radio into my pack, "We need to move."

By midmorning we were marching again, though it didn't seem

like morning or marching. It was more like trudging through a hurricane. The storm I'd been waiting for had arrived with a vengeance, sending sheets of stinging rain into our faces. The swampy ground flooded in minutes, making the march more like a swim. I looked up at the boiling storm clouds through squinted eyes. They showed no sign of letting up. Pulling my drenched hat a little tighter, I slogged forward into the gale.

It was almost noon before the storm let up, giving way to a slight sprinkle that peppered newly formed pools with small, ripple-causing drops. A dazzling double rainbow spanned the slowly clearing sky, and the insects were resuming their chorus.

"Let's hold up here for a minute," I said.

Grateful for a break in the march, Roberts, Collins and O'Brian all shed their packs and found a relatively dry log to sit on. I hung my own pack from a sturdy looking branch and joined them. The decomposing wood gave a little under our weight, threatening to collapse entirely into a pile of rotted pulp.

"Whew, the heat doesn't wait very long," O'Brian said.

He was right. The sun had not reemerged more than fifteen minutes ago, and already the saturated air was turning into steam. It was the worst kind of heat too. Swamp heat always is.

"Hey," Roberts said, "What do you suppose we're in the middle of anyway?"

At first it seemed like a dumb question, but then I realized what he was talking about. All around us was the evidence of what looked like a mass extinction. Forms of life I had never seen before, most of which no longer existed, lay forever preserved in rock fossils. Entire trees lay across the watery ground, every detail captured in stone. The ossified remains of reptiles, amphibians and even a few mammals lay scattered across the petrified forest. Large pools of oil, born from the decay, rose to the surface of the muck.

"Boy oh boy," I said, "Gatling would have loved this."

I picked up rust colored rock and turned it over in my hand. A palm-sized hornet-like insect had been entombed in its center, leaving a perfect print of its crisp features behind.

"What do you suppose happened," O'Brian asked.

"Most likely a mudslide." Roberts said "The geology could have been different here in the ancient past and this was most

154

likely a valley that got the bitter end of a few tons of soil."

I gave him a puzzled look, surprised by his answer.

"What?" he said, "I dated a paleontologist once, chaps. No need for concern; I'm not turning into a bloody...a bloody...Gatling, yeah that's the word."

I smiled. I could have stayed here all day, taking in the melancholic beauty of a forest frozen in time. There was no telling what discoveries were lying here, no way to know what secrets were entombed within stone, but sadly, no one on Xavier gave a damn.

"Come on," I said, "We've got to go."

"Can I have just a minute, Captain?" Roberts asked, "Let me find one good souvenir to give my little boy, in case he ever makes it here."

I gladly granted him this request. I even placed the wasp fossil in my pack to keep for myself.

Roberts quickly settled on the preserved remains of a tiny, carnivorous plant and slipped it into his pocket. I gave one last look at the remarkable scene. A spectral of colors moved across the oil's shiny surface, and a flying insect landed at the tip of a fully preserved tree. Then I turned away, walking out of serenity and back into reality.

"If there was one species I could rid Xavier of entirely, do you know what it would be?" Roberts said.

"What?" I asked.

"These bloody insects."

"Insect is a Class," O'Brian said, "Not a species."

"I said I dated a paleontologist, I didn't say I was one."

While incorrect and exaggerated, Roberts did have a point. Constant buzzing, constant biting, and a few other choice annoyances were all the millions of insects in this swamp were good for, and they performed their tasks relentlessly. O'Brian had even managed to angry what looked like the descendent of the fossil I had found, resulting in an egg sized whelp on his forearm.

Roberts slapped another biting pest off of his neck, "I swear chaps if I get sick and die from Xavier's rendition of malaria I'm suing the military for every cent they've got."

I didn't even bother to point out the obvious as I sometimes wondered if it's intentional with Roberts.

"I don't think you have to worry about it," I said, "Xavier malaria has to have been covered under at least one of our forty-three vaccinations."

Roberts didn't look convinced.

"How far off are we?" O'Brian asked.

I looked at the worn out map Sergeant Tanner had given me and tried to make sense of it.

"It's hard to tell," I said, "But I think we're about a half days march away."

I handed the map to Collins.

"Wouldn't you say that was the hill we just passed?" I asked, pointing to a raised area on the map that indicated elevation.

She took a close look at the map, her eyes skittering across the worn paper, then glanced back over her shoulder, even though the hill was well out of sight.

"Yes, I think it is." she said, handing me the map.

I nodded, "A half-day march is about right, so long as we don't stop again."

"You know," O'Brian said, "It's actually nice having the Marsh tribe all in one spot where we don't have to worry about them."

"That only means we'll have to worry about them that much more when the time comes to get the Scroll," I said.

He frowned, "Yeah, but for right now it's kinda nice, lads."

It did make for a much more peaceful march. I was noticing things about Xavier I never had before. Seeing various scenes from Xavier's flora and fauna, such as a mother bird no bigger than my thumb diligently feeding a nest full of babies half that size, gave me hope the planet might be habitable after all.

"Why do you think they would rally together like that?" Collins asked, "I can't see why a tribe too primitive to even fashion weapons or clothing would care about the Scroll."

"I don't know," I said, "I'm not even going to take a guess."

"I will," Roberts said, "I propose that rather than valiantly defending the Scroll, the beasts are merely gathering there for some kind of jolly reunion, ya know."

"Maybe if you would put as much effort into marching as you do coming up with these absurd ideas, we would get a lot further." Collins said.

Roberts faked to be hurt, then replied, "You wouldn't like me serious."

"I'm not so sure I like you anyway," she said.

This time Roberts didn't mock offense. He gazed distantly into the dense forest.

"I've only got two modes, chaps, joker and killer. Ones a lot more enjoyable than the other."

I recalled the way he fought in both of our interactions with the Eastern Empire soldiers, battling his way out of there like a madman. I felt at that moment as if I understood Roberts a little better. His antics served to erase his memories and cover the killer inside of him. I sighed, we all had one or we wouldn't be here.

Collins, however, wasn't going to take him seriously, "You're kidding yourself right? My cat was a better killer than you could hope to be."

"Why missy, I'd challenge your cat in a contest of killing any day of the week."

Collins smiled, then pulled out her photocopy of the map, "I think we'd better pick up the pace a little if we want to make it by nightfall."

I glanced at my watch, then leaned over and looked at her map. "She's right. We'd better get moving."

The swamp seemed to grow thicker, more water and less soil, with every step we took. Undoubtedly the small deluge that had moved through earlier had a hand in this. At any rate, our pace had been slowed incredibly. I lifted my legs straight up and down in the knee deep water, not daring to think what might be slithering around them. Thick brambles of dead brush replaced luscious grass as we continued deeper into the swamp.

"I'd hate to think about having to cross this with the Marsh tribe infesting it," Collins said.

"We wouldn't have made it twenty yards in this stuff," I added.

I looked around at the countless places a Marsh creature could have concealed itself. Several half submerged logs, covered in thick algae, would have worked perfectly, as would a few of the denser thickets of swamp brush.

"You know, I wonder if we should trust that report completely," Roberts said, "After all, there is a chance that a few of them hung back."

"Maybe," I said, maneuvering under a bundle of overhanging vines, "I'd like to think they wouldn't tell us something like that if it wasn't one-hundred percent true."

Roberts frowned, "It wouldn't be the first time they didn't tell us the whole story."

"That's just speculation," I said, even though I agreed.

"I'm going to keep my eyes peeled that's for sure," O'Brian said.

I could tell he had moved his rifle into a more accessible position after hearing our conversation. That was okay though. A slight sense of paranoia could keep you alive on this planet. After all, Roberts was right; it wouldn't be the first time they didn't tell the entire story.

Gradual was the best way to describe the receding water level, but with every mile of thick brown slush we sloshed our way through, it grew shallower. By twenty hundred hours we were back into ankle deep water. The sluggish progress the knee-deep water had forced was having its consequences, though. A glance at the map, then at the sinking sun, told me there was no way we could make it to the rendezvous point by nightfall.

"I sure would have liked to have regrouped before we made camp," Collins said.

"Me too," I said, "But we might as well start looking for a suitable spot."

"Cap'n," O'Brian whispered.

I turned to see him lying prone in the swamp water, his scope pressed to his eye. I jerked my binoculars up and scanned the direction he was looking in. It only took me a second to spot what he was looking at. Movement, I couldn't tell what or how many, but *something* was clamoring around about a hundred yards to our east.

I shouldered my rifle and sank into the watery muck, "Get low and get ready."

Chapter 25

Warm water lapped against my suit as I lay down in the ankle deep swamp. Using my elbows and knees to pull myself across the slimy mud, I slowly positioned myself behind a fallen tree. I placed my back against the rotting wood, causing strips of wet bark to fall down my back and into the shallow water. Slowly, I glanced back at O'Brian. He had not moved an inch. His eye was still pressed gently against his scope, his fingers swiftly adjusting various knobs on its neck. Small ripples of water, driven by the after-storm breeze, splashed against him, but he paid them no attention.

"Conformation?" I whispered.

He didn't move an inch, but his lips mouthed the word, "No."

I thought about peering over the log to look again for myself, but didn't want to risk the movement. It had been risky enough crawling over here in the first place. After a minute of tense stillness, O'Brian slowly raised his dripping hand out of the water and cupped it to his ear. I trained my hearing, listening intently for whatever sound he'd noticed. Over the never ending chorus of swamp bugs, I was barely able to make out the din of someone speaking English. O'Brian took his eyes off his scope and rose.

"We're clear, lads. They're on our side."

We hadn't walked fifty yards before we were stopped by a steely and calculated corporal. His sharp brown eyes never broke from mine, nor did his gloved finger move from the trigger on his shotgun.

"State your name, rank and orders," he said, looking at me and paying no attention to the others.

"Captain Michael Dawn. Orders are to rendezvous with SEAL Team 11 for a joint operations undertaking."

He lowered his shotgun and grunted, "You're in the right place at least."

He turned and started walking away.

"Why didn't you follow standard approach protocol?" he asked, without turning around, "I would have killed you all if I hadn't been expecting you."

"The rules are different on Xavier, Corporal," I said, purposefully reminding him of his rank, "Humans are the good guys."

He spat, his back still facing us, "Not anymore."

I knew he was referring to the Eastern Empire, however, I could tell by his tone things must have gotten worse.

"The next time you approach a friendly, activate your locater beacons. Got it?"

"I know the procedure, Corporal,"

He snorted, "Apparently not."

Roberts must have had enough of the brash corporal's mouth. He grabbed him roughly by his shoulder and spun him around.

"Now you listen here, chap…"

Before Roberts could finish, the wiry haired soldier threw a wild left hook at his chin. Roberts reacted immediately, parrying the strike and sending a thudding punch of his own into the young corporal's side. I heard a whoosh of air leaving his lungs, but he didn't go down. Instead, he lunged forward, sending a powerful kick flying towards Robert's knee. The impact from the steel-toed boot would have easily broken his leg, but Roberts blocked it nicely with his foot before combining a lightning-fast series of jabs and crosses. The stunned Corporal stumbled backwards under the blows, before falling into the swampy water.

"Had enough?" Roberts asked, standing over the defeated corporal.

"I think he has," a voice to my left answered.

I turned to see a burly colonel sloshing over to where we were.

The young corporal started scrambling to get up, sputtering off words at the same time, "Sir, um these men…"

"Shut up, Mulligan," the colonel said, "You'd better get back to camp before I beat you myself."

The shamed soldier, got up and shuffled off, strongly favoring his left leg.

"The name's Colonel Steve Fisher," he said, extending a salute that I hesitantly returned, "Sorry about the welcoming committee. The only reason Mulligan was keeping watch in the first place was I wanted to punish him for spouting off."

He shook his head and sighed, "I guess I should have thought that through better."

"By the way," he said, nodding towards Roberts, "That was some whoopin' you put on him. They don't teach you to box like that in the service. Where'd you pick that up?"

Roberts beamed, "I was a three time middleweight champion of the UK before joining the service."

Colonel Fisher nodded, "Impressive."

He turned and started walking towards the camp.

"Come on," he said, "I've seen strays that looked better nurtured than you lot. Let's get ya'll some food and dry clothes. Besides, I think there's a few of your bunch that might enjoy seeing ya'll again."

After walking about thirty yards, I was beginning to wonder where exactly this camp was. All I saw was thick foliage and swampy water. Suddenly, I noticed the swamp ahead looked a little strange. The depth seemed to be a little off, the color a little hazy.

Colonel Fisher walked up to this peculiar area and reached out into nothing. I heard a slight unzipping sound as thin air parted open like the flaps of a tent.

"After you," the colonel said, standing by the bizarre opening.

I stood gapping, trying to figure out what was going on, when Collins stepped forward.

A thrilled smile spread across her face, "It's an invisibility cloak!"

"Invisibility dome, actually," Colonel Fisher said, "We employed it so we could set up a full scale camp."

"How does it work?" I asked, still in awe.

"It's shaped in such a way at both the micro and uh...large levels that the light on any side of it is reflected over and to the other side. Makes the thing and what it's concealing look like it isn't even there."

He motioned with hands for us to enter, "Come on boys...and miss," he said, as if he just noticed Collins. I saw his eyes glance up and down her a few times before he continued.

"Let's not stay out here all day."

The instant I entered the dome, I was bewildered that it had hidden *so* much *so* well. At least twenty full sized tents were set up at the dome's further most edge. At its center was a large fire, curiously, not giving off an ounce of smoke. Peculiar, one-man vehicles were parked at another corner. I peered up. Large light fixtures lined the black edges of the dome's ceiling, casting an artificial glow. Again, I was taken aback by the dome's dimensions. The ceiling was at least three-stories high, and it's diameter around a hundred meters. Colonel Fisher must have caught my stare, because he answered my question without me asking it.

"It has to be taller than the trees or else their image will be cut off."

I nodded, not completely understanding, but pretending like I did. The next thing I noticed was the ground. Rather than swampy water, we were now standing on a solid floor. Somehow, I refused to believe that the only dry portion of the Marsh territory happened to be the exact same size as their dome.

"What's going on here, Colonel?"

Colonel Fisher chuckled, "I've got far too much to tell and far too little time to tell it. Why don't we get you some dry clothes, somewhere to rest and a warm meal, then you and me can take a little stroll and I'll explain."

I nodded, "Sounds good."

He gave a smile that reminded me of a deceitful politician, then walked off, but not before taking one last look at Collins... a look I didn't fail to notice.

I watched him leave, watched every step he took.

"I don't think I like him any more than the screw-brained corporal Roberts worked over," I said.

Collins flashed me a suggesting smile, "I wonder why?"

We stood there for almost five minutes before a six foot private with buzzed black hair and Native American features strolled over.

"Follow me," he said, not making eye contact.

We let him lead us through the center of the camp, past various tents, latrines and numerous soldiers, each engaged in lively games of poker and telling wild tales of their sexual endeavors, most of which were probably lies. Finally, we arrived at a small patch of tents, made of thick green vinyl and shaped like wide based pyramids. He motioned towards two separate tents, one almost twice the size of the other. In the largest, I could hear a small clamor of conversation

"There's a few more of your squadron in there," he said, pointing at the larger tent, "Though I'm not sure how many you're expecting."

"What's with the other tent?" I asked.

"Colonel Fisher requested it be moved here for her," he said, motioning towards Collins. She looked at me then shrugged.

"Food will be here shortly," he said, then turned to walk away, but Roberts stopped him.

"We didn't catch your name, chap."

The private turned back around, then hesitated.

"My name is Chinmay Yang," He said, then, as if he was accustomed to explaining this, he elaborated.

"The first name is Cherokee, like my mother. My father was Korean."

Roberts stifled a laugh.

"How 'bout that, chaps?"

"That's nice, Roberts," I said, then turned to catch Collins before she went into her "private" tent.

"I need to talk with you later." I said.

She nodded then disappeared inside.

"You know something odd," I said.

"What?" O'Brian asked.

"We're supposed to be meeting with SEAL Team 11, right?"

"Yeah?" O'Brian said.

"How come none of these men are even dressed like Navy, much less SEALS?"

O'Brian adjusted his cap, then narrowed his eyes, "I don't know. I just don't know."

"I hope Colonel Fisher is in a mood for answering questions," I said, staring into the distance.

I gripped the tents cool zipper between my thumb and forefinger, then gave it a slight tug. There was a metallic ripping sound as the zipper's handle slowly carved a circular opening in the tent's side. I pushed the thick flaps aside and was greeted by a burst of enveloping warmth and flickering light.

"Captain," Rice said, "You made it,"

"Yeah, I guess I did. Who else made it?"

"Everyone except Collins, O'Brian and Roberts." he said.

"We're right here, lad," O'Brian said, entering the tent along with Roberts, "And Collins is outside."

I saw relief wash over almost everyone's face, the same relief I'd felt when he gave his first answer.

"That makes everyone," I said.

Smith stood and gave a quick salute, "Glad you found us, sir."

I returned his salute and said something, but my concentration was fixed on the eccentric fire at the tents edge. Everything about it was wrong. Its flame was solid white, as was its illuminating beams. There wasn't a trace of smoke, and the heat was somehow…different. Gatling must have seen my confusion, because he spoke up.

"There's something weird going one here. I'm talking like bad re-runs of 21st century sci-fi weird."

"I'm supposed to have a little chat with Colonel Fisher this evening. Hopefully he can elaborate."

"Speaking of little chats," Gatling said, "I need to talk with you sometime tonight."

Great, I thought, *three private meetings in one night.*

"Alright," I said.

"I'm serious, Captain," Gatling said, "It's important."

"I said I'd be there."

Gatling seemed satisfied, at least mostly, and he went back to playing a casual game of checkers with Stillworth.

"Where's the change of clothes they were talking about?" I asked.

Stillworth motioned to the tent's left corner, without taking his eyes off the wooden checker pieces. I walked over and picked up a sack that had my name written across it in black marker. The clothes inside were ridiculous in appearance and composition, strongly resembling the GI's martial arts students used to wear, but with the slight military touch of brass buttons on the shirt's midsection and around the cuffs, along with a pale green coloring that matched our tent. With a chuckle, I slipped out of my sopping, wet uniform and into the fresh garment.

At least it's comfortable, I thought, fastening the first four buttons, but leaving the next two undone.

It was only then that I noticed the rest of the squad was wearing the same attire.

"I need some rest," I said, only imagining what else I might have missed.

Rice pointed towards a cozy looking cot at the tent's edge, "That one's got your name on it, Captain," and he meant literally, "Might as well get some sleep."

I nodded then slipped beneath the cot's soft sheets. After sleeping on the ground for almost two weeks, the freshly made bedding was bliss. I leaned my head back against the pillow, yawning deeply. The last image I saw before drifting off was the pure white flames of the fire dancing back and forth like the transparent ghost of some scorched being. It was an image that haunted my dreams.

Chapter 26

The steamy aroma of a wonderfully hot meal drifted through the air, filling my nostrils, enraging my hunger and waking me almost immediately. I slowly rose, stretching my arms out like a small child. I sat there in the bed for a second or so, savoring the conclusion to the best sleep I'd had since starting this mission. It was a quarter after eleven, meaning I'd slept for almost two hours. Another waft of the savory aroma drifted through my senses, causing me to exit the cot's comfort entirely.

"Better get some, Cap'n," O'Brian said.

I wandered over to a small stainless steel cart that looked like a surgeon's trolley. On top of it sat a steaming pot of meat stew, a few chunks of toasted bread and a jug full of iced tea. I glanced around to make sure everyone had eaten, then greedily shoveled the remainder onto the final plate and poured myself a glass of the tea. My eating habits for the next few minutes must have resembled that of a wild animal. I quickly downed the large bowl of soup, only bothering to use my spoon on the larger chunks of meat that didn't drain so well. After I had finished off the soup and bread, I quickly tossed down the glass of tea.

"Good nosh, huh?" Robert said.

I nodded, then got up.

"If you'll excuse me, I need to talk with Agent Collins," I said, heading towards the tent's flap. I saw Gatling frown, obviously irritated. I couldn't help it though; I needed to talk with her, needed to get a few things off my chest before I dealt with Gatling or Colonel Fisher either one. I grabbed hold of the tents zipper and hastily exited.

Collins' tent was only a short distance from ours, but still I felt exposed, like I couldn't get there fast enough. I reached the entrance then made sure no one was watching.

"Ashley, it's me," I whispered.

As soon as I spoke, she quickly opened the tents flaps and ushered me inside, closing them behind her. Her tent was almost an exact replica of the one the rest of us were staying in, just scaled down. She greeted me with a slight kiss, but it didn't feel right. There was far too much on both of our minds. I listened as she voiced the same concerns I harbored, the uniforms they wore, the dome, the fire and the colonel.

"Did you see the way he looks at me?" she asked.

I nodded, instantly becoming ashamed for not doing something about it.

She shook her head in disgust, "It's like he's a starving animal or something."

I wrapped my arm around her and sat down on the edge of her cot.

"Don't worry," I said, "He won't try anything. If he does you have my permission to take him out." I said, only half joking.

She smiled, "I know he won't."

I wrapped my arm around her a little tighter, and she leaned her head against my shoulder.

Suddenly there was a slight wrap against the tent's frame.

"Miss Collins, are you in there?"

She pushed my arm off of her then looked at me concerned, before answering him.

"Yes, I'm here."

Colonel Fisher unzipped the tents flap without further permission, then entered. A bottle of wine was in his left hand, only the second I'd ever seen on Xavier, and there were two glasses in his right. He started to say something to Collins, but then he saw me. His lighthearted smile quickly faded into a scowl.

"May I ask what you think you're doing here, Captain?"

"Strategizing with a key member of my force. May I ask you the same?" I said, motioning towards the wine.

"You know, a fellow could really get the wrong idea here," he said, ignoring my question, "In fact, I think there's quite a few MPs out there that wouldn't look to highly on an officer relaxing on a cot with a comrade of the opposite sex."

"I told you what I was doing. She's on my team, and I can speak with her at any time I see fitting. By the way, you still didn't answer my question."

"I was just dropping this off," he said, "I had no intention of staying."

"Hmm, a whole bottle of wine just for her? Are you trying to get her drunk? And what's with the second glass you're holding? Is it just for decoration?"

Colonel Fisher turned red; his hands gripped the bottle's neck almost hard enough to crush it.

"I've had quite enough of this, Captain," he said, "I'm a man of my word, and that's the only reason I'm still willing to speak with you later."

"I believe duty might be another reason, Colonel."

He ignored me.

"I'm leaving. Meet me at my quarters in thirty minutes. Maybe that'll give me some time to conveniently forget a few things."

"Maybe you'd both better go" Collins said, ushering us both towards the exit.

"I'm very sorry about this ma'am," Colonel Fisher said.

"I'm an agent, Colonel," she said, "Not a ma'am."

He pursed his lips, then left the tent. As soon as he wasn't watching, she gave me an apologetic look for forcing me out.

"It's okay." I whispered, "The situation called for it."

I left her tent then zipped it closed behind me.

I didn't feel like going back to our tent. I didn't feel like talking with anyone. I shoved my sweating palms into my pocket and shuffled past the main tent. There was a slight hubbub of an argument coming from inside and I stopped to listen. I couldn't tell what they were saying, but it was between Roberts and Gatling, which meant it was probably lighthearted and nonsensical. I walked past the tent, heading towards the patch of vehicles I'd seen earlier. I could feel cool air seeping through the dome and could barely hear the never-ending chirps. The large florescent lights still shone down from the ceiling, though they had been dimmed considerably for the night. I was vaguely gazing at them when the tip of my boot caught on something. I stumbled forward, barely able to retain my balance. I was expecting to see a pack, an ammo box, or some other item someone had thoughtlessly left behind, but instead, it was a rock.

Someone didn't do a very good cleanup before they laid down their little floor.

I reached a hand down and grabbed hold of its rough edge. A

slight tug slowly morphed into an enormous heave, until I had exhausted my efforts, and still the rock wouldn't budge. My eyes narrowed in confusion, and I knelt down to take a closer look. The plastic looking floor around it was the same dull green as everything else in the place, yet it was just transparent enough to see through. Rather than merely sitting on top of the floor as I had first thought, the rock was encased within it. I started peering through the floor at other places, which revealed the same story. Blades of grass, other rocks, even insects lay trapped beneath and within the bizarre floor. It was like a discolored ice storm had blown through, encasing everything in slick sheets of green. I'd had more than enough of this place and its eccentricity. I rose from my knees and headed back to find Colonel Fisher.

I didn't get thirty yards before I realized I didn't have a clue where I was going. All around, there were soldiers gathered near the strange white fires, carrying on the same cluttered conversations, but they disregarded me entirely. I decided to compel them to speak. The distance to the nearest group was about twenty yards, and I jogged towards it. Even when I closed within a few yards, close enough to feel the *different* heat coming from the blazes, no one acknowledged me. No one even stopped their conversation. "

Where's Colonel Fisher?" I asked.

Nobody answered. Most of them just continued talking. I could feel my anger rising, could feel my hands starting to sweat again.

"I believe you're supposed to stand at attention when an officer is present," I yelled.

They stopped talking, a few even looked up at me, but most didn't. I thought I was going to lose it. I felt like beating every one of them until they talked. I clenched my fists, with the intentions of doing just that, when a baby-faced private spoke.

"We're not under your command, Captain, In fact, we're not even…"

He would have continued, had he not noticed the reprimanding stare given to him by his sergeant.

"You speak when you're spoken to, Private." The sergeant said.

I'd had all I could take. I tore my pistol from my belt and pointed the muzzle at the sergeant.

"Someone better start speaking…right now!"

The sergeant stared indifferently at the gun's muzzle, no sign of fear in his eyes. After a few seconds his gaze switched to something beyond me.

"There's no need for that, Captain." a voice from behind me said.

I turned to see a tall, black man that all of Xavier presumed dead, standing a few feet away.

"Put down the gun, Captain Dawn," he said, "We're all on the same team here."

"Ge-General Tipton? I thought…"

"Just put the gun away, and I'll explain everything."

I stared at him for a second, trying to read him. Never breaking my gaze, I slipped the gun back into its holster, though I made sure there was not an ounce of trust in my eyes.

"Come on," he said, "I think it's time we talked."

The general led me across the camp, up to a small building at its edge. Bits of green paint were flecking off the door, and its brass handle looked like one you might see back on earth attached to an ancient convenient store. General Tipton grabbed hold of the handle and gave the door a tug. Timbers groaned and metal scraped against metal as the door creaked open. A dim wash of light poured out and onto the fabricated metal porch.
Tipton stood to the side and motioned inwards with his hand.

"After you, Captain."

I ascended the porch's three steps cautiously. Once I reached the building's entrance, it took even more encouragement to get me inside. My trust for this place and the people who occupied it had reached a dead zero. I quickly took stock of the room's contents. At its center was a circular table about five feet across. A thin layer of dust was the only thing evident on its surface, other than a few deep scratches and strips of peeling varnish. Three small chairs that looked worse off than the table formed a triangle around it. At the edge of the room were several bookcases, lined with all varieties of dust covered volumes. I didn't see any doors that could lead to other rooms, but I didn't expect to. The building had looked fairly small from the outside.

"Have a seat," General Tipton said, sliding one of the chairs from beneath the table.

I slowly settled into the wooden seat, somewhat concerned that it would break. General Tipton reached up and grabbed a small chain that was dangling over the table, and gave it a pull. An overhead light flickered on, causing the aged room to take on a far more inviting appearance. He pulled a chair out for himself and sighed.

"I hear you've got a lot of questions, Captain."

"You heard correctly. I hope you're prepared to answer them."

He spread his hands out in a welcoming gesture, "I'll do my best."

I had so many, in fact, I had a hard time deciding which to ask first. After a few seconds of silence, I began.

"I thought you died three years ago. There was a funeral. It was broadcasted on every station. How are you even here? It's like I'm looking at a ghost."

"I didn't die three years ago, Captain," he said, "I was merely transferred. My death was staged so that people wouldn't ask questions."

"So the Quadrate is still in place?" I asked.

"I'm still calling the shots as much as ever, along with Ridley, Stacks and Young of course. Any other questions?"

I paused, trying to think of what I wanted to ask next.

"I was told we were supposed to meet with SEAL Team 11," I said, "and so far I haven't seen a soldier here I could identify as even being in the Navy."

General Tipton sighed, "Well we're most certainly not SEALS."

"Well what are you then?" I asked, "And how were you able to set up such a full scale camp in so little time?"

"The camp was set up three years ago, Captain. It's a permanent installation." he started to continue, but then stopped.

"Let me start from the beginning," he said, "In the past, as new technologies emerged, they were given to select groups of soldiers who would use them, and tell whether they were indeed effective. About four years ago, however, the rate at which military technology was increasing began to outpace that of soldier willing to field test it. The devices became more and more complicated and numerous as the years went on. Eventually, soldiers refused to use them until they had been properly tested by someone other than themselves. As you can imagine, this created quite the problem. That's when the DoubleA created the E.T.A.D., or Experimental Technologies and Applications Division. That's where you're currently stationed. We, myself and the men you've met, are the individuals who make up the entirety of this division, and almost everything you see within the camp itself, is experimental equipment we are currently testing."

He paused and then looked around the rickety room, "Almost everything, that is."

"The floor?" I asked.

"A substance that sprays on liquid, but turns solid in seconds."

"The fire?"

"The logs are coated with a gel that makes them burn hotter, give off no smoke, light in pouring rain, and remain undetectable by infrared."

Things were definitely starting to become clearer, however, I still had questions.

"Once again, I was told we were supposed to meet with SEALS. Can you explain that?"

"You weren't lied to, Captain. SEAL Team 11 will be arriving here shortly, if they can make it through. Once they do, we will continue the mission you started. If they don't make it, we will continue it without them."

"One more thing, Colonel. Why do your men behave so strangely?"

He sighed, "Some of them don't take to well to the drugs."

I straightened up in my chair, "What drugs?"

He sighed again, waiting for a few tense seconds before replying. "This planet has taught us a very cruel lesson, Captain. Sometimes no amount of firepower can take place of physical abilities. The primitives on this planet are ten times more physically adapt than any army we've ever dealt with, and we're on their home turf. We had to compete somehow, had to fight fire with fire, you see."

"What are you saying?" I asked.

Tipton paused, "Not long after the Xavier Project began, the military started…enhancing its soldiers."

"You mean supersoldiers? I said.

He nodded, "Injected nanobots, physical enhancement drugs,

172

endurance drugs, the whole nine yards. The program was called C.A.M.D.O.S.. Stands for chemical and mechanical development of supersoldiers. "

I took a deep breath, trying to process what I was hearing.

"You don't believe me do you?" he asked.

Before I could answer, he pulled a thin knife from his belt and traced a deep cut across the top of his forearm, keeping a straight face the entire time. No sooner did he lift the blade from his skin, did the cut begin healing. Within seconds, you couldn't even tell he'd been wounded in the first place.

"A dose of Creecriium permanently deadens pain receptors, other than a slight tugging to signal injury. Nanobots in the blood stream detect and heal the damaged cells within seconds."

I slumped back in my chair, unable to believe what I was hearing, unable to believe what I was *seeing*.

"Me and my men are the second phase of this enhancement." he said.

I paused, "If E.T.A.D. is the second phase, who was the first?"

General Tipton sighed again, this time remorsefully.

"You were, Captain. You and your squad."

Chapter 27

My head was spinning; I thought I was going to get sick. Still, I clung to the hope that I'd misheard him. After a few seconds of silence, I forced myself to speak.

"Wha-what did you say?"

"I said that you, the members of your squad and a few other men and women, were the first phase of enhanced soldiers."

Another wave of nausea spread over me.

"I don't believe you, General."

He chuckled slightly, "Come on now, Captain. It's not that hard to see. Why would the world militaries send regular soldiers on the most important mission in this project's history if supersoldiers were available?"

"But…I can't do that," I said, pointing to his healed wrist.

"Of course you can't," he said, "I'm the second phase, the more advanced model, if you will. But you *can* do things an ordinary human can't, Captain Dawn, including healing abilities. I heard you suffered a pretty nasty fall right before you were chosen for this mission. Am I right?"

I nodded.

"Did any of your doctors happen to remark on how quickly you healed?"

Again I nodded, thinking back to my short conference with Dr. Clemson.

"Do you think that was a coincidence?"

I wasn't sure what I thought. My mind was too busy trying to disprove what he was saying to think about anything else.

"Why hasn't Gatling made remarks on our healing abilities?" I asked.

"Because Dr. Gatling knows about the enhancement program. He helped create it and was the first human it was given to. That's one reason why he was chosen."

I was starting to believe, starting to force myself to accept this.

"Look, Captain, healing isn't all this program does. Corporal Rice told me that he had run ten hours straight to get away from the DoubleEs. Ten hours without stopping through a swamp! Do you think a normal human being could do that?"

"I don't know what a 'normal human being' can do, General. Apparently I'm not one."

He noted my sarcasm with a frown.

"But you were, Captain. The enhancement was given to you on the *USS Pandora*. You never had it before."

I stretched my mind, trying to remember the day we'd arrived, trying to remember if I'd felt more powerful than I did on earth, but I couldn't recall anything.

"That's it?" I said, "That's the only reason we were chosen?"

General Tipton looked me in the eyes, holding his gaze before responding.

"No. The first phase of enhancement was given to over two hundred soldiers. Each and every member of your squad was chosen for a specific reason, a specific talent or trait he or she possessed. I know Gatling's reason. He is the only Dr. that could keep up with you all. He has extensive knowledge on almost every aspect of this planet. And he knows how to care for enhanced soldiers. I don't know what the rest of you have, that the others didn't, that was Stacks' assignment, but the sooner you find out the more likely you are to survive. I can tell you this with certainty, however. You and your squad's abilities are not limited to the technology that's in your veins. In fact, there was one, a Russian I believe, that received no enhancement whatsoever."

"Yakutsk." I said.

"I assume he couldn't keep up?" General Tipton said.

"No," I said, quick to uphold his honor, "He fought just as well as any of us, if not better. I would have never been able to tell a difference."

I told him about Yakutsk's death, of how the Scorpions had somehow found him worthy to fight in the arena.

General Tipton listened carefully until I finished, then began to speak again.

"Yakutsk was 'found worthy' because he *didn't* have the enhancement. The Scorpions can smell the drugs, Captain. It's like they somehow know what we're doing, and they despise it. The fact that he was fighting amongst you without enhancement made him honorable in their eyes. If Yakutsk had not been with you they probably would have killed you all on the spot. In fact, it's very likely that this was the reason for his being chosen for the mission in the first place."

I recalled how Yakutsk had sensed his death coming, the lack of surprise on his face when he was forced to fight.

"He would have known, wouldn't he?"

General Tipton nodded, "Most likely."

I sat back my chair, trying my best to process all of this. General Tipton rose and started heading towards the door.

"One more thing, Captain. I was informed that the Scrolls were now inside a DoubleE death case. My men are already at work on getting it open, and when they do, I'll see that the Scrolls are placed with your other belongings."

"You won't be keeping them?" I asked.

He shook his head, "These items are Stacks' baby. Just make sure you get them to him. For now though, get yourself some rest. We'll most likely be heading out tomorrow."

He creaked open the buildings door and held it there as I walked out.

I stood outside the building, not sure where to go. Anywhere with other people, even my own squad, was not where I wanted to be right then. Unfortunately, there wasn't a spot in the base that wasn't crawling with soldiers. One look into the lackluster eyes of a young major, squatting next to his flickering white fire, convinced me that my men were the best company I could keep, seeing as privacy wasn't an option. I trekked across the base's floor, keeping my eyes at my feet the entire time. My head still whirled with mixed and jumbled feelings, most of them never forming into a legible train of thought. I felt lied to. That wasn't a new feeling, but this time it was worse. I felt completely owned by the military. My own body had become theirs to modify, without me even knowing it. I couldn't even imagine how they'd done it. Could they have put all General Tipton was talking of through our vaccinations? It was the only thing I could come up with.

I had just about reached our quarters when I noticed light coming from Collins' tent. This time I didn't care if someone saw me. I strolled over to the entrance and announced myself.

"Ashley, can I come in?"

I had to wait a second this time before I saw her shadow walking towards the tents' entrance.

"Michael? Are you sure you should be here?"

She grabbed me by the arm and pulled me into the tent, closing the flap behind her.

"What's going on?" she asked.

"I had to talk to you. There's something I need to tell you."

"What?" She asked.

I wanted to tell her everything, if for no other purpose than to get it off my chest, but stopped. How could I tell her? How could I tell her that she wasn't completely human? The truth was I couldn't. I couldn't let Collins, or any of the others, know this...ever. I told her about Tipton and E.T.A.D. and explained a few of the camp's stranger aspects. I even told her what the general had said about each of us being chosen for a specific ability we possessed, but mentioned nothing about the enhancement program.

When I finished, she smiled and placed her hand on my cheek, "I'm glad you came by."

"So am I, I feel better," I said, and this was completely true.

"You need to get going though," she said, "Before someone sees you."

My mind agreed with this suggestion completely, but my heart could not have disagreed more. For all the world, I wanted to stay here with her until morning, but the dangers in doing so were too severe.

"Good night, Ashley," I said, exiting the tent.

"Good night, Michael."

There was no light or noise coming from the larger tent, as I ambled over to its entrance. Upon reaching it, I slowly unzipped the flap, trying not to wake anyone. Inside, it was completely dark, and I began stumbling through the shadows to find my cot. My leg bumped into something, causing an audible thump, and I paused, hoping no one would wake.

"Captain? Is that you?"

Through the darkness I could barely make out Gatling sitting up in his cot.

"Yeah, it's me."

177

"I need to talk to you, remember?"

I had forgotten, but I remembered then. I certainly didn't feel like talking to him and even felt somewhat betrayed by him. Right then was not a good time.

"Gatling, I've had a rougher day than you could possibly imagine. Could you please just let me get some rest and we'll talk in the morning?"

He threw the sheets off of his legs and got up.

"Forget it," he said, noisily rummaging through his pack. His hand came across a sheet of paper and he shoved it into my chest.

"Take this and read it at your convenience, whenever that might be. I only hope it isn't too late."

"I'll read it tomorrow, Gatling. I swear."

I folded the paper and put it into my pack before crawling into my cot.

The thunderous roar of gunship blades tearing through the air brought me awake. I flipped the sheets off and jumped from the bed.

"Everyone up," I said, while stripping off the ridiculous clothes they had given us, "I have a feeling we're moving out."

I plucked my uniform off of the tents ceiling and quickly put it on. Someone, I assume Private Yang, had taken the time to clean and dry it, making the familiar fabric feel better than it did the day I'd left.

"We'd better hustle." I said, zipping up my combat suit.

"We're right behind you, Cap'n," O'Brian said.

I slid my rifle from beneath my cot and slung it around my shoulder, before heading out. Turning to my right, I saw Collins, uniform on and weapons equipped.

"Ready?" I asked.

She nodded.

A voice came over a loudspeaker system positioned around the dome.

"All soldiers need to meet at the dome's center for briefing ASAP. Come armed and ready to move out."

I gave a slight nod to Collins and the rest of the squad that had exited the tent.

"Showtime." I said.

The jog to the dome's center took less than a minute, but felt incredible. The wonderful night's sleep, the familiar feeling of my uniform, and flowing blood the sprint had generated, combined to revitalize me in an extraordinary way. I strode within a few yards of the makeshift podium General Tipton's assistants were busy putting up, then stopped. The rest of the squad was not far behind, arriving within seconds to stand alongside me. Soldiers began filtering in, group by group until a sizable crowd had formed around the podium. After a very short wait, General Tipton emerged from his quarters and took his place at the podium.

"Men and women of E.T.A.D., as well as our guests," he said motioning towards me and my squad, "We will be bugging out promptly at the end of this briefing, in order to participate in perhaps the most daring undertaking of your lives. The objective is to provide cover for Captain Dawn's squad in their attempt to retrieve an object of interest. The enemy standing in our way is the Marsh tribe. I wish I had the time and knowledge to tell you more, but sadly I have neither. Fight hard and die courageously, men!"

Colonel Fisher took over after General Tipton exited to the left.

"Move out! Single file through the East exit, pronto!"

Within a minute, the entirety of E.T.A.D., as well as my squad, had gathered outside the dome's eastern edge. I could see sunlight glinting off a Gunship about fifty yards ahead, and could still hear its churning blades, though the noise had lessened considerably after the craft had landed.

"Prepare for boarding, single file!" the colonel said.
We hustled and bumped into a crude line that, after a moments delay, began moving. I marched in unison with those around me, until I'd reached the Gunship's open hatch. A fully suited gunner was crouched at the entrance, ushering the line forward with his hand.

"Come on! Move it along."

I scaled the metal steps leading up to the entrance, my boots carrying on the same continuous clang that'd begun once the line started moving.

"Hold up, Captain." the lieutenant said through a microphone equipped flight helmet that made his voice sound almost automated.

"General Tipton wants to see you once you board. He has a private compartment at the ship's south end labeled Compartment 32."

"Got it," I said, and entered the craft.

The interior of the ship looked exactly like that of the first Gunship I'd traveled on, with long rows of seating running through the middle, and minigun ports every ten or so feet along the edges. I quickly made my way to the back of the craft, pushing and shoving through hordes of E.T.A.D.S. and SEALS. The crowd slowly diminished as I reached the ship's south end, allowing me to start searching the numbers on various compartments for 32. It didn't take me long to realize they were going in order, and within seconds I head traced my way from 29, to the brass 32 that hung above a small door at the craft's very end. I gripped the door's handle and opened it, not bothering to knock. General Tipton was sitting on a steel bench that was at the edge of the small room.

"Sit down," he said, beckoning me towards the bench, as there was nothing else in the compartment, "We don't have much time."

I took a seat on the bench, and listened intently to what the general had to say.

"I want to fill you in a little better on what we're up against, and what everyone's role in this operation is." he said.

"I'm all ears, sir."

"Good. The first thing I want to tell you is the same reason that the Marsh tribe has flooded to this particular spot in their territory will cause them to be twice as aggressive as usual." "What reason's that?" I asked.

"About four days ago, our researchers detected that *something* had released a literal ton of sexual pheromones over this area. Since the Marsh tribe participates in migratory breeding at a location and time designated by female pheromone releases, everyone last one of them has flocked to the place."

I nodded.

"The point of this is that they are going to be even more violent than usual. The second thing I need to tell you is the only place the Scroll could be in this particular location is at the bottom of a lake."

"What?" I asked.

Tipton sighed, "I wish it wasn't true, but it's the only possibility. That's where the SEALS come in. Their job is to dive to the bottom and retrieve the Scroll while the rest of us keep as many of the Marsh tribe off their backs as possible. Remember, Captain, these monsters are amphibious and are more than capable of killing underneath the water, making it *crucial* that we keep them out of the pit while the SEALS do their job. One last thing on this topic. Your man Jackson is going to lead the dive."

"General," I said. "I want my men with me at all times."

"I'm afraid that's not an option," General Tipton said, "Due to the confidentiality of the Scrolls, Jackson will be the only diver that knows exactly what he's looking for and how to treat it. His being down there with them is crucial."

"Where is Gatling going to be during all this?" I asked.
General Tipton folded his hands across his lap, "I apologize for not telling you sooner, but Gatling was given orders to stay at the base."

"Alone?" I asked.

"Don't worry, Captain. *Nothing* has discovered that base in the three years it's been there. You don't have to worry about him. He'll be waiting for you when you get back."
Suddenly, my memory was jogged.

"I need to show you something," I said, handing him the chip we'd retrieved from The Demon Brute.

He took it and turned it over in his hand.

"It looks kind of like a control chip," he said, "Nothing really that special about it, except that it doesn't look like one I've ever seen before."

"What does it do?" I asked.

"You can pretty much make someone do anything you want with it if you plant it in them," Tipton said, "It disrupts the electrical signals to their brain, and replaces them with whatever signals you want. Where did you find it?"

"This one came out of a Brute known as The Demon, but there was one like it in the leaders of every tribe we've encountered. I was wondering if you knew how they got there."

He shook his head.

"All I can tell you is that we didn't plant it" he said, "But I intend to find out who did."

181

He put the chip in his pocket, somewhat to my disappointment.

"One more thing," he said, "I want to apologize for my men's behavior towards you and your squad, including the incident with Colonel Fisher. Like I said, the drugs can really get to their heads sometimes."

I quickly accepted his apology, not wanting to get on the subject of myself and Collins, and why I had been in her tent. I got up and started to leave, but General Tipton stopped me.

"I almost forgot," he said, "Give this to Private Roberts when this is all over."

He handed me an envelope, neatly sealed with his signature at the top.

"May I ask what it's for?" I asked, putting in my pack.

"It's nothing really," he said, "Just a short note and my contact information. I heard about the beating he took out on Corporal Mulligan, a more enhanced soldier than Private Roberts remember, and I want for him to be able to reach me should anything...*interesting* happen."

I would have liked to have asked him what his definition of *interesting* was, but I didn't get the chance. The ship suddenly came to a stop, and a voice I recognized as Sergeant Tanner came over the speakers.

"All personnel prepare to exit the craft!"

Chapter 28

I left the compartment and began jostling my way back to the center of the crowded Gunship. After a few minutes of seeing no one familiar amongst the swarms of soldiers, I was beginning to give up on finding my squad, until I caught a glimpse of O'Brian. He must have seen me too, because he motioned for me to come over. I worked my way through the crowd until I had reached the Gunship's edge, making it to within five yards before realizing that the entire squad was there, gathered around a large porthole cut into the ship's wall.

"Take a look, Cap'n" O'Brian said.

Roberts moved aside, allowing me to look through the dusty glass. Soft, green foliage lay trampled under a sea of Marsh creatures. Spanning the ground like a horrific blanket, the mud drenched monsters were slinging sludge, fighting amongst themselves, and breeding. At the center of their gathering was a pit of muddy water, about the size of a small lake.

"Prepare to exit craft," a voice said.

Jackson's face drooped, "You're kidding me! They can't set us down there!"

Rather than reply, I turned and briskly made my way up to the pilot's compartment. Standing next to the small, sealed, door that led into the cockpit was a clean-shaven private, with rat-like eyes and a tazer rifle slung across his arms.

"You can't go in there," he said, as I reached the door.

I had neither the time nor the inclination to deal with him. Utilizing the strength enhancement the military had so thoughtfully afforded me, I grasped him by the shoulder and roughly flung him aside.

If I don't get court-martialed it'll be a miracle, I thought as I opened the door.

Sergeant Tanner was seated behind a massive array of buttons and levers, engaging various ones that I could tell were making the craft lower. I tore a headset off of the wall and quickly put it on.

"Come on, Sergeant, why can't you light 'em up? Dropping us

down there first is murder."

He spun his chair around, obviously surprised.

"How'd you get in here?" he asked.

"It's not important. What's important is that you're about to send this entire force to their deaths when you could kill every Marsh creature down there."

"I'm sorry, Captain," he said "But if I opened fire now, the hostiles would just dive right into the water. Once you guys are down there to keep that from happening, I'll give 'em all they can handle. You can count on it."

He was right. Intervening now would undermine everything we were trying to accomplish. I turned away from the pilot's compartment, a tight ball forming in my stomach.

"What the hell did you think you were doing?" the soldier with the tazer rifle said as I walked out.

"Look" I said, "If me and you both make it out of here alive, then you can press charges, but I wouldn't get your hopes up."

He sighed and shook his head, "Don't worry about it."

The Gunship had hovered close enough that the violent commotion of the Marsh tribe was barely audible over the craft's blades.

"SEALS! Aten-hup!"

I turned to my left and saw a middle-aged Platoon leader with the SEALS trident on his uniform. He had cleared a small area and was addressing his men.

"Employ dive gear pronto!"

It was then I noticed the SEALS had already been wearing a full wetsuit, perfectly camouflaged with the Xavier swamp and with two compact oxygen containers sewn into the back. The only portion of the Platoon leader's order that needed completion was the application of the dive mask, and they performed this task in seconds. I looked around the faces of the valiant SEAL Team 11, the only team sent to Xavier. My admiration of what they were about to do was profound. I do not know if I would have had the courage to dive into those murky waters, but I certainly appreciated the horror in doing so.

Sergeant Tanner's voice came over the speaker, breaking my stare.

"E.T.A.D. and Squadron One, gather at the left exit portal and prepare for deployment."

"I didn't know we had a name," Roberts said, appearing by my side.

"They've gotta have something to put on our tombstone," I said.

We made our way over to the others. Smith and Rice were peering out of the exit's window, their hardened faces slowly melting into fear. Suddenly, the portal hissed open, blowing exhaust into our faces and causing me and the others to stumble away from the exit.

"E.T.A.D. and Squadron One, exit craft!"

I gripped the thick line in my hands and prepared to slide down into Hades. I gave the shiny cable a quick jerk, testing my grip, then snapped a carabineer on for good measure. After mumbling one final prayer, I pushed off.

The slide down was much faster than I'd hoped it would be, and I jerked the trigger on my pistol repeatedly, not able to aim properly due to the speed. Mud and grass spewed up from the impact of rounds that landed harmlessly, but a few found their target, causing two Marsh creatures to splash to the ground with blood spilling from their heads. The watery landing loomed closer until I was only ten feet away, and heartbreakingly, my pistol was empty. At least five Marsh creatures were waiting furiously for me to land, and there was no way I could stop their murderous intentions. I threw my pistol at them and tore a knife from my belt. Just before I reached the cable's end, something buzzed past my cheek. Bits of skull and brain matter flew from the head of a large female Marsh creature. In the seconds before my feet hit the ground, bullets began overlapping and clearing a small hole in the hordes of mud covered monsters. I didn't dare to look up, but I knew what was happening. At least three other soldiers had mounted the gunship's exit cable and were firing down into the melee. Those that had not were providing fire from the edge of the portal. The Marsh creatures below me scattered, just as I landed on the soft ground. I unclipped myself from the cable and tore my rifle from its sling. A quick jerk of the trigger and I was spraying rounds in a full circle. The Marsh creatures ducked and stumbled away, desperate to avoid the deadly swarm of lead. I heard a loud thud to my left and turned to see General Tipton rising from his knees. It took me seeing another two E.T.A.D. soldiers falling from the sky and landing unharmed to realize they were jumping from the craft, now hovering at least fifty feet from the ground. General Tipton jerked a red and silver carbine from his pack and opened fire. The explosive report of my rifle joined the sharper and faster fire of his weapon in an effort to keep the hordes of Marsh creatures at bay. I heard the slide of gloves against the cable behind me and soon our fire was joined by that of Smith's four round bursts. More E.T.A.D.S. dropped from the sky and the rest of the squad slid down the ship's cable so that within seconds, a hundred or so soldiers were on the ground, blasting away at the relentless Marsh tribe.

"We've got to get to the water's edge!" General Tipton yelled over the roar of the battle. I drove my bayonet into midsection of a charging Marsh creature and gave it a sharp twist, before heading towards the lake.

The position we had held had been one of strength. However, moving towards the water had turned the tide in favor of the Marsh Tribe. Out of the corner of my eye, I saw a group of E.T.A.D.S., at least four men strong, get blindsided by a small wave of Marsh creatures. Their horrified cries were quickly silenced by a swift barrage of filthy claws and teeth. My heart bled for them, and in an act I knew I would regret, I turned back, gunning down their killers in a decision fueled only by revenge. Before I could turn back around, a force that felt like a speeding truck slammed into my back. I went flying forward under the momentum, landing face first in the muddy ground. My eyes filled with the wet silt and I could taste bitter dirt in my mouth. I tried to rise, but something enormous was pinning me down. A thick, webbed hand smashed against my helmet with a wet slap, whipping my head sideways against the ground and sending a shattering wave of pain through my skull. Two more powerful thuds from the Marsh creature's claws and my dented helmet flew off, rolling lazily across the ground before coming to a stop. My arms had been sandwiched between my chest and the ground, and I struggled desperately to free them. However, it was hopeless. I felt the creature's weight shift as he prepared to strike me again. This time, it would be fatal. I gave one last surge of strength, but couldn't so much as budge the beast from my back. I felt his mass shift back downward as he brought his hand down in an ark, but in the seconds before he decapitated me, I heard the familiar sound of bullets striking flesh. The Marsh creature toppled, and I seized my chance. With a sharp tug, I freed my hands and rolled over onto my back. My vision shifted from mud, to the enraged face of a male Marsh creature. Three ragged holes riddled his muscular chest, blood pouring from each one. His crocodilian face tightened into an enraged grimace, and he brought his toothed jaws down towards my face. In the seconds before he ripped the flesh from my skull, I drove the karambit's talon-like tip into his lower throat. His downward bite came to a stop, the tip of his vicious snout only inches from my nose. A thick trickle of blood ran from his neck, down the knife's blade, and onto my upper chest, joined by that still flowing from the bullet holes. Yet he lived. A deep growl escaped his throat, and he pushed his head downward against the blade, his slowing snaps edging closer to my face. Just as I could feel the air off of his snapping teeth, could feel saliva mingled with blood, splash against my skin, I gave the karambit a half-circle jerk. His eyes went misty, and the massive creature toppled to the side. With a sickening squelch I pulled the knife from his gushing throat and rose. I knew I was under the immediate threat of an attack, and the rifle I had been clutching the entire time flew to my shoulder. It only took a second, however, to realize that soldiers and Marsh tribe alike had moved their battle elsewhere, closer to the lake's edge I assumed, leaving nothing but carnage in their wake. This left me to wonder whose three shots had saved my life, a question, whose answer, was heartbreaking. Ten or so feet to my right, and lying on the ground, was Rice, a large sidearm still clutched in his hand. He dropped the pistol into the mud and wept tears of pure agony. A ragged slash traced its way from above his left ear, all the way down his neck. From where he'd crawled across the ground was a path of blood and entrails. I felt sick to my stomach, and my head was spinning. Everything around me began to seem like a bad dream. I stumbled to his side, falling to my knees before him

"Easy Rice," I said, "Just let go,"

"It w-was my j-job, Captain. To k-keep you alive. They-they said that's why I was chosen. I-I couldn't leave you."

Out of the corner of my eye, I saw the body of the Marsh

creature that had done this to him. A wave of guilt, flooded over me. Had he stuck with the others, he would have lived.

"Go," he said, as his eyes glazed over, "Don't waste this."

I nodded and rose, causing a tear to splash into the ankle-deep water. As much as I wanted to stay with him, if I was to stay alive, I had to hurry. Catching back up would not be easy.

I had not gone ten meters when a brilliant streak snaked through the sky and hit the ground ahead of me. The projectile exploded violently, sending the scorched remains of Marsh creatures sailing into the air. Before they had time to land, another missile impacted to my left, this time much closer. A wave of blue and yellow flash-fire threw me to the ground. I felt the heat of the blast singe my suit, and could feel clumps of misplaced dirt raining against my back. The fact that the Gunship was providing cover fire meant two things. For one, it meant that enough soldiers had formed a defensive around the lake to eliminate the threat of the Marsh Tribe taking refuge in its depths. Second, it meant that I would have to dodge their fire all the way there. I rose from the ground and took off at a dead run. Another missile, this one exhibiting an odd green trail, smashed into the ground behind me. Rather than produce a fiery explosion, the rocket's impact sent billows of dark green gas spewing from the warhead. The ominous vapor quickly enveloped a trio of Marsh creatures, causing them to all but disintegrate under chemical burns. My feet flew forward, faster than I knew to be possible. I hurtled over the bodies of Marsh Creatures and humans alike, desperate to escape the fatal mist. Up ahead I could see a large wall of transparent shields, encircling the pit. The men behind them were pushing franticly against a mob of enraged monsters that were trying to break their barrier. Vapors of the deadly poison floated onto my exposed neck, singeing my skin in a painful burn. Without thinking, and without hesitation, I rushed through the hordes of Marsh creatures and hurled myself over the wall of shields.

Chapter 29

My legs crashed into the top of the wall, yet I would have flipped on over harmlessly had the transparent defenses been what I thought they were. Upon contacting the shield's surface, a jolting shock rippled through my leg, all the way to my head. I felt my body go into seizures as I thudded against the ground. My head was pounding and all I could see was a brilliant light. Voices murmured around me, but they sounded distant and almost surreal. Suddenly, the light vanquished and the tremors stopped. I turned just in time to see what I assumed was an E.T.A.D. medic pull a pronged device from my leg and shove it back into his coat.

"Better get up, Captain," he said, "Lying there won't help."

I slowly rose and scanned the area. An entire wall of E.T.A.D.S., each brandishing some kind of force field shield, had encircled the lakes perimeter. Those that were not forming this defensive wall were chunking sophisticated grenades over its top. I flinched at the whistling sound of a mortar round leaving its tube. The red ball streaked upwards in an ark before falling to the ground and imploding, sucking at least ten Marsh creatures into its fiery vacuum. The Marsh Tribe seemed to be at a loss on what to do. Every so often, a brave one would press forward, only to be thrown violently backwards upon touching the walls sparking surface.

"Captain, I thought we'd lost you."

I turned to see General Tipton holding an armed grenade in his hand.

"What can I do?" I asked.

He smiled, then chucked the cylindrical explosive over the wall. It landed with a clink then started whistling like a teapot. Within seconds, the device shorted out, sending long tendrils of electricity through the ground and causing six Marsh creatures to fall dead.

He spat on the ground, "Never gets old. As far as what you can do, relax. The Gunship should be dropping the SEALS down any time now, and we've got the place locked up tighter then Alcatraz. Not one of those fools is getting through that wall, you can bet on that."

As if on cue, streaks of black fell from the ship's compartment and landed with a splash. After the SEAL Team had been deployed, the Gunship circled around and resumed raining down torrents of lead from its miniguns.

"Not a bad setup, huh?" Tipton said, "We haven't had one causality since we employed the shields.

I shook my head, watching the bewildered Marsh tribe struggle to get over the wall without being shocked to death.

"Nothing to do now but…"

Suddenly, a deafening report sounded over our heads, causing more than a few soldiers to hit the ground. I flicked my eyes upward, thinking that the Gunship must have exploded. It was still there, but it had ceased firing. What I saw next, was petrifying. One by one, the electric shields flickered off, leaving the men who'd wielded them with nothing but a saucer sized handle. It took the Marsh tribe only seconds to realize their problems were solved. Like a deadly, green tidal wave, they rushed forward.

"Open fire!" someone screamed as I threw my rifle to my shoulder.

Overhead, another explosion sounded, this one sending chunks of debris falling amongst us and killing at least one man. I chanced a look up, though I kept the trigger jerked back the entire time. The Gunship was spinning out of control, and plumes of fire roared from a crumpled hole in its side. In the distance I saw a triangular craft speeding forward. Another circular missile exited its weapons bay and slammed into the burning Gunship, this time, causing it to disintegrate into a heap of burning steel. I knew the craft would not stop there. I knew we were its next target, but at the moment, the hordes of Marsh creatures presented a far more noticeable threat. Though we fought like madmen, hacking and blasting at everything we saw, the Marsh tribe was forcing us back towards the water. A few soldiers at the innermost portion of the circle were pushed over the edge by the hordes of retreating men and into the murky depths. The Marsh tribe drove forward from all sides, their throaty howls almost deafening as they dispatched those who stood and fought, and forced those who didn't ever so closer to the lake. We had to stand our ground; it was our only chance.

"Come on men! Drive forward! Drive forward!" I screamed at

the top of my lungs as I rushed towards the swarm of blood-soaked Marsh creatures.

I could see Smith, Roberts, and a few of the E.T.A.Ds (including General Tipton) follow my lead. This small group of men, rushing into the face of the Marsh Tribe, caused a profound domino effect. By the time I reached the battlefront, the entire force of soldiers had expanded outward like a ripple in a pond. I fired at head level as I neared closer to the army of Marsh creatures, dispatching over six before they hit me. The force of the collision between myself and one of the Marsh creatures sent me sprawling backward, but I was back on my feet in an instant, thrusting viciously at his face with my bayonet. The anguished creature shrieked as the foot long blade plunged repeatedly into his eyes and mouth. The second he fell, I was gunning down the one behind him. E.T.A.D.s piled in around me, opening fire with their blaster-like carbines. In seconds, the tables had turned, and the Marsh tribe was now being forced back, though the causalities they were dealing with their flailing arms and snapping jaws were immense. Just as we had pushed them back about six or so meters, something that sounded like the stststststst of a sprinkler split the air. I glanced up, just in time to see a small swarm of projectiles snaking their way from the triangular craft's weapons bay like wasps from their nest. The spray of missiles streaked downwards, impacting in deadly explosions that killed both man and Marsh creature alike. One of the slender rockets nosed into a pile of dirt, not twenty meters away, close enough for me to hear its impact just before it exploded. I threw my hands around my face and dove into the watery ground, just as I was enveloped by a wave of heat and shrapnel.

My vision came into focus after what I assumed was a short period of time, a minute maybe. Blood poured from the side of my head where a piece of flaming metal had grazed me and into my eye. Every bit of my body that had not been protected by my suit was blistered. I painfully rose, scared to death that my back had been broke. Both our force and the Marsh tribe had been decimated. Burning bodies of both species lay scattered like burned cookies that'd been thrown away. Through the drying blood on my left eye, I saw Roberts lying face down in the dirt.

Behind him was a Marsh creature unlike any other. He was almost twice as large, and every move he made screamed dominance. A small spot beneath his massive head flashed blue. However, he was also injured terribly. His entire body was riddled with gunshot wounds, though the blood on his claws and teeth showed that the battle had not been single handed. In his hand was a branch, as big around as a saucer and with a sharpened end. I watched helplessly as the powerful beast raised the spear high and chunk it at Robert's exposed back. It sailed through the air at an unbelievable speed, but rather than strike Roberts, it hit something else. A large figure had thrown himself forward, like an athlete diving for a ball, and had taken the weapons force in the side of his chest. The creature paused, giving me my chance. Painfully, I drew my sidearm and emptied the entire clip into his back. The monster stumbled, not even fifteen more ragged holes able to bring him down swiftly. Finally he fell, splashing down into the murky water. Agonizingly, I rose. A wet cough caught my attention. Lying next to the creature's make shift projectile, I saw General Tipton. The entire log was protruding from his chest and by the way he was bent, I could tell his back had been broken as well. I stumbled over and knelt down beside him. The nanobots in his body were trying feverishly to repair the damage, but his injuries were too grave.

"Th-there's three vehicles about a half kilometer to the west," he said, "Take your men…and the Scroll and get out of here."

He pointed to the lake. I turned to see Jackson and a few other SEALS emerging from the muddy water. In his arms was the fourth Scroll. I knew I shouldn't question General Tipton's selfless act. I knew I should just admire his bravery, but something in me had to know why he, one of Xavier's top generals, had sacrificed himself for Roberts.

"Why?" I asked.

He turned towards Roberts, who was now coughing out dirt and rising from the ground.

"Captain, what's flowing through his blood is far more important than any chemical that's flowing through mine."

With that his eyes glazed over and death claimed its prey, leaving me to wonder what his last words had meant. After flicking his eyelids shut with my fingers, I rose and went to gather what was left of my squad.

192

To my elation, every one of them, save Rice, had made it out alive. However, there was no time for celebrations. Overall, the Marsh Tribe had fared better than we had, and those that were uninjured were taking great pleasure in dispatching the remainder of our force. With speed most certainly not born of energy, we headed west.

A quick six-hundred meter run and I saw a glint of light reflecting off steel. A camouflaged tarp, very low tech for the E.T.A.D.S., was thrown over three vehicles. Jackson grabbed the tarp's corner and jerked it off.

"Holy smokes," he said.

"I'm driving," Collins said, stepping towards the vehicles. I stood my ground, admiring them from a distance. Undeniably, they were impressive, though what they were exactly was beyond me. They were about three meters long and a meter and a half across. Two thickly studded wheels and a massive kickstand supported their jet black body. At their top was a large hatch, and beneath it I could see three seats and an assortment of controls. An ultralight minigun was mounted on its side and a chain of stubby pistol rounds extended from it and into the vehicle.

"You sure?" I asked Collins.

She flashed me a smile, "Absolutely."

"Let's move then. Collins, you take Smith. I'll drive the second one and take Jackson. O'Brian, do you think you can handle one of these?"

He smiled, "Yes, sir!"

"Good, you take Roberts."

I heard the clamor of the remaining Marsh creatures in the distance.

"We'd better get moving, too,"

Once the hatch closed, the controls on the inside came alive, engaging with a touch, or even a voice command. The dim light and numerous touch-screen buttons made me feel like I was flying a spacecraft. I pushed my thumb against a flashing green button and the engine hummed to life. I quickly tried to figure out the other controls. The gas, brakes, and steering were obvious, not differing from anything else I'd driven other than the fact that the steering wheel was small and octagonal.

"Where are the gun's controls?" I asked.

"Back here," Jackson said smiling.

I turned back to see a rather large screen with crosshairs at its center. Jackson was holding a triggered joystick in his hand and turning the gun's view back and forth.

"Go easy with it," I said, putting the vehicle in gear via the touch screen.

My foot slammed onto the accelerator and we were off. Before I could even realize our speed, the vehicles digital dial had reached one hundred and twenty. I let off a little until we were back down to a hundred.

"Think she'd do what's on the speedometer?" I asked, motioning towards the seven-hundred at the dial's end.

"I know I don't want to find out." Jackson said.
About that time one of the other vehicles flew past me. I had a guess it was Collins.

"How is this thing gonna make it once we reach thicker stuff than this grass?" Jackson asked.

"I dunno, but apparently it will. They wouldn't have left it for us if it couldn't make it."

I pressed the pedal a little harder, climbing to one-thirty, tearing towards the E.T.A.D. camp.

It turned out the slick cycles had no problem tearing through the thick foliage and even thicker mud. Within fifteen minutes, we were nearing close to the base. I saw a dead tree, split at its top about a hundred yards ahead. This was my landmark. I let off the gas and let the vehicle coast to a stop beneath the tree's rotting branches. The hatch slid open with the press of a button, and I swung my legs onto the ground. A second later and the other two vehicles pulled up beside me. Roberts exited the first one, his carefree smile already returning.

"That was incredible, chaps," he said.

"Go get Gatling and let's get out of here," I said, motioning towards what I knew to be the dome's surface.
He nodded and quickly found the entrance. In an instant he disappeared behind the invisible fabric.

194

I glanced down at my watch for the fourth time, growing more impatient by the second. It had been fifteen minutes since Roberts went in. I tossed a piece of grass I had been chewing on aside and stood up. Just as I started towards the dome's entrance, a wide eyed Roberts burst out.

"He's gone," Roberts said.

"What do you mean he's gone?" I asked.

"Gatling. He's gone!"

Chapter 30

We searched the base for over an hour, combing every inch for signs of struggle, a note, anything that might give us a clue to where he might be, but found nothing.

I wiped beads of sweat from my brow and sat down by the cold ashes of a burned out fire. It wasn't long before the rest of the squad joined me.

"One of two things happened," Collins said.

I raised my eyebrows, too tired to speak.

"Either he was captured…or he went AWOL."

"Why would he go AWOL?" I asked.

She shrugged, "I don't know, but the Marsh tribe sure didn't get him."

"I think Gatling had about two billion reasons to go AWOL," Stillworth said.

It took me a second, but I realized that Gatling was the one who'd been given charge over the DoubleE money.

"That doesn't sound like him," I said.

I could tell that none of the others harbored the same trust in his motives. After a minute, I questioned them myself. Perhaps greed really could get to the best of us.

"He mentioned wanting to talk to you, Captain," Smith said, "What did he have to say?"

I shook my head, still staring at the gray ashes, "I never got the chance to talk with him."

That's when I remembered the note he'd given me. I shrugged off my pack and rummaged through its many pockets until I found the crumpled piece of paper. I unfolded it and read it carefully.

Summary of a scientific study conducted by Charles A. Gatling.

Hypothesis: Extraterrestrials, indigenous to the planet Xavier997, have been visiting the planet Earth for at least thirty years, probably longer.

Supporting evidence:
1. Many UFO sightings reported before our visitation of Xavier997 have matched the strange crafts we have engaged on this planet. This could be coincidental.
2. Technologies harbored by the tribes are eerily similar to that of ancient mankind. The possibilities of how these devices came to match one another are both frightening and too open ended to be discussed in this report.
3. Many of the tribes themselves resemble creatures from legends and myths. For example, the Brutes bear much resemblance to a Minotaur, and the wolf tribe to werewolves. It is possible that these legends were born from ancient interaction with the tribes; however, this too could be coincidental.
4. A peculiar white fur was found on the back of a Brute known as The Demon. Samples of this fur were tested by myself at the E.T.A.D. base, using the most advanced equipment available. The results of four consecutive tests all confirmed the DNA, with 99.999% accuracy, to be that of Ursus Maritimes (Commonly known as a polar bear).This species has been extinct for thirty years, and was most certainly not brought here by us. This is not a coincidence, and there is no explanation that can be produced other than something personally came to our home planet and abducted this specimen.

In conclusion, I am forced to believe that Xavier997 has been visiting us, long before we visited it.

Dr. Charles Gatling

I flipped the paper over, to see if there was more, but found nothing. No one spoke after reading it; they simply sat in silence. It wouldn't surprise me if it was true, yet none of this made sense. Reading that note had done nothing to help solve his disappearance. I shoved it back into my pack.

"We've wasted enough time here." I said, "Whatever's become of Gatling, there is nothing we can do."

"Hold up," Collins said, "We've got to restock. I'm completely out of ammo and anything electronic was fried by that first explosion."

"What do you suppose that was?" Jackson asked.

"Some kind of localized EM bomb," I said, "It isn't the first time they've started their attack like that. On the issue of restocking our gear, we shouldn't have any trouble salvaging what we need from this place."

During our search for Gatling, we had located a steel building at the dome's north edge that we presumed was the base's surplus storage. Collins was confident that she could crack its electronic lock in minutes.

"How?" I asked, staring doubtfully at the green number-pad at the door's edge.

"First we'll do this," she said, and pulled a tiny spray bottle from her pack.

She squirted the blue liquid sparingly across the number-pad's surface, causing the numbers 1 6 3 and 8 to glow a slight orange.

"It reacts with the oil on the buttons that have been touched repeatedly," she said, shoving the bottle into her pack.

"Impressive," I said, "So it's a four digit combination?"

"No," she said, "it's a five. The six is glowing twice as bright as the others. It's used twice."

I nodded, "So now what? That's still a lot of possibilities."

"Well, for starters, the three is the first number; it has the most deposits on it next to the six, meaning it's the first one they touch."

"So *now* what?" I asked again.

"Now I just work with what I've got and start guessing."

She punched five numbers in, then jolted backwards.

"What on earth," she said, "The thing shocked me."

She blew a strand of hair out of her eyes and quickly punched in another combination.

"Yikes! Ooh that hurts."

She started to punch in another guess, but stopped when she heard Roberts snicker.

"Won't you let me try, miss," he said.

"Have at it." she said, stepping away from the lock.

Roberts confidently strolled up and punched in a combination. The lock hummed for a second, then clicked open.

Collins stared dumbfounded at the open door.

"How?" she asked.

Roberts handed her a small slip of paper with the numbers 36861 scribbled across it.

"It was on the dash of my vehicle." he said, smiling.

Collins gritted her teeth, then barged into the building.

Inside was a treasure trove of advanced weaponry, and I felt like a little kid at a toy store. I snatched a thick bandolier of grenades, no two alike, and slung it around my shoulders.

"You think the Cabinet of Military Affairs would look very highly on this stuff leaking out?" Smith asked, in a voice that suggested he didn't really care what they thought.

"Screw them," I said, "General Tipton left the combination for a reason."

"Look here, lads," O'Brian said, "I think I'm in Heaven."

I turned to see him proudly hoisting a weapon no bigger than an assault rifle, yet was obviously a sniper. It had numerous dials across the scope and stock and was sporting a bright green barrel. O'Brian slung it over his neck, tossing his damaged rifle aside, and then grabbed a carton of ammo. I picked up one of the carbines that must have been standard issue judging by all of the E.T.A.D.S. I'd seen using them.

"Everyone take one of the carbines, and a sidearm," I said, "After that it's up to you. Just don't go overboard."

I shoved a pistol with a stubby barrel and a ghost-ring sight into my belt and watched as Smith silently gawked over what looked like a miniature rocket launcher. Roberts picked up a railgun carbine. Jackson chose a hefty device with a shotgun-sized barrel and Collins picked up a pistol-sized weapon with a black sphere embedded in its receiver.

"Get something, Stillworth," I said, "We haven't got time to waste."

He had already gotten a carbine and a sidearm, like I'd said to do, but nothing else.

"With permission, sir, I would rather keep my rifle."

I gazed at Stillworth's worn rifle, noticing for the first time the J.S. carved into its stock. I looked back up at his face, noticing also for the first time a second pair of dog tags hanging next to his own with the name Jonathon Stillworth engraved across them.

"You can keep it, Sergeant. What is its caliber?"

199

"385 leopard." he said.

"See if you can find some ammo and let's get out of here."

Like I'd suspected, Stillworth didn't find any rounds for the apparently outdated rifle. He had two full clips left, though, and a half-full one in his gun.

"How are we getting to the Wolf territory?" Jackson asked.

"I'm sure we can find something to get us out of here," I said, looking at the various vehicles lined up along the base's northeast end, "If not, we'll just use the cycles we came in on."

"Let's see about an upgrade," Collins said, as she took off walking towards the northeast.

We counted five different varieties of transportation lined up against the dome's wall. There was a round vehicle with thick tracks and enormously thick armor, which would have been great if it would go faster than twenty miles per hour. There were three forms of aircraft, which would have been perfect if any of us knew how to fly. Other than that our options looked bleak.

"You're RAF right, Roberts?" O'Brian said, "Think you could fly one of these?"

"I'm a paratrooper, chap, not a pilot. I jump out of the buggers, not fly them."

"I had flying lessons as a civilian," Jackson said.

"Frankly, I'd rather stay out of the air anyway," I said, "Most likely we'd just be shot down."

"I don't know if we have any choice," Collins said, "Those cycles are not going to take us all the way to the Wolf tribe. We nearly tore ours up just getting here."

I frowned, staring at the three crafts we had to choose from.

"You really think you could fly one of these?" I asked Jackson. "I'll do my best."

"That was not what I wanted to hear," I said.

"It's all I can promise." he said, "As long as they're not too different from the aircraft I've flown, we'll be fine."

Again, something I didn't want to hear. They looked *very* different from anything I'd ever seen.

"We might as well give it a shot." I said reluctantly.

"So which one of these fine crafts is going to be our grave?"

Roberts asked.

I looked over the three choices. They were all relatively small, with the smallest being a helicopter looking craft but with the rotors being on its belly.

"How about the chopper?" I asked.

"I never said anything about having chopper lessons," Jackson said.

"Is there a difference?" Stillworth asked.

"I wouldn't know," Jackson said "I've never flown one."

"This one looks like it could outrun almost anything," Roberts said, pointing to a rocket- like craft.

Smith raised his eyebrows, "Speed's a nice perk, Captain."

There was no arguing with that. If whatever was flying the triangular crafts couldn't catch us, they couldn't blow us to shreds. I looked the plane up and down. It resembled a rocket that had been given wings. It had one large thruster at its back, an acutely pointed nose, and large wings coming from its midsection. I looked at Jackson doubtfully, but he was smiling.

I shook my head and sighed, "Might as well."

The inside of the craft contained ten seats, all lined in a row, with the front one being placed behind the ship's controls. The walls and floor were completely lined with screens that showed the outside view, making it look like we were floating on thin air.

"Ya'll ready?" Jackson asked.

"How are we going to get out of the dome?" Roberts asked.

"One way or the other," Jackson said, starting the craft.

When he did, I noticed the top of the dome open up like an observatory, revealing a noontime sun.

"I guess that's how," I said.

Jackson engaged the craft's belly thrusters, causing it to lift a couple meters off the ground, while remaining horizontal.

"You know, it looks simple," he said, eyeing the controls, "The steering wheel's mounted like a joystick. I think all of the movements are controlled through it except for the belly thrusters."

"Good," I said, "Maybe we'll live."

"We'll see," Jackson said. He jerked down and back on the wheel, causing the craft to soar up and out of the dome.

It took him only a few minutes and two near nosedives to get the plane figured out. As he'd reminded me, it was currently used by E.T.A.D.S., not for the Air Force. At the moment, we were high above the clouds, and cruising at an unbelievable speed of 14,000 mph, which was good, the Wolf Territory was clear on the other side of Xavier and near the planet's North Pole.

"How are we going to find the Scroll anyway?" Collins asked, "I doubt the GPS is working."

I'd forgotten, but suddenly Roberts lit up. After a few seconds of digging through his pack, he produced a laminated piece of paper and handed it to me.

"I found it in General Tipton's quarters. It's not exactly marked with a key or whatnot, but I think you know what the purple dots represent."

I did. For every place we had found a Scroll, there was a neon purple dot on the map Roberts had handed me. At the very center of the Wolf Territory was one of these dots, the location of the final Scroll. I pushed the map into my pocket and closed my eyes. The idea of looking out into oblivion as we sped along didn't thrill me. Besides, I could use the sleep. We had a long ways to go.

Chapter 31

I slowly woke, rubbing my eyes with my hands. Upon looking down, I nearly fell out my seat.

"That's some kind of a way to wake up," I said, staring at the seemingly thin air beneath me.

Jackson laughed, "Startles ya, huh?"

"No kidding," I said, still watching the moonlit landscape rush by.

"How long have I been out?

"'Bout twenty-five minutes," Jackson said.

"What? Why's it dark?"

Jackson laughed a little, "We're on the north end of Xavier; it's always dark."

I was still confused. Had we really got there so quickly? I did a couple calculations in my head and sure enough at the speed we were going it would only take about thirty minutes to fly all the way across Xavier.

"Don't you think you'd better slow down," I said, "We're probably getting close."

"I'm not even controlling the thing," Jackson said.

Now I was really confused.

"What do you mean you're not controlling it?" I asked.

Jackson chuckled a little, enjoying the fun at my expense.

"As soon as we got out of the dome, the craft switched into autopilot. Scared me at first. I wasn't sure where it was going to take us, but it's headed right where we need to go."

"E.T.A.D. must've had the crafts preprogrammed," I said.

Jackson shrugged; his hands were off the wheel and behind his head.

"I suppose. It's a good thing though. Once that dial got above nine-hundred I started getting pretty nervous. I don't think I could control it at this speed for nothin'."

Suddenly the dial arced to the left, the numbers it was pointing to swiftly decreasing with every second. Just as the craft started descending Jackson turned back and gave a toothy grin.

"We're here," he said, in a singsong voice.

"Everybody up!" I said, mostly talking to O'Brian, who was sound asleep.

"Holy…" he said, sprawling back in his seat and away from the crafts floor.

"Gets ya don't it, chap?" Roberts said.

"Listen up, guys," I said, "We've got less than a minute before this thing drops us right on top of the Scroll. I don't know what's down there, but get ready for anything. I want sting-operation extraction. Get in, get the Scroll, and get back to the craft. Got it?"

They all nodded, their newly acquired weapons clutched in their hands. The craft continued to decelerate and descend, until its belly thrusters engaged. Slowly, it hovered down at an angle until hitting the ground with a bump. The doors hissed open, letting the arctic air rush in.

"Everybody out," I said, and exited the craft.

I quickly buttoned my collar around my neck. The tortuously cold wind blew tiny projectiles of ice into my exposed skin, adding to the pain of the cold.

Through squinted eyes, I couldn't see more than a few feet in front of me. In the seconds I'd been outside the craft, my lashes had already frozen together. I glanced down at my watch. The screen had cracked, and the dials were frozen, but the thermometer had broken at negative ninety-five degrees Fahrenheit.

"Get back in!" I yelled over the wind, "We wouldn't last ten minutes out here!"

I followed Jackson, the only one, besides myself, who'd exited the craft, back through the open doors. The instant we were inside, I gripped the smooth handle and slammed it shut, sending bits of ice sliding down the plane's cylindrical sides. My hands and face were painfully red. I slowly moved my fingers, trying to work some feeling back into my numb hands.

"What are we going to do?" Collins asked, "We can't stay in here forever."

"We can't stay in here for more than twenty minutes, if I had to guess," Jackson said, "After that the doors are gonna freeze shut."

I shook my head, trying to think, "They sent us here, right?" Roberts cocked his head, "Who's *they*?"

204

"E.T.A.D. They left the cycles, they gave us the combination, they even programmed the aircraft to take us here. Surely they would have planned for the conditions we'd face."

Jackson frowned and glanced toward the areas of the craft where the outside cameras had already been burst by the cold. "If you think they left something, you'd better look fast."

We scoured the ship for half an hour, but couldn't find a thing. "Cap'n," Jackson said in a very nervous voice, "We don't have much time."

I didn't look up, but I knew things must have been getting worse. My hands flew across the craft's interior, turning it upside down in search of something the E.T.A.D. might have left. I was starting to give up. Most all of the outside cameras had burst and I could feel the temperature dropping. Leaving wasn't an option. I doubt we could have even gotten the craft started. After all we had survived, we were going to freeze to death inside an airplane. I tried to blow some warmth into my icy hands, all but giving up. Suddenly, I realized our stupidity. Anything we needed would have been in the storage building. That's why they gave us the combination in the first place. I gazed over at Collins. She was still clawing desperately beneath the ship's seat. I felt like telling her to give up; it was no use. Yet in the moment of my deepest doubt, a spark of hope shined. Collins' hand fumbled across a tiny handle on the craft's floor. With a tug, one of the broken screens slid back, revealing a compartment barely big enough to fit a man and overflowing with thick, vinyl-like fabric. Collins and Roberts began tearing them out, throwing one to each of us. I caught one of the folded packages and quickly unfolded it. The white and grey lining had two dials embedded in the shoulders, betraying it immediately as a temperature control suit.

"Get 'em on," I said, "We are *very* short on time."

I gave the outside zipper a sharp tug. It had taken at least five minutes for us all to get the complicated suit on, and with every second that passed, our chances of getting out grew slimmer. I quickly twisted the first dial to thirty-three degrees Celsius. Instantly, wonderfully warm air rushed through the suit's interior, flooding precious warmth into my body. I switched a dial on my new helmet, turning on a microphone.

"Time to go."

Once more, Jackson and Smith pushed against the craft's door, but it didn't budge. A thick sheet of ice had entombed the craft, sealing it shut. Jackson looked at me and shook his head.

"It's no use," he said, "She's not going anywhere."

"To hell it's not," Stillworth said.

He stepped forward, then, balancing himself against one of the seats, slammed the bottom of his boot into the door. Metal clanged loudly, and shards of glass fell from a broken screen, clattering to the floor and revealing a slight dent in the shiny steel. Again he slammed his foot into the door, enlarging the cavity, but doing very little to budge the icy deadlock the weather had placed on the door's seal. After three more kicks, I could see his ankle starting to swell, but yet the door showed no sign of opening. With one final surge and a grunt of exertion, Stillworth planted foot against steel. This time though, the result was different. A rush of frosty air flitted across the craft's floor, gently lifting a scrap of paper before setting it back down again. At the bottom of the door, the frozen seal had been broken.

"Move aside," Jackson said.

No sooner had Stillworth stepped away from the door, Jackson slammed his full weight into it. The metal groaned a little, parting further from the craft's floor. One more combined assault by Jackson and myself, and it came completely open, falling off of its mechanical hinges and onto the snowy ground. Even through the thick suit, the screaming wind sliced through, chilling me to the bone and prompting me to turn the dial on up to thirty-five degrees Celsius. A strange darkness, akin to a winter twilight, cloaked the tormented landscape. Sheets of pellet-like ice assaulted us without mercy. The only visible features of the arctic landscape were jagged boulders and scraggly hardwoods, their lifeless branches straining under the weight of ice.

I kept a gloved hand locked around the E.T.A.D. carbine. Everywhere I turned, I saw an ambush waiting to happen. Gatling had mentioned before his disappearance that the Wolf tribe sees in infrared. With our temperature control suits pumping heat out like ovens, we would look like a spotlight to any Wolf within a mile.

"Which way?" Smith asked.

206

"Don't know," I said, still staring at a distant snowdrift.

"Cap'n," O'Brian said.

I turned to see him pointing at a grey rise in the snow. Closer inspection betrayed the mound of rock as a narrow cave. I narrowed my eyes upon its jagged opening.

"On me, guys. Let's get in and get out."

My insides churned, threatening to expel every bit of their contents. Another waft of decaying flesh floated out of the cave, causing my head to spin. Roberts was bent over, hands on knees, retching onto the frozen ground.

"Don't these suits have air filters," I whispered into the in-helmet mike.

"Bioweapon filters, Captain," Collins said, stepping towards the cave. "They have bioweapon filters, not air fresheners."

She put up a tough front, but as she neared the entrance, I saw her turn visibly greener.

"Get up, you sorry wretch," Smith said, dragging Roberts up by his collar, "There's no time for that."

I turned back to the cave's entrance and steadied my nerves. Behind the crevice of that opening undoubtedly lay horrors that even the most morbid of men could not imagine. Yet this desolate crack in the ground was also the most likely place to find the final Scroll. I muttered a quick prayer, a humble plea for my continued survival as well as a request for the ability to block from my memory whatever repugnant scene lay ahead. This request, so unlikely to be granted, almost triggered a cynical smile. Every grisly image I had ever seen was engraved into mind. For every one existed a separate nightmare that would torment my sleep, and I was about to add another. With the flick of a glove I motioned for the squad to proceed.

"Single file behind me," I whispered, "Keep your weapons at ready, and watch your step."

I carefully avoided a large icicle and entered the cavern. Instantly, the faceplate on my suit adjusted, turning a fuzzy yellow before clearing into a crisp vision that allowed me to see deep into the bellows of the pitch dark cave. The first thing I noticed was the bodies. Strewn everywhere, splattered against the wall and lining the walkway like forgotten road kill, lay the mangled and torn remains of at least a hundred human beings.

"Smith," I said, "Find out who they are."

He shouldered his carbine and knelt beside the one of the dismembered remains. Grabbing the dead man by his shoulder, Smith deftly flipped him over on his back.

"Eastern Empire," he said grimly, "Chinese to be exact."

"And the others?" I asked, already knowing the answer.

"All DoubleE." Smith said.

"And they got what they came for," Collins added, pointing to a barren pedestal, not ten yards away.

"No," I said, "No no no no."

"Young and Chambers had better get brushed up on foreign relations." O'Brian said, "That's the only way we'll be getting our hands on that Scroll."

I took one last look at the carnage, at the long claw streaks across the wall, then turned away.

"Let's get out of here. We'll regroup and contact Stacks. Providing the radios still work."

I somehow felt compelled to return to the craft, even though the logic in this maneuver was shrouded. Kneeling next to the ice-entombed metal, I jerked the E.T.A.D. radio from the shoulder of my suit.

"Slim chance the temperature didn't break the thing, even less that the satellites are still up and working." O'Brian said.

"Keep your fingers crossed," I said, and pressed the button on the receiver. The mike crackled and hummed, making a noise that threatened to fizzle out into static. When I thought it was going to do just that, a faint voice sounded on the other end.

"This is Cha'lie two requesting you identify you'self,"

"This is Captain Dawn, Eighth Battalion Army Rangers,"

"Go ahead Cap'n and pa'don the formality. Fo' some reason your signal was scrambled. I didn't know who you might be."

I started to tell him that the radio was from the E.T.A.D. and was probably scrambled intentionally, but decided that anything related to their organization was far too classified for him to know about.

"Put me through to General Stacks. It's urgent."

There was a small pause, and I could hear a faint commotion in the background.

"The general is in the middle of a highly impo'tant conference, Cap'n. I don't think now's a good time."

"Dammit, Scott," I said, "I don't care if he's talking with President Young himself."

"Well, actually he is."

"Put him on the line, Scott, for crying out loud."

"He's gonna be mad, Captain." Private Scott said.

"It won't be the first time."

He sighed, "Give me a minute, and I'll go get him."

The line went silent for a good three minutes, giving me plenty of time to envision the surrounding rocks and trees as bloodthirsty Wolves. When Stacks did pick up, however, not a touch of annoyance was in his voice.

"I believe I can guess the problem, Captain," he said.

"I wish you could General, but whatever your thinking it might be, I'm afraid reality is far worse. We have every reason to believe the DoubleEs have taken possession of the final Scroll."

Stacks gave a deep and throaty sigh that suggested far too little sleep.

"I've known about the success of their endeavor to steal the thing from underneath us for about an hour now. Contact with Eastern Empire leaders has proved impossible, and unless foreign relations take a turn for the better, I'm afraid we might have to face the possibility of doing without the final Scroll entirely. The good news is their declaration of war has fizzled out now that they've got what they want."

"How are we going to get out of here?" I asked.

He gave another long sigh, "I assume the craft you flew in on is inoperable."

I glanced at the cracked and frozen ship.

"Froze to hell." I said, "No irony intended."

"I figured as much," Stacks said, "I've arranged a StarfireX for your pickup."

"When will it arrive?" I asked anxiously.

General Stacks paused then sighed in a way I found tragic.

"There's been a complication. Someone has hacked into the Air Force's main data base and screwed the autopilot and communication functions on all of their crafts. President Young has declared the entire fleet grounded until the problem is resolved."

I swallowed hard.

"How long will that take?"

"We've got the best tech team we could find working 'round the clock, but it'll be at least two days."

Before I could process what he'd just said, a howl tore through the air. This cry, so tortured, so full of hatred and pain, terrified me, personifying every sound that has ever haunted our imaginations into one blood-curdling roar.

"General," I said, "Two days is starting to sound like a *very* long time."

Chapter 32

"Form a defensive…now!" I said, snapping the squad into action.
"O'Brian, I want you and Smith to see if you can get on top of
the craft. The rest of you entrench around it."

O'Brian gripped the craft's slick sides and tried futilely to scale
on top.

"Let me give ya a leg-up," Smith said.

He grabbed the bottom of O'Brian's boot and hoisted him on
top of the craft with ease. O'Brian, in turn, grabbed hold of
Smith's hands and helped him up.

I glanced at the remaining squad, waiting anxiously for orders.

"I want the rest of us to form the tightest circle we can manage
around the ship's edge. If something so much as sneezes out there,
we're gonna know about it."

Collins positioned herself in the point closest to me,
purposefully I supposed. She traced her glove tip around the
strange reaction chamber in the center of her newly acquired pistol.

"I don't like a thing about this," she said.

"Tell me about it," I said, "What besides the obvious is
concerning you."

She shuffled her position, without peeling her gaze away from
the ominous horizon.

"For starters we're out here with an arsenal we don't have a
clue how operate."

I flipped the E.T.A.D. carbine over, examining its controls.

"It's got a trigger doesn't it? Seems simple enough to me."

She frowned, "Maybe. I still don't feel comfortable with them,
and that's problem enough as far as I'm concerned."

I started to press her further. Collins would not be bothered by
insignificant chinks in our defense and anything that was serious
enough to catch her attention should be addressed. Unfortunately,
my thought process was interrupted by another heart-stopping
howl.

"Three a-clock!" O'Brian yelled.

"O'Brian, get an ID on the target, ASAP!" I said.

O'Brian's eye shot to the scope of the E.T.A.D. sniper.

"Two Wolves in front, another one trailing five meters behind…and they're moving this way fast! Permission to fire Cap'n!"

"Granted, light 'em up."

The second the words left my mouth his rifle bucked. A blue flash lit up the air, followed by something that sounded like the crackling of electricity. The streak sizzled through the sky, followed by a dying yelp. Smith's finger was already hammering on the trigger of his carbine, sending a wall of rounds sailing forward, and quickly dispatching the other two Wolves.

"I think were clear," Smith said.

O'Brian gave a sardonic chuckle that threatened to morph into a sob.

"Oh I wish to heaven you were right, lad."

Suddenly, glowing yellow eyes emerged from all sides, like sinister beacons, sitting on top of dark black shadows. One by one the Wolves materialized. Their discolored fur was raised, making them appear even larger. Beneath their bloodthirsty eyes was the most nightmarish set of jaws that could be imagined. Their yellowed canines dripped with saliva and blood, and were bared in a snarl. Simultaneously, they commenced a growl that would have sent an entire pack of rottweilers scampering in fear. Under the heightened senses of adrenaline, I could see their wicked claws digging into the snowy ground, seeking the traction to pounce. Every fiber of their being seemed to exist for the sole purpose of slaughter. I could visibly see their eyes narrow the second before they charged. All at once they came. From all sides and angles they flew forward, and I was shell-shocked. My eyes were locked with those of a particular Wolf. He had graying fur with wisps of faded purple. Across his brow was a brutal scar that still festered with infection. Yet the malice in his eyes showed that whoever had caused that wound had died before any blood hit the ground. In that instant, I was certain that this creature would be the one to carry out my long-due death. A fate, I was finally willing to accept. As in the past, however, I was wrong. A brilliant flash of yellow tore through the dark air, followed by a deep hiss. The streak of fire snaked its way across the sky, before nose-diving into the snowy ground. The Wolf's searing, yellow eyes never left mine;

his charge never ceased, even as the mushroom of dark red energy enveloped him, burning the flesh from his bones.

The report broke my trance. I quickly cursed myself for being so weak then slung the carbine to my shoulder. My sights drug across the head of the closest Wolf, and I jerked back on the trigger. At least eight spurts of blood flew from his head and back before the creature crumpled. I swerved the carbine to the next target, just eight meters away, then sent a two-second burst into his chest. I knew there couldn't be many more left. The blast had taken out at least half of them, and those remaining were dropping swiftly under the spray of gunfire. The distinct clanging sound of a railgun report, followed by a spray of fur, bone, and blood signaled the death of the final Wolf.

"Steady," I said, my carbine still at my shoulder.

"Something's wrong," O'Brian said, his eyes still glued to his scope.

"There were eleven pairs of eyes," he said, still not looking away from the night vision optics, "Eleven sets of eyes and only ten dead Wolves out there."

"Jackson's missing," Collins said, swerving around the corner of the craft.

"Captain!"

I turned and saw Roberts, pointing his sidearm at the snowy ground. Thick splotches of blood, crimson red, not like the bluish-red blood of the Wolf tribe, lined the ground. A drag trail of the same blood led into the distance as far as night vision could pick up.

"Collins, come with me," I said, "The rest of you stay here."

"Don't you think it might be a trap, Captain?" Smith said.

"I know it is," I said, "And so does Jackson. That's why he's shut his mike off. He doesn't want us to be drawn out by his screams"

"What are you doing then?" he asked.

"Fighting fire with fire. Collins, I want you to circle the trail around the right side, and be ready."

An explorer on earth once said that there is nothing more eerie then the howl of the arctic wind. With every step I took being planted in the lifeblood of my comrade, with every move I made

213

being undoubtedly noted by a very smart monster, and with the my only hope of survival resting on Collins' ability to know my intentions without me ever telling her, I realized how true this was.

Slowly, the blood trail began to grow thicker, meaning the Wolf was slowing down. A scraggly tree, with a large rock at its base, came into vision. The deep trace of crimson led through the snow, before stopping behind the rock. I tried to swallow, but found my throat incredibly dry. The E.T.A.D. pistol was in my hand, its large, ghost-ring sight focused on the rock. Every step I took grew heavier. From behind the boulder's concealment, I could see the spiked fur of the Wolf. I heard a deep groan, the groan of a man still alive, but at death's door. When I was close enough to see Jackson's bloodstained hand splayed across the ground, I knew it was time to spring the trap that was set for me.

"Jackson! Are you there?" I said, knowing the consequence my words would bring.

From behind the boulder, the Wolf rose. His clawed hands hung from his sides, still dripping with Jackson's blood. On two legs he stood about eight foot tall, reminding me for all the world of the werewolves of folklore. He knew he had me. He didn't even bother to make his ambush swift. Even if I were to open fire, the Wolf would close the distance in an instant. Death was of no concern to this creature, for judging by the SEAL knife protruding from the base of his neck, it was inevitable. His teeth spread into a terrifying snarl. Suddenly his front paws hit the ground, and, with a thud, he dropped onto all fours. He was a heartbeat away from killing me, a breath away from his ambush being a success, but the second he dropped to his feet, I saw Collins standing behind him. The reaction cylinder on her sidearm was glowing black, almost like the shimmer of oil. The barrel was lowered on the back of his head. Just as the first bit of snow flew up from the Wolf's paws, she pulled the trigger. What looked like a jet black icicle exited the weapon penetrating through his skull and out his jaw. The Wolf died without a shudder, what momentum he'd had the time to build carrying him only a few inches across the snowy ground.

"Get to Jackson!" I yelled, rushing towards the tree and rock.

It was worse than I'd imagined. If the Wolf had harbored any interest in keeping Jackson alive, he'd only intended to do so for minutes more. I could see the color draining from his eyes, as the last of his blood flowed from the ragged gashes on his neck. I knew something should be said. I knew there must be some comfort I could offer him, but I could think of nothing. I saw his trembling lips form a smile.

"Cap-Captain."

I nodded, a tear forming in my eye.

"D-do you believe in someplace other than this?"

I nodded again, though I wasn't sure I did.

"I-I sure h-hope your right then. I'd really l-like to g-go somewhere n-nicer than h-here."

"You will soldier. Just go to sleep and it will all be better."

He took a trembling breath, then closed his eyes for the final time.

"Help me get him back to the craft," I said to Collins.

The squad was gathered in a tight circle, watching me and Collins carry Jackson between us. Their faces were grim, their jaws clenched tight with pain. All at once, O'Brian cracked.

"What is happening!" he yelled.

Smith tried to restrain him, but O'Brian threw off his grasp.

"*This*," he said, pointing at Jackson's shredded remains, "Is not what I signed up for."

At this point my own rage boiled over.

"Then what did you sign up for, Corporal? Do you even realize that all your screaming is probably directing every Wolf on Xavier to us?"

O'Brian shook his head, his own anger declining, "Doesn't matter anyway, lad. Do you really think we can make it two days out here? It hasn't been two hours and already we've lost a seventh of our force. We're disorganized, unprepared, physically and emotionally drained, and armed with weapons we don't know a thing about."

"So we fix it," I said.

O'Brian stared back down at Jackson's body, his hand quivering slightly.

"After the first shot, I couldn't figure out how to rearm the weapon. I saw the Wolf coming for him, but there was nothing I could do. He had trusted me, Captain. He'd trusted me to have his back, and I couldn't even jack another round to keep 'em alive."

"Don't do that to yourself, O'Brian," I said, now understanding the source of his emotions, "There was nothing you could have done."

He didn't say anything, just stood there staring at Jackson's body. Smith emerged from behind the craft, his radio still clutched in his hand.

"I just got off with General Stacks, sir," Smith said.

"What did he have?"

Smith frowned, "Good news and bad news."

"Let's hear the good news first. I'm sure we could all use some."

"The tech team has isolated the virus in the Air Force's systems and projects being able to eliminate it by twelve hundred hours tomorrow."

I showed no emotion, but was inwardly rejoicing.

"There's more good news," he said, "The DoubleA managed to hack a small surveillance satellite, and Stacks has a team of strategists watching our every move."

"Good," I said, "As long as we have a line of communication with them I'm sure they'll help us in every way possible."

"Now for the bad news," Smith said, "According to them, that group of Wolves that attacked us was a scouting party from a pack called the Darkfurs. The entire pack should be arriving within twelve hours."

I swallowed hard, "How many?"

"Surveillance suggests they number around a hundred." Smith said.

I took a deep breath, "Stay online with Stacks' strategists. Relay anything they have directly to me. O'Brian, see if you can figure out how to work these weapons. The rest of you help me set up some defenses. We've got a lot of work to do."

Chapter 33

"You're sure this will work?" I asked Stillworth.

"Absolutely," he replied, without looking up from the wires he was splicing together, "When you hit the switch, it will blow like TNT."

"I wouldn't walk out more than ten meters if you're heading south," Collins said, strolling up with an empty bag in her hand, "I scattered a few dozen poison tipped caltrops in that area."

"Good," I said.

Smith walked over, the radio in his hands.

"Sir, Stacks' team suggests placing O'Brian at the top of a split rock they located about two hundred meters east, once the fighting starts."

I nodded.

"Where's Roberts?" I asked.

Collins frowned and pointed to a small rise in the terrain about fifteen meters north. Roberts was perched on top, studying a scrap of paper.

"What's he got?" I asked.

"I'm not sure," she said, "I saw General Tipton hand it to him once the E.T.A.D. walls went down."

I saw Roberts pull a shiny cylinder from his pocket and flip it over in his hands. After studying it intently, he stood up and walked our way.

"I guess we're about to find out," I said.

"Maybe," said Collins.

Roberts set down and started helping Stillworth.

"Anything important?" I asked.

"Huh?" he said, looking up from his work.

"The note you were reading, was there anything that might help?"

Roberts quickly shook his head then went back to bolting down the lid on Stillworth's contraption.

"Are you sure nothing's wrong?" Collins asked him.

"Look, chaps, there's nothing the matter that getting out of here alive won't fix. The bloody problem is I don't think that's gonna happen."

I turned away. If I'd really thought that was what was bothering him I might have done something, but I didn't believe him. Roberts had faced death countless times before, and each time that I witnessed, he did so with the same carefree demeanor. Something was different this time. Apparently, Collins caught on as well. I saw her about to press him further, but interrupted her before she could.

"Collins, come help me, I've got an idea."

"Do you think any will still work?" she asked, staring at the lines of mostly shattered cameras.

"I doubt it," I said, "But it's worth a shot."

We searched the craft's edge for a camera that had not been destroyed by the arctic temperature.

"Ashley," I said.

"Yeah?" she said.

"I know as well as you do that Roberts is lying, it doesn't take CIA training to realize something is wrong with him. I don't think we should press him about it though."

She ignored my second statement and focused on the first.

"Yeah, well maybe CIA training would have helped you notice that the shiny metal thing he was holding was a syringe. Or the fact that he ditched his firearms inside the craft yet spent twenty minutes sharpening a metal rod. Whatever Tipton said to him sure has pressed a button."

"Just don't worry about it," I said, "When we get out of here we'll figure it out."

"*If* Michael," she said, "If we get out of here. At any rate, I think I found a camera that's still working."

"Good."

I set about dismounting the camera from the craft, the word *syringe* still haunting my imagination.

We decided to place the camera on top of the rise Roberts had been on. From the heightened elevation it would have a good angle on the rock O'Brian would be stationed on. I'd had reservations about positioning him by himself, but at least this way we could keep an eye on him, providing the camera and feed monitor continued to work.

"We'd better get back," I said, satisfied that the equipment was planted firmly in the ground.

"I guess," Collins said.

I could tell she was enjoying the peaceful rest as much as I was, but there was still a lot of work to be done.

"You do realize this is it, right?" she asked.

I gave her a puzzled look, so she elaborated.

"You realize if we make it through tomorrow we go home. This whole mess will be over."

"Or just beginning," I said.

She dismissed my pessimism and continued.

"What are you…what are *we* going to do?"

I would have liked to have told her exactly what we would do. I wanted to share with her my intentions right then and there, but it was neither the time nor the place to do so.

"We'll work it out, Ashley, I promise."

She frowned slightly, but I knew it was faked. Collins was far too experienced at reading people to honestly believe that was all I had to say. As the craft and the rest of the squad grew nearer, and though silence ruled the rest of our conversation, the impact of her words still rang loud and clear. I'm not sure if it was her intentions or not, but she had revealed her hand. Collins was already planning a future, *our* future, and as bad as I wanted to share her optimism, I was still not convinced we would have one. As though she could read my mind, Collins added onto her last statements.

"Don't read too much into that," she said, just as we reached the craft, "I know that right now the only concern is getting out of here alive."

I smiled, "Didn't say I was."

Three hours from the last attack and the place was finally looking like the fortress we needed. The entire perimeter of our entrenchment, barring two well rehearsed escape routes, was lined with tripwire grenades and poisoned caltrops. O'Brian had managed to learn the working of our weapons to the point of field stripping them and had given us each brief instructions on the basics. Even Roberts had gained a small amount of optimism, though its only noticeable effect was the fact that he had reclaimed his weapons.

"Whatever's eating him, I hope it doesn't jeopardize our cause," Collins said, watching Roberts intently sharpening his knife.

"I could try straitening him out, sir," Smith said.

"No," I said, "Leave him be. "

Stillworth walked up, covered in dirty ice and with a wrench clutched in his hand.

"Craft's ready, Captain," he said, thankfully oblivious to our conversation.

"You're sure it will work?" I asked, "Are you willing to bet your life on it?"

He spat out a bit of dirt, "Captain, I *wish* that the only factor my life was hinging on was that thing detonating."

I nodded, finally satisfied that Stillworth had done his job well.

"How much fuel is left?" I asked.

"Fifty-five percent capacity." Stillworth replied.

"How much of a bang should that give us?" I asked O'Brian.

"Fifty percent capacity, that means fifty pounds of lightening300 rocket-fuel. Ignited, that should give us a blast radius of about a hundred meters."

Smith chuckled, "Do you have a calculator planted in your head or something?"

He laughed, but I realized that this was a real possibility considering the fact that we were all C.A.M.D.O. experiments.

"How about we take a half-hour R&R then get back to work."

"Are you sure that's a good idea, sir?" Smith whispered, "We have a very dangerous deadline here."

"I understand, Sergeant, but keeping our force in fighting condition is crucial as well."

I glanced over at Roberts. He was once again studying the note that Tipton had gave him. His face was torn into an expression that threatened to break into sobs of remorse or shouts of rage.

"Get some rest, guys." I said, starting towards him.

It was time to figure out exactly what that letter said, before it got us all killed.

The tip of Xavier's crimson moon, Advenacruor, was slowly

peeking above the horizon as it continued on its eternal path across the heavens. The icy ground crunched with every step I took, reminding me of my year's stay in Alaska. A brilliant meteor streaked across the sky, landing somewhere that appeared so close, it was frighteningly beautiful. Yet Roberts was oblivious to both it and my approach. Over and over, he flipped the syringe in his hand, watching dim rays of red light reflect off its shiny surface. Even as I slowly lowered myself down next to him, he didn't take his eyes off of the needle's tip.

"What did it say?" I asked, hoping the straightforward approach truly was the best.

He ignored me, though he did set the syringe aside.

"Look," I said, "What General Tipton did for you was the most courageous and selfless act he could have offered, and you can't blame yourself."

He shoved the syringe into his pocket and swiftly turned to face me.

"You don't have a bloody clue what this is about, and in reality, Captain, you couldn't be further off track if you wanted to be. I'm glad that the good general took that spear. He was a selfish, lying fool, and if me living hadn't been in his best interest, he never would have gone with us in the first place. Actually, it's his reason for saving my life, his justification for the sacrifice that *bothers* me. I'm finding the reason for my entire existence so appalling that I wish he'd just let me die."

He paused for a second, staring into space.

"It doesn't really matter though, does it?" he said, "After tonight I'll be nothing but a story that hardly bears telling. In fact, Captain, why don't you just take this."

He shoved Tipton's letter into my hands, then looked me in the eyes.

"I want you to know. I want you and you alone. But if you read this before my time is done, or share it with another soul, then you've proved that any ounce of friendship and loyalty we might have gained over the course of this god-forsaken mission was nothing but an illusion."

"I swear it, Roberts, and you swear to me that whatever this is about, you won't let it distract you."

He smiled, the twinkle finally returning to his once cheerful

221

eyes.

"I swear it, chap. Remember, I only have two modes, and those slobbering puppies are going to get the *very* bitter end of the second one."

I gave him a hearty pat on the back then turned with the intention of finding Collins. This intent, however, was quickly hindered when I saw the look on Smith's face.

"Captain, you'd better come fast," he said, "General Stacks is on the radio and it's urgent."

Just as I turned to leave, a tortured howl echoed in the distance.

Chapter 34

I rushed to the radio Smith had left lying on the ground. The receiver was strewn into the snow, suggesting that he'd come to get me without even bothering to put it up. I snatched the cold handle from the ground and shove the mike to my ear.

"Captain Michael Dawn, over."

"Captain," Stacks said, "There's been a serious mistake. The Deathclaw pack altered its course about an hour ago and headed your way. I'm not sure when they'll get there, but it could be any minute."

"I think they've arrived," I said, listening to another string of howls ripple through the night air.

"Why didn't the satellite pick them up before now?" I asked, hastily loading my carbine with marble-like rounds, while pressing the receiver between my head and shoulder.

"I-I don't know," he said, "It's still not picking them up. The only way we know they were there in the first place was because we managed to get one of our own satellites online."

"General, did you ever find out the owner of the satellite you hacked?"

"No, we assumed it was Eastern Empire. Why?"

"I think its screw-ups may have not been accidental." I said.

I heard a series of short, angry barks, followed by the rippling explosions of our tripwires.

"I got to go, General."

"Wait a second. I've just been informed that the hacked satellite is equipped with weapons, we'll be able to provide you cover, Captain."

My heart sank. Everything had just become terrifyingly clear.

"No! You've got to shoot it down!" I said, "Now!"

Before he could reply, a set of paws slammed into my side. I went sailing towards the ground, with my attacker driving me down even harder. The snow mingled with hard ice barely served to cushion my blow as both my breath and a puff of snow exited into the air. Before teeth or claws could find their target, I shoved the end of my pistol into a patch of fur and jerked the trigger. Flesh and blood flew in all directions as the hefty sidearm bucked my arm backwards. My attacker stumbled off of me, a slight yip leaving its throat. With a sharp turn, I flipped onto my back to face the predator. Bluish- red blood streaked down the fur of the Wolf's back leg. Her eyes locked onto my throat and her teeth bore into a bloodthirsty snarl, but before she could pounce, a streak of electricity mingled light smashed into her chest, crumpling her instantly. I silently thanked O'Brian, then rose to my feet. The radio was still lying unscathed beside the craft, even though the squad was tramping all around it. I knew the chances were slim that General Stacks was still online, but I had to try. Our lives were hinging on it. I scrambled to the receiver and jerked it off the ground.

"General! General Stacks, do you copy?"

The only noise that followed was the eerie static that resonates from destroyed communications. I heard paws pounding into the ground and hastily turned to face a bluish-grey female that had managed to make it through the tripwires. She had halted hard, rising onto two feet about ten meters away. However, she was not looking at me. To my left, and about three meters closer to the Wolf than me, was Collins. Her face was tightened in concentration as she sent three black bolts into the head of an oncoming Wolf. I swerved back to the female, just in time to see her drop back onto all fours. The barrel of my carbine flew upwards, in deadly race to reach the Wolf, before she reached Collins. The second the red-dot sight grazed the bottom of her tensed underbelly I squeezed the trigger. A burst of six or so rounds flew from the barrel, finding their target in seconds and leaving it in shreds. The large female slid forward on the ice, coming within inches of bumping Collins in the legs. The reports of the tripwires grew more and more spread apart, signaling a treacherous shift in the battle. The hordes of Wolves surrounding us were closing in, more confident now than ever in their ability to make it through unharmed

"Form a circle!" I yelled to the squad.

They quickly shuffled from their positions to form a tight defensive around the craft.

"We can't last here!" Smith said.

224

All around, the pack was coming together, their large, yellow eyes glowing like beacons in the snowy darkness. Their multicolored fur swayed and rippled under the force of the arctic wind. Whatever reservation that was keeping them from charging was the sole reason for our being alive. I glanced down at the live feed monitor to make sure O'Brian was okay. Thankfully, he was, but I feared that wouldn't last.

"O'Brian," I said into the helmet's microphone, "You've got to get as far away from here as you can. Any second that satellite's gonna blow us to shreds."

"Can't do it Cap'n." he replied, "I'm not leaving like that."

I saw movement to my left and suddenly understood why the Wolves were just standing there, waiting. Twenty yards to our right, a monster unlike any other in the pack was moving through their ranks. He walked upright far more adeptly than any of the others. His long, ripped arms swayed with each step, and ten, razor-like claws dangled from their ends, gripping and relaxing in rhythm. Thick cords of blue veins, visible beneath bushy grey fur, snaked their way through his flexed muscles. His neck flashed blue, but I hardly noticed it at this point. Overall, the creature stood almost two feet higher than any of the others, making him a horrifying ten foot tall. Every member of the pack stepped aside as he made his way towards us.

"O'Brian," I whispered into the mike, "If you're not leaving, now would be a really good time to give us a hand."

In reply, a report sounded behind us. A streak of light, sparking with energy, burned through the air, just meters above our heads and heading straight for the chest of the alpha Wolf. Just as the bolt reached him, a flash of brown dove in front. The projectile smashed into the martyr Wolf, killing him instantly, but leaving the alpha unscathed. Once more, O'Brian fired, and once more, a different member of the pack dove in front, more than willing to sacrifice itself. The alpha let out a deafening howl, then charged. His massive jaws were opened, his five inch canines begging to taste blood. In the seconds before he reached Smith, the monster rose upright. Still flying forward, he raised one arm above his head, then brought it crashing down. Smith tried to scramble away, but it was no use. I winced my eyes shut, but not before catching sight of *something* flying towards the Wolf. A flash of grey slammed into the monster's side, tackling him to the ground. Smith's savior was on his feet before the Wolf, standing over his crumpled foe with a sharpened rod in his hand. I stumbled backwards in shock, suddenly realizing that the creature before me was Roberts. He had grown over two feet taller. His skin had turned a dull bluish-grey and his eyes a misty white. At his feet lay his shredded clothes and the metal syringe, now empty. He towered over the Alpha Wolf, the rod raised high above his head. With a roar of exertion, he brought the point down. Yet before it could find its target, Roberts was toppled by an unseen attacker. A pudgy female had managed to bring him down and save the pack leader, but her efforts would not extend much further. Roberts, or what he had become, grabbed her head and twisted it sharply, snapping her neck with ease. Just as Roberts rose to his feet, he was brought back down by the now recovered alpha. The two hit the snowy ground with an audible force, rolling forward in a tangle of fur and skin. Once their momentum was spent, the Wolf quickly flipped on top of his adversary. His clawed paw came crashing down in effort to quickly dispatch him, but Roberts caught the Wolf's strike with one hand, stopping it entirely. A swift, yet forceful blow to the snout sent the creature toppling off of his stomach. Unfortunately, the speed at which he recovered must have caught Roberts off guard. The beast whirled back around, dragging his claws across Roberts' muscle strewn chest. Blood spilled to the ground, but Roberts didn't seem to notice. He jumped into the air and rained two heavy blows onto the Wolf's snout. Gore and gristle flew from his nose as it snapped sideways under the force of the blows. Before he could recover, Roberts was on him again, tackling him to the ground. Roberts dealt two more punches to the Wolf's eye before the odds turned. All of the aggression and rage that Roberts possessed could not make up for the obvious size difference. The Wolf dug three claws into his shoulders and flipped him to the side with ease. Roberts went sailing through the air, landing at the spot where the battle had begun. Before he could rise, the Wolf was on him again, picking him up with one hand, then throwing him forcefully back to the ground. I saw Smith raise his carbine, but I quickly stopped him.

"If you fire, they'll kill us all!" I said, pointing to the hordes of wolves that were watching their leader battle.

The Wolf brought a deadly torrent of strikes down upon Roberts, sending blood flying with every blow.

"Get out of here!" I heard Roberts yell, in a voice that still bared resemblance to his own.

I gave him a nod, then turned and ran. The ground flew beneath me as I raced away from the craft. It took only seconds to reach the rock at which O'Brian was stationed. The rest of the squad was right behind me. I turned back to the scene, compelled to witness Roberts' final moments. The Wolf was still raining down strikes on his chest and face. There was a pool of blood beneath him that, having lost as much, would have killed a normal man three times over. Yet, Roberts still lived. His hand was groping for the sharpened rod, just barely out of reach. I could see his strength faltering as his efforts to retrieve the rod grew less and less vigorous. Finally, as his last breath escaped him, his fingers found the shiny metal. Roberts brought his arm up with force, and with one final surge drove the point into the monster's throat. The rod impaled the Wolf fully, driving through his windpipe and out the back of his head. His yellow eyes lolled backwards as he reluctantly gave up his life. The rest of the pack stood in shock; A few howls of pain echoed from them as they gathered around their dead leader. Sorrow, however, was quickly replaced with rage, and they turned their attention toward us.

"Hit it, Stillworth," I said, my eyes locked on theirs.

He brought the ends of two wires together, causing a small spark. The electricity raced back along the lines, far quicker than the pack was racing towards us. It reached the craft's fuel compartment before the first Wolf had even put ten meters between itself and the rocket-like transport. The potent fuel ignited, triggering a ground shaking explosion. Raging plumes of fire went in all directions, engulfing the entire pack in the blazing inferno and burning them to ash. I felt a wave of intense heat against my face and turned my eyes away. When I looked back, all that was left was a circle of melted snow and burning debris.

"We've got to go," I said, thinking back to the armed satellite above us.

"Where?" O'Brian asked.

"Anywhere but here."

Surprisingly, we fled for over an hour, with no sign of an attack from the sky, or from the Wolf tribe. By the time we'd reached a suitable stopping point, I was almost convinced that neither would be a threat.

"We'll camp here," I said.

The squad, eager for rest, threw their packs down onto the ice. "Do you think the DoubleA will be able to find us?" O'Brian asked.

"According to Stacks they've got a satellite online," I said, "As long as it stays that way they can find us anywhere."

I sat down and stared into a small pool of glacier water. My glassy reflection stared back, the pain of loss most evident on its face. Roberts had been more than a comrade; he'd been a friend, a never ending source of humor, and time after time, the only thing keeping me from coming unnerved. Now he was gone, and no matter what he'd died as, his end was valiant. I pulled the crumpled paper he'd given me from my pocket and began unfolding it. As soon as the first crease was open, I heard a roar overhead.

"Everybody down!" I yelled, certain that the satellite's attack had finally come.

I sprawled onto my stomach clutching my helmet tightly to my head. The roar grew louder and louder with every second, causing me to tense with dreaded anticipation. Whatever weapon they'd chosen to launch, our chances of surviving it were zero. Suddenly, the roar died, leaving the area in silence, save the howling arctic wind. I lay there, still clutching my helmet, very unsure that we were safe. After four or five seconds, I heard O'Brian cry out with joy.

"It's a Starfire! We're saved, lads!"

I quickly raised my head, praying that he was right. Sure enough, the sleek descendent of the B2 Stealth Bomber was idling not ten meters away. A small door slid open, and a man in a blue flight suit ushered us in. I took off at a dead run towards the craft, not believing my eyes until my feet were planted on the studded metal entrance.

"First Lieutenant Rick Chapman, at your service, Captain," the man said, helping me into the craft.

"You sure are a sight for sore eyes, Lieutenant." I said.

"Glad to get you guys out of here. It looks like hell froze over out there."

I helped Lieutenant Chapman get the rest of the squad onboard before tossing my gear into the corner of the small craft. The shiny door slid shut automatically, little by little restricting my vision of the dreadful arctic terrain. I turned away, intent on finding somewhere suitable to rest, but Lieutenant Chapman stopped me.

"Captain," he said "There's someone in the pilot's compartment that wants to see you."

He motioned me towards a small door at the front of the craft. I started to open it, but the craft took off, causing me to have reservations about bursting in on the pilot. As though he could sense my hesitation, the lieutenant dismissed my concern.

"Go on," he said, "She's on autopilot. As a matter of fact, I'm the one who's supposed to be flying her."

I nodded and opened the door. Inside was a very familiar face. A streak of dried blood ran from his left eye, all the way down into his silver beard. However, this didn't stop him from flashing a toothy smile.

"Come on in, Captain Dawn. This has been a long time coming," said General Stacks.

"Too long," I said.

I sat down in the pilot's chair, careful not to touch any of the controls.

"Drink?" he asked, brandishing a bottle of whiskey.

"Please. I've got a lot of memories I'd like to erase."

He starting pouring the dark brown liquid into a glass, but stopped far sooner than I would have liked.

"There'll be a time for that, Captain, but, for now, you need your senses."

I took the glass from his hand and gulped down what little bit he'd given me.

"I thought President Young had grounded the entire fleet," I said, "What happened?"

Stacks took another swig of his drink before replying.

"Young's dead. Vice-President Winters made the call."

"Dead?" I questioned.

Stacks nodded, "A space-based debris laser tore our HQ to pieces not five minutes after I got off the radio. Only twenty-two, including me, made it out alive."

"The satellite." I said.

Again he nodded, this time with more remorse.

"I shouldn't have been so foolish. You were right, Captain. Everything about it was a trap and a good one."

"What's it doing now?" I asked, afraid of what else it might unleash.

"Floating around space in about a billion pieces. As soon as it was done demolishing our headquarters, the Navy launched an inter-planetary ballistic missile. Blew the thing to shreds."

Stacks poured himself another glass of whiskey, but offered me none.

"We are at war, Captain," he said, "The Cabinet declared it not ten minutes after Young's death. We are at war with an enemy we don't have a clue about."

He took a considerable gulp of his drink, then wiped his mouth on his sleeve.

"That's where the Scrolls come in," he said, pointing his glass at my pack.

"How long will it take to translate them?" I asked.

"A day tops."

I nodded.

"You'd better get some rest, Captain. You've earned it."

"I believe I will, General. It's been a long day."

He laughed heartily and opened the door for me.

"You bet it has."

I stepped out of the main compartment and closed the door behind me. The entire squad, or what was left of it, was sprawled out on the floor, sound asleep.

Lieutenant Chapman smiled, "They didn't make for very exciting conversation that's for sure."

I smiled a little, too tired myself to respond. Chapman took the hint and excused himself back into the cockpit. Finally alone, I huddled into a corner and pulled Roberts' letter from my pocket. My fingers trembled as I pealed back the neat folds and began reading.

Chapter 35

To Private Benjamin Roberts.
From General Joseph Tipton.

If you are reading this letter, it is only because I was certain that I would never have a chance to tell you this in person. The information I have disclosed may sound strange coming from a man you hardly know, however, I have known you and your family for a very long time. As a matter of fact, your father and I were classmates at West Point Academy. I wish to express my utmost regrets that he passed when you were so young. He was a great man and also the reason for my writing this letter.

In the year of 2047, an unidentified craft crashed in the middle of the Rockies and was found by a couple of hikers. After they reported the incident, including the mention of one or more bodies, the information was sent straight to the top. Despite what you hear about Area 51 and other sites, this was the first case in which an alien craft landed on earth with bodies intact. As you may know, your father's major was astrobiology, and he was good at it. President Dawson ordered that he be sent to study the bodies and that I be sent to oversee the site's security. To make a long story short, your father wound up embezzling a tissue sample for his private studies. He thought I didn't know, but I did. I sent an agent, disguised as a lab assistant, to monitor his every move. Not a week into his research, your father came upon a remarkable discovery. The alien cells were somehow enhanced. When dormant, it was hard to tell them from the cells of any other species, but when exposed to a particular serum, found inside a small gland at the back of the aliens' brains, these cells became extraordinary. They would heal themselves and any cell next to them. They became stronger, more efficient; they almost doubled in size. Your father was ecstatic at his discovery, but a week later, a different discovery was made, one far less welcome. At two years old, you were diagnosed with a rare but incurable strain of influenza. The world's best doctors gave you two weeks to live,

231

saying there was nothing that could be done. Your father was heartbroken. He immediately began testing the alien cells on chronically ill mice. After only two days, his hypothesis was proven. The cells, when in the presence of the serum, cured any and all types of injury and sickness. Before we could stop him, he injected you with the cells and a small dose of the serum. Within an hour's time, you went from dying in your bed, to playing in the yard. However, as you aged, we began to notice peculiar things about you. You were faster, stronger, and at times, smarter than kids twice your age. Unfortunately, your father never lived to see these results. You were sent to London to be raised by a man you believed was your uncle. I, with terrible regrets, must inform you that he was not. Mr. Bryce Saxon, operating under the alias of Gentry Roberts, was set with the task of bringing you up into a military career. You must understand that this man came to love you as his own child, and any fondness he showed you was truly genuine. However, he still had a job to do. Your involvement in combat sports, your first-class firearm training, and your eventual joining of the RAF was no accident, yet I must remark upon the way you have excelled. The feats that you have accomplished, while related to, were in no way limited to your injection. At this point, however, I am compelled to reveal the foremost reason for this letter. Beyond the purpose of disclosing information you deserve to know, I am writing to inform you of a very consequential, yet formidable option. I am sure you have noticed the syringe I included in this envelope. Contained within it is a dose of the serum required to bring the cells still within your body, out of their dormancy. The amount of the serum within the syringe is five hundred times the dose your father gave you, and I warn that the consequences of utilizing it are dire. Should the injection itself not bring eventual death, you will certainly wish it. I do not blame you if you find this information appalling and should you wish to destroy both the syringe and its contents, you have every right. You could continue to live an almost perfectly normal life and die a perfectly normal death, without ever thinking twice about any of this. If, however, you find yourself in a situation where death is inevitable, you must know that there is an option that will allow you to take every last one of your assailers with you. Is not that the dying wish of every soldier?

232

Sincerely and regretfully,
General Joseph Tipton

I looked up from the crinkled page, still in disbelief at what I'd read. I wondered who all had known of this. I tried to imagine what had happened to the alien bodies. If they were truly from Xavier, as they almost certainly were, why were they not being studied to further our cause? Perhaps they were lost or destroyed during the course of the Great War. It would remain unknown, yet the realization that something truly did visit us, whether they be from Xavier or not, was chilling. I put the letter aside and closed my eyes. Sleep would not be easy, but it was essential. After time, the soft roar of flight lulled me to sleep, just as it always does.

The jolt of landing, followed by a bustle of activity brought me awake. I rubbed the sleep from my eyes, and even though I was still drowsy, I could tell that the rest had been completely rejuvenating.

"Captain Dawn?"

My vision still coming into focus, I looked up to see a man with curly black hair and small round glasses that rested on the end of his slightly large nose.

"My name is Dr. Andy Evermore, Department of Linguistics. If you will excuse my alacrity, sir, but we must commence the translation of the Scrolls you recovered."

I had seen Stacks out of the corner of my vision, and I turned to him for conformation.

He nodded, "Go ahead."

I shrugged the pack off of my shoulders and unzipped the compartment I'd reserved for the Scrolls. The sealed containers spilled onto the floor in front of Dr. Evermore. His eyes lit up as he collected the Scrolls off of the floor, counting them as he did. "One, two, three, four…four? I understood there was to be five?"

"There were complications, Doctor." Stacks said.

Dr. Evermore raised his eyebrows, seeking a better explanation.

"Sorry son, classified. Just translate the ones we've got. Hopefully that will be plenty."

He nodded and exited the craft, Scrolls in hand. It was hard to let them go. We had worked so hard to get them. So much blood had been spilled, blood of both friend and foe alike. I watched until Dr. Evermore had exited the craft, until I could see the Scrolls no more, then sighed and rose. Attachment to my men and missions had always been a problem for me, but this time it was far worse. I was in love with Collins, considered a soldier now dead to be one of the greatest friends I ever had, and now I was feeling an attachment to those cursed Scrolls.

"Captain Dawn?"

Once again I looked up to see someone standing over me. This time, it was a woman in her late forties, with short brown hair that was barely long enough to be tied back like she had it.

"Can I help you?" I said, rising to my feet.

"Actually, I'm here to help you. My name's Dr. Sara Lopez. If you and your soldiers will follow me outside, my team and I can examine you all."

"I don't believe that's necessary, Doctor."

"I believe it is absolutely necessary," she said, "Despite the fact that you could be harboring unseen injuries, you will not be allowed clearance into the base until you have been tested for disease and radiation exposure."

I conceded and let her lead me out of the Starfire. The landing strip outside was a swarm of activity. Men in blue jumpsuits, with the Air Force insignia on their shoulders, were running around the craft, giving it every diagnostic in the book. A group of Air Force guards had encircled the landing zone, armed with stubby submachine-guns that looked like they would fire a million rounds a minute. Off to the side of the small runway was a team of doctors and nurses, I assumed under the charge of Dr. Lopez, busy setting up a white medical tent.

"Right this way, Captain," Doctor Lopez said, "By the time Nurse Potter takes care of the basics we will be ready for you."

She directed me and my squad to a line of small white chairs that had been hastily set up beside the tent. They had been lined from top to bottom with plastic sheeting, making me question if there truly was need for concern. As soon as I sat down, a curvy, blonde nurse strolled out of the makeshift tent. Her hair was sleek and long, bouncing lightly off of her rounded shoulders. She had light blue eyes and perfectly tanned skin.

"Agent Collins, if you would follow me inside we will take care of you first, then the men can all go at once." she said.

Collins smiled in a way that was almost fiendish. I could see the female rivalry in her eyes as she followed the nurse into the tent, quick to mimic her sexy stroll. I cleared my throat loudly, scattering the stares that had been locked on the two women, then scanned the area, looking for the camps main entrance. After only a second's search, I located it about eighty meters east, barely within sight. At either side of the panel and razor wire fence stood two guards, large rifles clutched in their hands. Overhead I heard a faint churning, and looked up to see three chopper drones. At what I presumed was the center of the base, I could see the tip of a SX77 Satellite Detector. No one gained access through any door without an eye and fingerprint scan, and guards were *everywhere*. In fact, it only took me turning around to find one near.

"Private, can you tell me what's going on here?"

He stood at attention, but did not look directly at me.

"Sorry, sir, I am not authorized to relay information to anyone lacking security clearance."

I considered pressing the matter, but decided not to.

"Captain Dawn, we're ready for you,"

I turned back around and saw Nurse Potter waiting at the tents entrance. She gave me a brief smile and wink, a gesture that was instantly noticed by Collins, and acted upon by a glare that told me that if I even gave this woman the time of day, that I was dead. I winked at Collins, but she didn't seem amused. I smiled slightly, finding her jealousy very attractive. Nurse Potter zipped the tent behind me as I entered, then directed me to a small bench.

"Take off your shirt, Captain."

I pulled my shirt over my shoulders and tossed it to the side.

"Now if you'll excuse me for a minute, Nurse Fearson will be right with you."

No sooner did Nurse Potter slip out of the tent, did a short pudgy woman in her mid-fifties enter the room. She had wiry brown hair, a barbwire tattoo, and in her hand was a needle. Before I could protest she shoved the tip deep into my arm and extracted a syringe full of blood.

Just when I thought doctor visits were looking up, I thought.

A few minutes after she left, two doctors entered and scanned me and my clothing with a clunky handheld device that was supposed to beep if any dangerous particles were present. Much to my relief, it remained quiet.

"Ok, Captain, you're done," one of the doctors said, "If you will step this way, I will sign your medical clearance and give you the key to your quarters. General Stacks has already vouched for your security clearance, so you will be free to go *almost* anywhere you please."

"What about the others?" I asked.

The doctor shuffled nervously before replying.

"Umm, all of them passed medical clearance; however, security clearance was not given to Sergeant Stillworth or Corporal O'Brian."

I could already feel my anger rising.

"Why?" I asked, trying to control my volume.

"Please, sir, if I knew I would tell you. You'll have to talk with General Stacks."

"I will be, Doctor. You can count on it."

I threw my shirt back on and exited the tent.

"Where can I find General Stacks?" I asked a guard who was standing at attention beside the main entrance.

"Do you have security clearance, sir?" he asked, his bushy mustache the only thing that I saw move.

"I'm Captain Michael Dawn. General Stacks was supposed to have vouched for my clearance himself."

The soldier nodded, then directed me to a small but heavily fortified building not twenty yards from the main gate.

"He's in there, Captain. He said you'd most likely want to see him."

"Thanks, Corporal."

He pressed a combination into the gates lock and swung it open. Just as I stepped through, he stopped me.

"Sir, I apologize but we're required to confiscate all weaponry before allowing anyone entrance. Even Stacks had to give up his sidearm."

I cursed under my breath before dropping the E.T.A.D. pistol into a bin filled with firearms.

"Thank you, sir," he said.

I nodded begrudgingly before passing through the gate.

The jog to Stacks' quarters didn't take more than twenty seconds. Three guards standing by the entrance started to stop me, but made no attempt after recognizing who I was.

"I'm here to see General Stacks," I said, walking right up to the door of his quarters.

One of the guards, who I presumed was in command, pressed his thumb against a small touchscreen on the side of the door. The door clicked unlocked, then swung open.

"Right in there, Captain."

I stepped into the room, instantly welcoming the rush of warm air.

"Come in, Dawn. I've been waiting for you," Stacks said, a mug full of coffee in his hand.

"Want some brew?" he asked, sliding a chair out for me to sit in.

"No, but would appreciate a few explanations." I said, still standing.

His eyes widened slightly, obviously taken aback by my straightforwardness

"Well then, I'll see what I can do."

"Why were Sergeant Stillworth and Corporal O'Brian not given security clearance?"

General Stacks sighed, "Look Captain, before you blame me, I want you to know that it wasn't my call. Vice president, now President Winters issued an executive order requiring a reworking of our security systems. This included denying clearance to *anyone* not in the American Alliance military. "

"Sergeant Stillworth is an Israeli Commando, General. As far as I remember, Israel is part of the American Alliance."

"Not anymore." he said, "So much has changed since you've been gone. You must understand."

I sighed, conceding to the fact that this was out of my control.

"Where will they stay?" I asked.

"The European Alliance is sending the means for their transportation to *somewhere*. The transporter should be arriving any minute."

Upon hearing this I jumped from my seat and dashed out the door. The cool air hit me like an icy assailant as guards and razor wire flew past in a blur. I could hear the rhythmic whirl of jet engines, growing louder by the second, and by the time I reached the fence, a dark black craft, with European Alliance seal on its wings, had landed on the base's runway. I laced my fingers into the fence, watching as Stillworth and O'Brian boarded the transporter. Just before they disappeared into the fuselage, they turned and saw me. A solemn salute was all that passed between us, yet contained within this simple gesture were words that could never be spoken aloud. I held my hand up proudly, as did they, until the doors on the craft shut entirely. The thruster at its back roared with flame, speeding the vessel into the sky. I turned away, struck, once again, with the sorrow of lost friends. Once more, I felt completely alone amongst a crowd of faces. Perhaps the eccentricity of the E.T.A.D. camp was not the only reason I'd felt so distanced. Perhaps this world truly had changed greatly since I'd been gone, and now I felt as an outsider amongst my own people. I shoved these thoughts from my mind, far too forlorn to think about something so disheartening and headed for my quarters.

I rolled over on my cot, trying to ignore the urgent nudging, hoping it would just go away.

"Captain Dawn, You've got to get up, sir. General Stacks has sent for you."

I sighed and sat up, facing a tall young private with a button nose.

"It's five in the morning. What could he possibly need?"

"I don't know, sir, but he said for you to go to the office of linguistics immediately."

I jolted awake and jumped out of the cot.

"Thank you," I said, throwing on my uniform as I headed out the door.

Chapter 36

The sun had not yet risen, but the camp was well lit with the faint glow of lampposts. Overhead, the pale white moon, Albus, was nothing but a tiny sliver of a crescent and was constantly disappearing beneath the clouds. Gravel crunched beneath my boots as I trekked towards the center of the camp. My heart was racing, but my mind was racing faster. To finally see what secrets lay beneath the Scrolls was something I considered without equal. The building I was to reach was now in sight, and I picked up my speed. At the door were two lackluster guards, their weapons drooping at their sides. Without question, they stepped aside when I neared the entrance. I reached out and turned the handle, but, without surprise, found it locked.

"What's the combination, Private?" I asked the guard on the left.

"Doesn't have one, sir," he said drowsily, "You scan your eye and thumbprint to get in."

I stepped onto a small plate and pressed my eye up to a peephole in the door. A red light flickered in the opening, then turned green.

"Now your thumbprint," the guard said, pointing to a small touchscreen just above the doors handle.

I pressed my thumb onto the glowing red display and waited. After only a second the screen turned green, and the lock clicked open.

"Congratulations, Captain," he said, almost sarcastically, "You're one of the very few allowed in there. You'd better hurry though. She'll lock back in a few seconds if you don't open the door."

I nodded and swung the door open. Instantly, I felt as if I had interrupted a conference rather than join one. Everyone inside had ceased whatever conversation they'd been engaged in and peered awkwardly at me. General Stacks, however, quickly vanquished this impression.

"Have a seat, Captain; we've been waiting for you."

I ambled over to the large steel table at the room's center and was suddenly struck with who all was present. President Winters, General Stacks, Chief of Extraterrestrial Policies, General Ridley, Chief of extraterrestrial technologies, Dr. Hernandez, Chief of Extraterrestrial Studies, Dr. Chang, as well as Xavier's chief of Extraterrestrial Linguistics, Dr. Huff, were all seated at the table and focusing on a large screen at the room's side. I pulled a chair out and slowly sat down.

"Dr. Huff, would you mind explaining our situation to Captain Dawn."

He cleared his throat and stood, "Certainly, General. As you might have expected, the department and I were most eager to begin the translation of the manuscripts you retrieved. Regrettably, upon our breaking the seals in which they were encased, we did not find what we were expecting."

At this Dr. Hernandez stood, "The items you retrieved, while certainly bearing much resemblance to, are not scrolls at all."

"Are you saying we brought back the wrong thing?" I asked.

"No," General Stacks replied, "What he's saying is that what you brought back is not what we were prepared to deal with."

Dr. Hernandez paused to be sure that Stacks was finished, before resuming.

"These...*items*, if you will, contain levels of technology that would take us years to decipher, and that's not all."

Dr. Hernandez picked a small remote up off the table and switched the screen over to a picture of one of the four Scrolls. Rather than being made of the ancient and yellowed paper I was expecting, the Scroll was an electronic cylinder. Down its sides ran four bright blue lights. Dr. Hernandez pressed a few buttons on the remote, causing the picture to morph into a projection.

"Now, will you take a look at this and tell me what it looks like to you." he said, grabbing hold of the projection and turning it until I was facing the Scrolls base. I studied it for a second, noticing the electronics that were enclosed within a small indentation on the round surface.

"It looks like an outlet of sorts." I said.

"Exactly. As a matter of fact, there was an opening in the bottom of the seals so it could be connected without ever being opened" said Dr. Hernandez, "Now the question remains, and this is the reason we've brought you here, what did they plug into?"

I was dumbfounded, not having the slightest clue as to what these things might connect to. After a few seconds of awkward silence, I was struck with realization.

"You said that the Scroll could be connected while they were still encased?"

Dr. Hernandez nodded.

The pedestals, I thought. It was clear now. The wires I'd seen, the way the Scrolls had all been placed on top of a pedestal, the way they had clicked when I removed them, I even had the faintest recollection of seeing a small, key-shaped, object protruding from the top of an empty pedestal. I quickly relayed this information to everyone present.

"Do you have documentation of these devices?" Dr. Hernandez asked, "If you do, my team and I might be able to replicate the receptor in a matter of hours."

"No," I said remorsefully, "But I know someone who might."

After only a minute, Collins walked through the door, her hair in a mess and sleep still in her eyes. Upon realizing who all was there, she gave me a look of pure spite and started franticly tidying herself.

"Don't bother, Agent Collins," General Stacks said, "We just need to ask you a very crucial question."

At this, Dr. Hernandez took over.

"Upon retrieving the Scroll from the Scorpion territory, did you happen to photographically document the scene?"

Collins sniffed mockingly, "Of course I did. Where do you think I was trained? Girl Scouts?"

The doctor's eyes lit up, "May we please have access to the photographs?"

She nodded and began rummaging through the pack she'd been told to bring. After only a moment, she pulled a handful of pictures out and handed them to Dr. Hernandez. He rapidly flipped through them, growing more and more excited with each one he saw.

"These will work perfectly. Combined with the information we can gather from the receiving end of the connection, this should be more than enough for us to duplicate the receptor."

He summoned for his small team of engineers and scientists to follow and headed out the door.

"Now what?" I asked Stacks.

"Now we wait."

I let out an exasperated sigh. After watching the clock tick away for five tedious hours, I was starting to think their attempt had failed. Just as I was about to rise and go back to my quarters, Dr. Hernandez burst through the door.

"I believe we've done it," he said, dark circles under his eyes.

"How did you manage it so quickly?" Stacks asked.

At this, I was surprised, but I realized that to replicate alien technology, five hours was impressive.

"It's really a rather simple device," he said, "Nothing compared to the Scroll itself."

"Does it work?" Stacks asked.

Dr. Hernandez shuffled a little, "We haven't exactly tested it yet. We imagined that you would want to be present when we plugged the Scroll in."

Stacks nodded, giving Dr. Hernandez his approval. The doctor produced a device about the size of a small lamp and placed it on the table.

"She's not pretty, General, but I think she'll work." he said

"That's all that matters," Stacks said.

Dr. Hernandez took a deep breath. He was sweating, and I could tell he was very nervous about how his device would perform. General Stacks must have noticed this as well.

"Calm down, Mark, and plug the thing in. If it doesn't work it doesn't work."

The doctor nodded, and after an anxious sigh, he clicked the first Scroll into the receptor. After only a second's wait, the Scroll's blue lights grew noticeably brighter, and it started to hum. I watched with gripping anticipation, yet after waiting for an entire minute, the contraption did nothing more.

Dr. Hernandez looked concerned, but suddenly lit up.

"It makes sense actually," he said, "I don't recall Captain Dawn mentioning the device doing much of anything when he obtained it, and apparently it had been connected. It has to be activated somehow."

He stared at the apparatus intently, his fingernail in his mouth.

242

After a second, he reached out and gave the scroll a sharp turn. It clicked twice, then began to hum louder. A bright blue hologram flickered to life, projecting from the Scrolls top.
General Stacks spoke without taking his eyes off of the foreign symbols and lettering scattered across the projection.
"Get the linguistics team back…now."

"Well," Dr. Huff said, "I'm not sure whether I should be disappointed or delighted."
"Would you please elaborate?" Stacks said impatiently.
Dr. Huff frowned, "The language present on the hologram is the dialect of the Scorpion tribe. I can translate it electronically in about thirty seconds, however I was rather hoping for a challenge."
"We don't have time for challenges, Doctor." Stacks said.
He nodded and started scanning the projection with a small handheld device.
"Are you saying you believe the first Scroll was built by the Scorpion tribe?" I asked.
"Not at all," Dr. Huff replied, "I'm saying it was left for them."
After the device beeped, he placed it upright next to the Scroll and flipped a switch. An identical hologram sprang from its projector, except the alien symbols had been replaced with English.
"Incredible," I said.
Dr. Huff smiled, obviously pleased with my appreciation for what he'd done.
General Stacks scanned the projection then frowned.
"I want General Ridley and Dr. Chang to get back over here. Tell them they have two days to sort through the databases of the Scrolls and put together a profile on whoever placed them."
Just as the messenger turned to leave, President Winters burst through the door.
"General Stacks. Intel just informed me that the DoubleEs have located the city and are planning an all out invasion at fourteen-hundred hours."
Stacks glanced at his watch, then turned back to the messenger.
He shook his head and sighed, "Tell them they have two hours."

I watched as the two men worked feverishly, sorting through the Scrolls' databases, jotting down notes, and talking amongst themselves. Everywhere I turned, men and women were franticly conversing over radios and typing away at computers. I glanced at the doorway, just in time to see Stacks burst in.

"Do you have the report?" he asked.

General Ridley and Dr. Chang coughed slightly as they gathered their papers. Their faces were pale and beads of sweat rolled off their foreheads.

"Yes, I believe we have more than a profile for you, sir," Dr. Chang said, "We have the race's entire history at our disposal." Stacks nodded.

"Gentlemen." he said, "President Winters is currently online with the Cabinet of Military Affairs on Xavier. You have exactly ten minutes to convince him whether or not he should ask for a declaration of extermination."

General Stacks narrowed his eyes at them, "You must understand how important this is. If there is any hope of reconciling our relations with this species, based upon your analysis, you must point it out. It's going to be a shame if we have to annihilate the only race of intelligent life we have ever found."

General Ridley shook his head in disbelief.

"I'm not sure that will even be possible, Stacks."

General Stacks frowned, "I'll take care of that. Continue with your report; the clock's ticking."

Dr. Chang stepped forward, his notes in hand.

"There is, as we expected, a hyper-advanced race living in a veiled city at the planet's North Pole."

"What are they like?" Stacks asked.

"These creatures are very controlling, General," Dr. Chang said, "They thrive off order and dominion and will use unrestrained violence to achieve their wishes. In fact, the Scrolls themselves were placed in order to keep the tribes under their control. The various tribes worshiped this race as gods, and in turn, they were given the Scrolls as a means of guidance. As they evolved, they would learn to access more and more of the Scrolls' databases, allowing them to achieve feats they could have never accomplished on their own. Having this much reliance on the Scrolls forced the tribes to defend them with passion, and rather than conquering new lands for themselves, they stayed back and protected their life-sources. The race even handpicked their leaders to ensure they would remain defensive."

"How did they do that?" I asked.

"They would hand select a prospect at birth, then bring him or her back to their city," Chang said, "There, they would genetically enhance them so that no other tribe member would be able to challenge their command. After that, they implanted the new leader with a control chip so that they could manipulate his or her every move."

"Did they manipulate the leaders to help or hurt the tribes?" General Stacks asked.

"Hurt," Dr. Chang said grimly, "All of their leaders were controlled to keep the tribes passive and many times to reduce their population. The Brutes were forced to take up self sacrifice in worship of their leader; the Scorpions had to fight in the coliseum to please theirs. The queen of the Supernest would kill much of her young and all of the adolescent queens. The dominant Marsh creature controlled breeding, and the Alpha wolf instigated countless pack wars."

"Is there any chance of reconcilement?" Stacks asked.

At this, General Ridley stepped forward, his face still pale.

"No." he said, "They despise us. We are all over that database, General, and none of it's good. These things, whatever they are, have been manipulating us since the dawn of man. They built the pyramids, a device that served many of the same purposes as the Scrolls. They communicated with numerous leaders, ranging from Julius Caesar to Napoleon Bonaparte, all the way up to President Tyson, trading technology for control over their decisions. They have started wars and caused disasters. They have handpicked our leaders, just like the tribes, and killed those they found unacceptable. Their hand has been in every aspect of our history, and for all practical purposes, they are responsible for our downfall."

"We believe they are planning an eventual invasion of earth, sir" Dr. Chang said.

General Stacks sighed and shook his head, "If they wanted our planet, why have they waited so long? Why not just destroy us somewhere around the stone age when we couldn't have put up a fight?"

"They were giving us a chance." Dr. Chang replied, "After World War One, these beings made the same decision we are now making about them. They decided humanity was too volatile for slavery and ordered our extermination."

"Slavery?" Stacks said.

Dr. Chang nodded, "Once they realized we could not be forced into servitude without constant uprising, they began manipulating us towards annihilation. As far as I can see, they've done a good job of it. They started the Second World War and shortly after gave us nuclear technology. They are responsible for the outbreak of 2021, The Great War, the impact of the asteroid Goliath, and most every other event that has brought us to our knees."

"I've heard enough," Stacks said, "Get me President Winters."

"Wait, Stacks, there's more." Ridley said, "Our arrival has caught them completely off guard. They never suspected that we would achieve interstellar travel as quickly as we did, and our presence on their home planet has left them with only one option."

He paused and swallowed hard.

"According to an update to the Scroll's archive, by next month, they plan to wipe our presence from Xavier entirely before doing the same on Earth."

"Get me Winters," Stacks said to his secretary, "I'm going to advise a declaration of extermination."

"Are you joking?" Dr. Chang said, "This race is light-years more advanced than we are. Their lifespan is almost a thousand years, and even death by unnatural causes is almost unheard of. These beings are practically gods!"

"There's only one God," Stacks said, "And they are not Him."

He turned to me, just as Private Scott handed him the radio.

"You'd better suit up, Captain. I'm pretty sure it's gonna be all hands on deck."

"What do these things call themselves?" I asked, as I turned to leave.

"In our best translation," Dr. Chang said, "They're called Sirujians."

Chapter 37

By fifteen-hundred hours, I was standing in the snow, my rifle trained on what appeared to be thin air.

"All soldiers prepare for invasion," I heard through my helmet.

"Invade what?" a soldier to my right asked.

"Stay focused," I said, not taking my eye off the rifle's sights. Before someone could stop him, the young soldier stepped forward and reached out his hand. It extended forward for maybe a foot, before hitting an invisible barrier. The air sparked violently, burning off his hand and sending him into a fit of screams.

"Medic!" I heard someone yell, "Get him out of here. The rest of you get back!"

I saw a massive vehicle backing up to where we were standing. This was not really an odd occurrence; various transports and Bruin Invasion Tanks had been showing up for the past hour, emptying soldiers and training their weapons towards the same invisible shield. However, this one was different. Rather than weapons, it was equipped with what looked like a massive generator. The truck continued to back up, until a fist sized probe at the generator's back was touching the barrier. A lanky man with a small mustache and the Army Corps of Engineers insignia got out, slamming the door behind him.

"What's going on?" I asked.

"Are you the commanding officer, sir?" he asked.

"For this point of attack I am. Now what is this thing?"

"It's a XR300 pulse generator. We've got about ten of them that we're gonna connect to the force shield."

"What'll it do?" I asked.

"Hopefully fry whatever's keeping the thing up," he said, "Combined, these ten machines should generate around five trillion volts into the field. If that doesn't overload it, this thing's invincible."

"All soldiers at the ready and commence countdown," I heard through my radio.

At this, the lieutenant turned and engaged a switch at the

generator's side. Immediately it began to hum.

"Ten, nine, eight, seven..."

With every second the generator grew louder.

"Six, five, four, three..."

At this point the machine had grown so loud, it sounded as if it were going to explode.

"Two...one!"

With a heave, the lieutenant threw a second switch at the generator's side. A blinding pulse of electricity shot from its probe and into the shield, separating into a thousand tendrils of electricity that coursed up the domed shield like reversed lightning. The barrier glowed a bright blue, absorbing more and more of the energy until it could take no more. Suddenly, the field exploded, sending every one of us diving face first into the snow. Hastily, I rose, the tingling of electric shock still rippling through my body. I blinked twice, my mind not believing what my eyes were telling it. The barrier had disappeared entirely, revealing the astonishing amount it had hidden. Buildings, taller than earth's skyscrapers rose into the clouds. Hovering around them like angry bees were aircraft of all shapes and sizes, the only ones I'd seen before being the triangular attack planes. However, the most unbelievable sight was beneath them. Formed together in a rough line, and numbering around ten thousand, stood the city's inhabitants. In a way, the creatures were almost mystical. Their grey skin was stretched tight across their body, and from it hung two barbed arms. Their chest rippled with muscle, yet broad ribs were still visible. Thick bone extended from their brows, all the way around the skull, slightly shading the most inexplicable eyes one could imagine. They were solid white and glowing, highlighted only by a crescent of solid black, which ran along their tops, and all of them were looking at us. I slowly shouldered my rifle, as did most every other soldier there, though I was terrified with the prospect of a firefight. Most of them had already trained their vast array of weapons on us, and I could only fear what they might be capable of. To my dismay, hundreds more began to flood from a large building at the city's center. They seemed more heavily armored and their weapons were larger. They circled the first crowd and trained their armaments on us. These creatures appeared more than ready to fight an army three times their size, yet, for now, something was

248

holding them back. Suddenly, the crowd began to part, making way for eight figures, each clothed in solid white robes. At their center, was a being whose color was different than any of the others. He was a bluish grey, and his eyes appeared larger. I let my gaze drift into them, or rather he locked them onto mine. I was entranced, completely hypnotized by his stare. Every nightmare, every horrible sight I'd managed to forget, came rushing back. I felt my knees hit the ground, but I wasn't sure how they got there. My eyes remained locked on his, and though it was hard to tell, it appeared they'd grown brighter, glowing white like two full moons. A figure suddenly dove in front of him, obscuring my view and breaking the trance. Bullets riddled the body of the martyr, but before one could find its intended target, the leader was gone.

"Engage!" I heard someone yell.

I picked my rifle up off the ground, having apparently dropped it, then opened fire.

Rather than scatter, the enemy stood their ground, many of them returning fire. A ball of electricity flew past my side, smashing into the legs of the soldier next to me. He fell forward, his heart undeniably stopped by the jolt. I gritted my teeth and continued to fire. Just inside my field of vision, I saw the leader reemerge. I was careful this time to not make eye contact with him, but at least a dozen other men were not so lucky. Their stare was locked with his, their weapons pointed harmlessly at the ground. Before anyone could break the trance, they drew their knives and committed suicide, plunging their blades deep into their necks. I swerved my rifle towards the leader, but before my sights crossed him, he was gone.

"Charge!" I heard someone yell.

I took off running toward the still substantial group of aliens, hip firing as I did. At last, they began to scatter, most of them running away, but a few rushing straight toward us.

"All units, all units," I heard through my mike, "Primary objective status has been changed. We need all units to concentrate their efforts on eliminating the indigenous leader. We believe that the enemy force is receiving their orders from him."

I continued to charge forward, headed straight for where I'd last seen him. Suddenly, two enemies cut me off. I slid to stop in order to keep from running straight into them. They were both covered in armor and wielding horrendous weapons. One of them appeared to have some type of spear made of energy. The other's weapon consisted of four cylinders, each connecting to a nozzle like barrel. I jerked my rifle to my shoulder and emptied a full clip into the spear-wielder's face. Round after round slammed into its armored helmet, deflecting harmlessly to the side. The creature shrieked, then drove its spear into the paved ground at my feet. Waves of energy flew up from the impact, sending me sailing backwards. The instant I landed, the second assailant lowered his weapon on me. Just as he jerked the lever that served as a trigger, a figure flew in front, knocking the barrels aside. A spurt of superheated gas exited the weapon, the majority of it enveloping the legs of my rescuer. He fell to the ground, and only then did I recognize him as Sergeant Smith. My rage boiled over. I jumped to my feet and sent a round into each of the alien's unarmored knees. He shrieked and fell forward, dark blue blood pouring from his legs. I swerved my rifle to the spear wielder, but realized he was already taken care of. A small group of marines were swarming over his downed body, plunging their knives into the weak spots of his armor.

"Smith!" I yelled, rushing to his side, "Are you okay?"

"Sir," he said, "You've got to get as many men as you can muster and get inside that building."

He pointed feebly to a large, octagonal tower.

"We had a visual on the leader going inside."

"Are you alright?" I asked, knowing the answer already. Even if he were to make it out of here, both of his legs had been rendered useless. Even his fireproof combat suit was no defense against the scorching plasma.

"Medic!" I yelled.

"Sir," Smith said, "You know there aren't any medics around here. Now get in that building and kill that wretch before we both die in vain."

I noticed that his rifle had been melted.

"Take this," I said, handing him mine, "I'll be back for you."

Before he could protest, I turned and ran towards the octagonal tower.

By the time I arrived at its entrance, I had recruited over a dozen infantry men, as well as the four Marines that were accompanying Smith.

"Get it down," I said, staring at the circular, metal door.

A hefty Marine gunnery quickly wired a charge to its base. The rest of us backed off a few meters, our weapons trained on the door. He scurried back, a remote in his hands.

"Fire in the hole!" he said, and hit the switch. The explosion shattered the door with ease, but in its wake, left a cloud of dust that obscured our view.

"Steady," I said, the sights of my side arm locked at the dust cloud's center.

Suddenly the stillness broke, and a Sirujian came charging out, a three-pronged weapon in his hand. Before he could get two steps, his unarmored body was riddled with bullets. Two marines stepped over his body and bolted inside the tower.

"Clear!" they yelled almost simultaneously.

"Come on," I said, and rushed inside.

The interior of the tower was completely bare, save for a circular capsule at its center.

"Elevator maybe?" an Army major next to me said.

"Not unless it goes down," I said, "There's no connection for it to go up."

"Whatever it is," one of the Marines said, "It's our only way to anywhere in this place."

"Then I guess we'll find out." I said.

I stepped forward and wrapped my hands around the handle of the capsule's glass door. With a stiff tug, it opened. The interior was lined with various devices. Even the floor was made of a sensory material that glowed green when I stepped on it.

"Pile in," I said.

Hesitantly, the rest of the soldiers made their way inside.

"Which one?" I heard someone ask.

I turned to see the Army major looking at two buttons on the wall of the capsule. They were identical in size and shape, both being circles the size of a large coin, except in color. One was white, with a small circle of black at its center. The other was the opposite, being black with a white circle.

I frowned, "One guess is as good as the other. Are you feeling lucky, Major?"

He laughed, "I haven't felt lucky since I got on this planet."

251

"Me neither," I said, and pressed the white button. The capsule hummed, but only for a second before going silent.

"What do…"

Before whoever had started to speak could finish, a surge of agony ripped through my body. It felt as if every atom of my being had been torn apart. I saw a blinding flash of light, and then everything went dark.

When my vision came back into focus, I felt as if eternity had passed, though it couldn't have been more than a minute. I found myself in a second capsule, whose door, I quickly kicked down. I stepped outside, my pistol clutched in my hands. The room was around ten meters across and made entirely of glass. At its edge stood the leader. Again, the first thing I saw was his eyes, and again, they overpowered any will or intention I had, completely reducing me to a creature so pitiful, I couldn't even control my own actions. I fought hard to break his stare, fought with every ounce of my being to raise my pistol and fire, but it was no use. I could literally feel this being inside my head, could feel him controlling my every thought. Against every fiber of my will, I pressed the barrel of my pistol to my head. Beside me I heard gunshots, heard bodies crumpling to the floor, but it was if they were in another world. I could feel my finger pressing against the trigger. My mind, or what little I still had control of, reeled. I fought his command with desperation, yet I could not overrule it. My finger continued to apply pressure to the trigger, and I knew at any second, I would be dead. I thought of Smith and how I had failed him. I thought of Roberts and Yakutsk and Rice and Jackson, and all the others who'd died to get me here, in this spot, only to be defeated like a whipped pup. Mostly though, I thought of Collins, and how I would never live to see her again. Just as I applied that final inkling of pressure to the trigger, the final touch before hammer struck pin, I felt his control waiver, just enough. I swerved the pistol away from my head and towards his. The barrel flashed across him, just as the round went off. A ragged hole appeared in the being's head, yet his eyes never left mine. Even as their color drained, even as they died, I could see the emotions they radiated. Knowledge and fear, anger and, most strangely of all, compassion. I truly felt as if I was staring into the soul of a

252

deity. I could see what he saw, could hear his thoughts. Just as he slumped to the ground, he interjected his final meditation. *Have mercy on them* was all that passed before he was dead. I tore myself away, then headed back to get Smith.

Having survived another agonizing teleportation to the tower's base, I fled outside. The area was still in chaos. Overhead, the triangular crafts of the Sirujians were still engaging Gunships and Ravens, and on the ground, our troops were still fighting theirs. However, having only been outside for seconds, I could sense a shift in the battle. The Sirujians appeared disorganized, even dismayed. Some of them had dropped their weapons entirely and were fleeing left and right. I saw one of the triangular ships take a nosedive, though it appeared undamaged. I narrowed my focus and raced to where we'd left Smith. He was lying limp on the ground, and I feared him already dead. Just as my heart began to sink, he stirred. I pushed myself harder and slid down next to him.

"Smith," I said, rolling him over, "I'm back."

"Did you kill him?" he asked weakly.

I nodded.

"We've got to get you out of here." I said.

"Something saved me." he said, "They were gonna kill me, but something saved me."

"Shh," I said, "let's get you out of here."

"They-they were cloaked. They had yellow eyes." he said.

"It was a hallucination," I said, hoisting him over my shoulder.

Just as I did, my radio went off.

"All units. Bunkers will be dropped in all vicinities of the city. Get inside them ASAP. Following their drop, you will have one minute before the city is bombed. I repeat, the skies have been cleared for a bomber. We will be nuking the city in exactly one minute. Once the bombs detonate, all units need to activate their locater beacons. Do not attempt to exit the bunkers. You will be found and evacuated within twenty-four hours."

At that time, a sleek, black Raven flew over, dropping from its undercarriage a cubical bunker. The object tumbled to the ground, impacting not fifteen meters from where I was standing, and sending a shower of gravel into the air. I rushed to it, Smith still on my shoulders, then hoisted open its titanium door. After placing

Smith in the corner, I shut it behind me, leaving us in total darkness. Just as I did, it reopened, and three more soldiers poured in.

"I hope they've got plenty of these things," I said, haunted by the idea of our men being outside when the blast went off.

"Heck," one of the men who'd entered said, "This was the fifth one in this little area. I just hope these things can hold up."

"They will," I said.

I pressed my back against the cold metal, inwardly counting down the seconds. Suddenly, I heard a rumbling, like the sound of a million horses stampeding across the ground. Not a heartbeat after this, the bunker toppled, sailing sideways and throwing us like rag dolls, before finally coming to a stop. I hunkered down, my head between my knees and waited for the blast to dissipate. After an amount of time I could not judge, the rumbling stopped. The radio crackled with heavy static before Stacks' voice finally came through.

"All units, the place has been leveled. I repeat, no surviving indigenous present. All units remain sheltered and activate locater beacons. You will be picked up within twenty-four hours."

I breathed a sigh of pure relief, then activated my beacon.

Epilogue

Scientists explained that the effect was purely biological, that his eyes flashed a pattern that would hypnotize anyone who looked into them. They said that the effect was part of his domination tactics; however, it wasn't until a year later that I came to accept this. Friends had been lost, deeds done that I wished I'd never had to do. A species had been eradicated, and in all truthfulness, my heart bled for them. Yet standing here now, watching the skies, with those I love around me, I felt entirely healed. The Scrolls had taught us so much, the cure for cancer, the secret to sustaining the worlds we live on, and much more was still to be discovered within their infinite archives. In the year's time we'd had after the war, we had secured a three-million acre perimeter around the flatlands of the Brute territory. After eradicating one species, we couldn't bring ourselves to do it again, and had put our efforts into building a defense that no tribe could penetrate. One day, it might come to bloodshed, but for now, we were safe.

"You want some, Captain?" Private Hawkins asked, offering me a glass of champagne and interrupting my thoughts.

"I'm not a captain anymore, Hawkins,' I said, "I'm a civilian. And no, I'm through with the stuff."

He nodded and gazed up at the night sky. To our left a group of men were setting up a massive telescope.

"February 27th, 2072" Hawkins said, "The day we finally get to look back home."

I nodded, almost entranced by the thought.

"Can you believe earth's sun is only visible every fifteen years?" Hawkins said, "Kinda makes ya feel distant, doesn't it?"

"It sure does," I said, still staring at the sky.

"Take a look Mr. Dawn," one of the men setting up the telescope said.

I put my eye up to the lens and peered into the stars.

"You see the dim yellow one in the center?" he asked.

"Yes," I whispered.

"That is earth's sun."

I stared at the tiny, yellow dot, mystified by both the magnitude of what I was looking at, and by how insignificant it appeared. Around that speck of yellow, orbited a world ravaged by war, a world with nation and cities and people who all dream of one day coming here. I stared into the eyepiece until my tears fogged it over, then turned away. All around, I was surrounded by the people I called my friends. All of them were laughing and carrying on in such a lighthearted way that, besides Roberts, I'd never had the pleasure to see. I saw Smith, entirely healed and boasting to a group of young recruits. I saw Ashley, my wife, standing beside a fire, looking more radiant than she ever had. With no remorse, with no regret, I made a decision that never again would I question. This world, Xavier, was now my home.

JOHN A. ASHLEY

BEFORE THE
STORM

BOOK TWO IN THE
XAVIER SERIES

Three years have passed since the Sirujians were defeated and at last, the planet Xavier is at peace. A few light years away, however, lies a world that is not so fortunate. Earth—a planet ravaged by countless wars and totalitarian governments is on the brink of collapse, but even in these darkest days a slim hope shines. In a few short weeks, a lucky group of individuals will be chosen to colonize the promising world of Xavier997. Clay Morton and his fiancé Charity Collins are two of these hopefuls. Yet as the day of the Xavier Drawing swiftly approaches, an old enemy rises from the ashes, and this time in terrifying force. Separated during the chaos, Clay and Charity soon find themselves thrown into the ultimate battle for survival. Should they lose, so will all humanity.

For beneath the sands of a forgotten desert lies a force known only by them, a force that even the Sirujians fear and that has the power to be either mankind's salvation or their final destruction…

Learn more at www.scrollsofxavier.com